My Walls Speak

My Walls Speak

Carolyn Long Silvers

To order additional copies of this book, contact:
Xlibris LLC
1-888-795-4274
www.Xlibris.com
Orders@Xlibris.com
620605

Dedicated To

My husband Robert, who provided encouragement and support. His services of proofreading, fact checking, and instant spelling assistance are appreciated.

My great grandparents William and Helen Yingling who were extraordinary people and whose lives continue to inspire their descendants.

My mother, Maxine Yingling Long who taught me to love literature and encouraged me to write.

My children and grandchildren who are the center of my world and purpose of my life.

Lander Wyoming that is the setting of this story and was my home for over twenty years.

My Fanstory.com friends who mentored me through this project.

Contents

Chapter One

TRANSITION

"This may well be the first autobiography of a house"

This may well be the first autobiography of a house. It's difficult to know where to begin with my story. I could start at the beginning, or I could commence from the present and move backwards. I think, however, I will begin at the time of my breakdown, and with the events that led up to it. That would have been during a very sad time in the month of May.

Of course events occurred that inevitably led to my state of hopelessness. By 1990, the last descendants of the Yinglings, Kenyans, Greggs, and Carr had left the valley, placing the 160-acre ranch on the market. No one lived with me for fifteen years before that. For a while, some family members passed through for short stays during summer months or holidays. Eventually, even that ceased.

Then Dennis Dickenson bought the ranch. Of course, I was excited. It would be great having a family again. For years I'd watched my structure slowly go to ruin. My shingles often blew off in the wind, and my white paint chipped away. My outer walls exposed the drab gray color of bare boards.

New inhabitants replaced humankind. A large colony of field mice occupied my kitchen. A family of skunks settled in under my porch, and a lovely doe raised her young for several years in the apple orchard behind me to the north. Robins returned each spring, as well as crows. The large cottonwood trees became home to many varieties of chattering creatures.

I grew fond of these living beings, but they were not as dear to me as the repeating generations of the family I had sheltered for over one hundred years. I planned to embrace this new family with all the hospitality I could project. But it was not to be. As Dennis Dickenson walked around my perimeter, he rattled to his assistant:

"The well is good, the trees provide wonderful shade, and the apple orchard appears to be productive. Tearing down this old dilapidated building will provide a good site for the new hunting lodge."

I was shocked and insulted. He apparently did not know of the rich history I hold in my walls. I have a record of deeds, feelings, plots, and plans that have occurred over a century. Did he not realize that I'm the "Grand Lady of the Valley", a name attached to me years ago and still my identity among the residents of the area?

I was alarmed as he drove away in his red pickup. His conversation on that day informed me he was from another state; the history of this area mattered little. He planned to develop a dude ranch that would also serve as a hunting lodge. It wouldn't be profitable to restore me for that purpose.

I fell into despondency. I longed to talk to my sister, Aspen; her existence ended long ago. Where her rock walls once stood now lay a mound of rocky dirt, covered by the prairie grass that originally grew on her roof. Big Red, the barn, was unresponsive. He now barely existed, evacuated, even by the wildlife. It was time, I reasoned, that I too should return to Mother Earth. I resigned myself to the foreseeable future, but sadness as I'd never known before oozed from my wooden cells.

I gazed out, as I did frequently, toward the family cemetery near the orchard, at a dozen graves of my loved ones, buried over the first 100 years of my existence. Helen and William, my creators and builders, lay side-by-side, with stones bearing their names and dates of their births and deaths. The deep-set letters and numbers were hand chiseled by their son, who also rested there. The plots were now overgrown with tall grass, as tumbleweed entangled the stones. It was dear to me. When I no longer existed, who would watch over these memories, and love them?

A few weeks later, the women appeared. They walked around my premises and searched through my rooms. They were cheerful. I felt their respect, and their sensitivity to me in the conversation held in my now empty front parlor. I would later learn they were members of the local historical society.

"It would be a crime to tear down the 'Grand Lady, one said

"Certainly", the second woman answered, "We must find a way to detour this plan!"

The third woman, who was busy taking pictures stated, "We'll show these at the next meeting and arrange a committee to find a solution. Our vicinity can't continue to lose these wonderful old landmarks".

As they pulled out of my drive, I was ecstatic.

Yes, they would stop the death sentence pronounced upon me. I would be restored and live again. I watched each day with expectation.

With each sound of an approaching vehicle, I anticipated their return. But each time, it continued to passed on by. Then came the day when the big diesel truck, long flat bed, and workers, arrived. I realized then, that the historical society's solution was to me, worse than death.

Over the next 24 hours, men mercilessly ripped my aging frame from my crumbling foundation, and hoisted it onto the massive beams secured to the flatbed. They tore the climbing yellow rose vines that covered my south walls, and left them to wither in the late spring sun.

The workers trampled the remaining red tulips that graced the path to my front door, planted generations before. The creatures, my only companions, ran for their lives. The skunk family under my porch, however, put up a brave resistance, sending workers fleeing in all directions.

At last the truck started moving, pulling my quaking form behind. I sobbed and heaved with grief.

Where were they taking me? What's the reason? Was this just another way to destroy me, but with slow agonizing torture?

Creeping down the gravel road, pulled by the foul-smelling diesel, I watched my loved ones in their resting places slip further and further from me. The mother doe peeked out inquisitively from behind an apple tree. Crows flew in frantic circles above the cottonwoods and aspens, loudly proclaiming the alarm. Nevertheless, there was no reversing my destiny, now determined by the progress of the modern world.

After a while my panic turned to rage. I'd felt rage expressed by others, and had recorded it, but I had not experienced the emotion as my own.

How dare anyone be so bold as to disrupt time, and its natural progression? How could humans be so heartless as to remove a house from her family memories and cemetery? How could the last of my family carelessly sell me without assuring my survival? The notorious 'Grand Lady of the Valley' dragged from the valley is unconceivable.

By the time the truck had turned from the highway to progress ever so slowly down Main Street, in Lander, my anger completely overcame my reason. The ten block Main Street was cleared for my humiliating passage. With all the energy I could pull from my vast storage, I heaved myself from the trailer frame.

Never having physically attempted to move myself before, I had no idea how much propelled motion this would require. Therefore, I didn't manage to free myself completely. Rather, only one side, and about one third of myself, struck the pavement.

It caused a massive jolt to the equipment and a shattering noise. Window glass splattered to the ground. A worker yelled, "STOP!"

For hours they worked to reinstate me to my previous loaded position. I was uncooperative in every way I could conceive. I dropped my front door on the foot of the master mover, sending him to the emergency room with several broken toes. I hurled debris, loose shutters, and window trim, at spectators, and managed to break one shop window in the eighth block.

It was not a proud day, but at least I would convey my opinion of their thoughtless plan for my fate.

Eventually we were on our way again. I'd listened to the grumblings of the movers and the comments of the spectators while the project remained grounded in town. I learned the historical society had paid to have me moved to prevent the wrecking ball from its intended use.

There wasn't enough money to restore me at this time or to set me up in a respectable place as a museum. They would, however, set me on vacant property and wait for a later time to include me in a long-term plan of building a historical district for the community. Therefore, I was roughly unloaded, positioned on blocks, and left all alone on the desert edge of the valley, miles from my birthplace, and those I loved.

I settled into my new setting, and braced myself against the cold mountain winds that rolled in from the Wind River Mountains. On other days, the sun beat mercilessly on my roof, long accustomed to shade.

I gazed out over the dry unadorned countryside, already missing the familiar surroundings: the apple orchard, Big Red, the ruins of sister Aspen, the cottonwoods, and, of course, the graves in the aspen grove. Only the memories of a long happy past sustained me. Often I allowed them to lead me back to the days of my youth, my beginnings.

Chapter Two

BEGINNINGS-1875

*"It's because of anxiety that we have assurance,
and because of sorrow, that laughter is cherished"*

If houses had birthdays, mine would be August 27, 1875. That was the day William started the first fire in my hearth, and Helen boiled the first pot of water for tea. They spent the first night in my embrace. They were my mother and father, creators and builders, the purpose for which I exist.

Those who are sensitive to the memory vibration of buildings know that the fibers of each structure remain filled with embedded fragments of sounds, visions, feelings, even scents. Energy of spirits, rhythms of memories of those still living, those past, and those in transition, make up the composite of the memories I'm sharing with you.

Unlike your human mind, that can willfully forget unpleasant experiences, or reconstruct those that are regretted, my remembrances are solid. They remain as dense as the oak boards on my floors, as tight as the square nails in my rafters, and they cling to me like the plaster in the wooden ribs of my walls.

However, in 1875, I had no memories, only a wonderment as I watched my parents shape me into what they'd dreamed of, their perfect house. I have great sorrow for houses that are unloved, for until recent years I felt loved. I first felt it on this day. I know I was beautiful because Helen said so as she stepped inside and looked around at my completed state.

She'd watched and nurtured my construction from the first sawed board until the last driven nail. A few arguments occurred during my development. Very early, I remember Helen insisting on a certain placement of a wall, and William, in his frustration, explaining that her choice would not be structurally sound. In the end William had won, but not without compromising the placement of my hearth and chimney. Of course, the meaning of this was not clear to me; I didn't fully understand my life plan until my birthday, when William and Helen Yingling moved in.

Back then, Wyoming was young and settlers were few. Those who took up the challenge of homesteading had little time to build houses. Proving the land and setting up a quick cabin took most of the short summer. Storing up enough wood to heat the long dark days and nights of winter consumed the rest of their time. My parents were fortunate.

Helen's younger brother, Duncan Kenyan, and his wife, Amadhay, came north to assist them, and eventually proved their own land. Duncan had explored Oklahoma with a friend, found work at a trading post, and met Amadhay. He brought with them a used army tent obtained by trading furs. This served as home for the younger couple during the summer of my construction. The expected arrival of winter made my completion of great importance. My parents moved in with me, and the Kenyans moved into the stone cabin.

Amadhay was a quiet young woman, barely nineteen years old. She was Native American, with a slender build. Her long black hair and dark eyes were a strong contrast to Helen's red hair and ivory skin. Her name, she told Helen, meant "forest water." Helen thought it beautiful, but called her Maddie, as did Duncan.

I had the distinction of being the first of my kind. The nearest two-story family house was in Rock Springs. Even South Pass, except for its Grand Hotel, had nothing as nice as me. Not hurriedly assembled of mortar and stone like my older sister, Aspen. Instead, I was made of flat boards, wooden shingles, and I had glass windows looking out toward the snowy Wind River Mountain Range.

My older sister's stone walls were mortared, with a mixture of mud, grass, and dung, to keep out the wind and cold drafts. Her floor was the bare earth. Her roof was made of boards and prairie sod that grew grass when the rains came. I hoped she would not feel resentful of my long, covered, wrap-around porches. William used the last of his savings, brought with him from the east, to assure his wife and future children would have comfort.

My small, humble sister didn't mind. She was proud that she had protected the Yinglings during their first year in the wilderness, kept them warm throughout the hard winter, and witnessed the planning of me, before I had any existence at all. She looked forward to the Kenyans' move-in, and the memories they would make. She, of course, would record them.

My cabin sister had no formal name so I called her Aspen. She liked that. Although her tiny structure was mostly made of stone, aspen poles supported her roof, and trimmed her windows and door. She was a proud structure, so 'Aspen' she became.

Before the moving day my memories are scattered, intermittent, and a bit confusing, but after that, they are clear and vivid. That day started very early. The sun was turning the sky pink and gold as William began the task of fitting the glass panes into the windowsills.

Duncan had gone straight to the fields to stack hay, and move it by wagonloads to the barn for the winter. William would soon join him. Helen and Maddie cheerfully chatted as they moved items from Aspen, to me, as fast as they could carry them.

"Now you may hang those lovely curtains you worked so hard to make this summer," Maddie commented.

Helen smiled. Of course houses read thoughts as readily as we hear words. In house talk, it's called sifting. Helen's musings at that moment were of a large brick home and a plump older lady. I would learn later that the cloth for the curtains was a gift from her mother when she left her childhood home, in Maryland.

I instantly loved Helen. Her sunny nature was the inspiration William had relied on while designing and building me. A more demanding woman, and less flexible man, might have met with impasse and embedded negative vibrations in my development. But this was not the case. Much of my attitude as a 'happy house' is because of Helen.

This was the first day I could really study her. She had a delicate face that was usually smiling. And that was good, because when she felt sorrow, William was sorely distressed. Helen was 25 this day of my christening, and would soon deliver her second child. I knew she loved me, because she said so as she walked, skipped, and turned round and round, in my parlor.

She restrained her thick red hair recklessly into a knot at the top of her head. Not willing to remain secure, the curls released themselves, one ringlet at a time. These framed her pale complexion and gray blue eyes most becomingly. Helen was small in stature, but not in spirit. She didn't believe in the impossible most of the time.

As the two women unpacked dishes of various sizes and shapes, they placed them on the wooden shelves in my kitchen. Helen explained each one to Maddie. She hadn't used them while living in Aspen; she'd kept them safely packed away for this day.

"This piece belonged to my grandmother. She brought it from Scotland. Oh, just look at this green bowl! It was my Irish grandfather's favorite. Of course, we must put Willie's Mama's teapot in the front. Willie is her favorite child of the five, you know. At least it seemed that way to me."

As Helen unpacked the items from the trunk, Maddie carefully arranged them. Maddie's parents died from the fever when she was twelve. The kind owners of the trading post raised her, providing her some schooling, and work, at the post. She spent time with her extended Cherokee families as well, and learned much of their customs, legends, and skills.

She understood how meaningful these memories were to Helen. And of course, I recorded them accurately because it is my responsibility to keep up with this sort of thing; history, that is.

As the morning turned to a hot mid-day, the women began to tire. Their exhaustion caused silliness, and every mishap they encountered resulted in laughter. That is the moment I discovered that I like laughter. The way it rings through my rooms, bounces off my walls, and echoes everywhere, gives me great contentment.

The wood burning cook stove William ordered from the east arrived by freight wagon from Rock Springs. He and Duncan brought it, along with panes of window glass from Atlantic City, in William's wagon.

Helen hummed as she drove nails in my wall, '*My how that tickled,*' so that she could hang the iron pans and kettles around her new stove.

The women had difficulty fitting the wooden rocking chair through the door until they arrived at the idea they must turn it various ways to wiggle it through. Then the greatest challenge was tackled, the bed. Constructed of a board frame, its' attached legs held it above the floor.

The wives looped rope around the frame and pulled the winding as tightly as they could. Fresh straw, stuffed into a large linen bag, served as ticking for the mattress. This item created a challenge as it was awkward to drag through the front door and up the narrow stairs into the largest bedroom.

Helen's round protruding belly made her arms seem incredibly short and they collapsed on the stairs in a fit of merriment. Laughter was beautiful. I recorded it carefully; it might prove useful.

At this time, William and Duncan stepped onto my porch. Duncan gave William a quizzical look. William was smiling. He also loved Helen's laughter, and he was proud that they were moving in before winter. Duncan smiled; he was happy his young wife had found such a close friend and companion in his sister Helen.

Amongst the four of them, the overstuffed mattress took its rightful place. Helen dressed it with freshly washed, and sun dried, bedding prepared for this day, while the Kenyans busied themselves moving and arranging their few, but adequate, belongings into Aspen's waiting arms.

William splashed away the field dust using a basin of water on my porch. He then started a small fire in the hearth. He was gratified that my chimney properly pulled the smoke upward and out. Helen avoided the cook stove. The late summer heat was still too intense to cause such a rise in temperature so soon before going to bed. Rather, she brought the kettle and a pot, and placed them over the open fire in the hearth. The aroma of coffee was delightful; I absorbed it.

Duncan and Maddie returned, and the four gathered to have their first meal with me.

"I must build more furniture during the winter," William noted. "And we'll leave that little table in the cabin for the two of you. I'll build a bigger one for this kitchen."

That evening, sitting on the floor by my hearth, my family feasted on warmed over beans from the day before, cold cornbread, and hot coffee. It was a banquet for them. At last, we were all together. Later when my parents were alone, they cuddled together, watching the last of the embers fade.

Helen broke the silence, "Willie, I must confess something."

William, face relaxed as it had been thoughtful, "Darling, whatever could you have to confess?"

"I am fearful."

"About the baby . . . ." William's reply was a statement, not a question, because he knew what her answer would be.

"Having a child is so joyous," she continued. "Losing Eli was so dreadful!" Silent tears emerged and slowly wound their way down her cheeks.

William pulled her closer and laid his head on her disassembled locks. His face was sober and I sifted through his thoughts and memories. A few years ago, as clergy of the small parish in Iowa, he believed he had all the answers. Back then he would have provided assurance that prayer would guarantee this child would not die.

As a graduate medical student in Maryland, before meeting Helen, he would have had the self-reliance to offer encouragement. Medicine in the hands of a confident doctor could avoid such a tragedy. But despite all his training, he could not rely on any of it. To offer assurance, he must first believe it, and he no longer did, not in miracles, prayers, or medicine.

He gently wiped the tears from her cheeks and said softly, "Helen, I can only give you one promise. Whatever the future holds, in the best of times, and in the worse, I will be with you."

He picked up the candle from my mantle, reached for his wife's hand, and led her to the stairs.

I was stunned. For the first time in my young life, I felt anxiety, even sorrow. I didn't like it. I liked laughter better. Sorrow penetrated into my very foundation, and released negative vibrations that seeped through my entire structure. *I felt a chill.*

In time, I understood that life must have both. It's because of anxiety that we have assurance, and because of sorrow, that laughter is cherished.

In the coming years, I relied on that laughter, and replayed it over and over again.

Chapter Three

WILLIAM AND HELEN

*"I gathered and combined memories and information,
which in house terms is called meshing"*

It took me longer to get acquainted with William. He was not in my presence as continually as Helen. He also was not as expressive, which forced me to rely on sifting. Sometimes I needed to absorb his emotion to understand his thoughts. This is a skill that requires sensitivity, and focus, from a house.

I was still young and inexperienced. Often, just when I began a clear reading of William, Helen would start humming a delightful melody, and I would become lost in what she was doing.

I learned a lot about him in the stories Helen shared with Maddie as they worked side by side throughout the day. At other times, Duncan, as animated and inquisitive as his sister, wormed information from him. Still yet, Duncan, who also shared many of their experiences through acquaintance, discussed matters with Helen when William was outside, or busy elsewhere.

I gathered and combined memories and information, which in house terms is called 'meshing'.

William was a second child, as well as a second son. His family migrated from Germany before the Revolutionary War. In fact, the early Yinglings fought in that war. They arrived in America financially comfortable; they were merchants in the old country. In Maryland, William's father, Christian Yingling, joined partnership with the Kenyans, and established a mill. This venture was successful, and both families made gains.

Growing up around the mill, William was aware of Helen, five years younger. He avoided her in their youth, as she was an annoying child, rowdy, and playful, to a fault. It was she who started the hated-nickname, Willie. He insisted on the baptismal name, William, and throttled his siblings who dared take up the practice. However, time, and love for Helen, changed his attitude about the pet name. Her gentle way of using it was endearing.

The Yingling family was proud of the mill and its success. William, however, had a different dream for his future; he worked less at the mill, leaving his older brother, Joshua, to take over the responsibility. Christian, a firm father, demanded that his son be supportive of the family business while his mother, Margaret, defended his right to pursue a different path. In the end, William continued with his education.

William's perception of himself as being cut from a different cloth than Joshua started quite young. As a small child he quickly learned reading, writing, and sums, long before his older brother, Joshua. He loved the stories from the Bible, and read them to his younger brothers and sister. He enjoyed time in study, and learning new things.

The family attended the Methodist-Episcopal church. During his childhood, a missionary from an assignment in India spoke at his church. He talked about the shortage of medical services, the high death rate from disease, and the shortage of medicine. William determined on that day that he would become a missionary to India.

His mother defended his dream. "William isn't cut out for the mill," she insisted.

William became obsessed with this mysterious land. He had already contemplated a study of medicine. Now, he reasoned, with encouragement from the campus clergy, combining his studies to include seminary. This would ensure acceptance by a mission board to a post in India. He completed his studies at Drew Theological University.

Many were the hopeful smiles of available young ladies, in both communities, toward this tall, brown-eyed scholar. William, however, would not be distracted. He had a call, and he must answer it.

During the final year of study, a strange malady developed; a persistent cough that would not subside long enough to attend a day of classes was present. It sometimes caused wheezing and difficulty breathing. William's doctor treated him, but to no avail. This mysterious illness soon brought an end to his dream. The mission board would not commit to the sponsorship of an ailing man to a faraway land.

Angry and disappointed, William returned to the mill; he did bookkeeping, collected debts, and pondered what he would do to replace a life of foiled plans. There he took new notice of the now matured and beautiful Helen. At twenty, she was no longer a rowdy child, but a bright, happy, young woman; William was smitten. Even her insistence on calling him Willie was tolerable. They wed in the spring of 1870.

William's doctor, and the medical school professor, theorized that moving to a different climate might be helpful for him. His own research reinforced it. They reasoned environment most likely contributed to the illness of his lungs. To do this, and support a wife, he must have an occupation. This dilemma was resolved by accepting a post as pastor in a small parish in Kellogg, Iowa.

Moving westward, and settling into the parsonage with his bride, helped to dissipate his bitter disappointment from the previous year. His health improved. Then Eli was born. He was the light of their lives.

Sitting by the fire in the evening, watching Helen sing a lullaby as she rocked him to sleep, warmed the broken heart of the young reverend. His long held dream of India became a diminishing thought in the very distant past. His only concern was that the town had no doctor, and William soon found that the need for medicine was as critical as the need for ministry.

He tried to carry the responsibility of both. It was the summer of 1873, that the dreadful disease, diphtheria, took the town like a storm. Knowing how contagious the disease would be before the epidemic would pass, William quarantined the parsonage; he didn't allow Helen to leave, or permit anyone to come in.

William was up for long hours each day making the rounds to households touched by the sickness. Other days were involved in the funerals of those he was unable to save. Deaths were so rapid the undertaker could barely keep up with making caskets. William turned over the small wooden boxes, in which his medicines were shipped from the east, and he used them as coffins for infants. Helen cut up her wedding dress, and silk petticoats, to line the babies' caskets.

There were hours spent comforting the grieving. Some nights he could hardly stay awake to guide his horse home. It was his coming and going, he reasoned, that brought the illness to Eli. In spite of all William could do, using prayer and medicine, the two-year-old weakened and slipped from their love, and their lives. Following the funeral, William held the weeping Helen and vowed, "I will never preach, or practice medicine, again."

Heartbroken, the couple returned to Maryland. The mill was as dreary as he remembered it to be. William felt he had failed on every level, and he was humiliated that the town's people knew it. He was more than willing to move west again when he heard about the open land in Wyoming. A talk with his ailing father secured his bequest and his father's blessing. They kissed their parents goodbye and started a new life with William's share of the inheritance, provided to him even before his father's passing.

This is the reason my family came to settle in Wyoming: the place they would build me, and raise a child to carry on their dream. Months of listening, sifting, and meshing, made William's pain real to me. At times, when a cold dismal mood brought in the chill, I would know William was wrestling with his memories, broken vows, and regrets, and I recorded them.

Several weeks after that first day, William brought the cradle in. It had served both Helen and Duncan as infants, and was the bed for Eli during his first year. Although it had moved west, it was stored in the wagon, then in the barn, out of Helen's sight. William did not want sad reminders for Helen. He watched her closely as he positioned it before my fireplace. She surprised us. Stroking the pinewood for a short while, and wiping a tear, she looked up at William with a smile.

"What do you think, Willie? Will we fill it with a boy or a girl?"

"I'm sure it will be one or the other," he responded with a smile.

On that day, the air changed. A *new* feeling of hope presided. I liked hope. Hope makes days exciting, and nights restful. Maddie began working on a cradleboard for the baby. She convinced Helen that it provided a safer, and better, support for an infant, rather than holding him only in arms, or laying him on a surface.

Helen knitted every idle moment: sweaters, booties, caps, and coverlets. She was thankful her granny had insisted on tucking the fine yarn in and around the dishes in her trunk. It was difficult to find yarn out here in Wyoming. Although some ranchers raised sheep, and raw wool was available, it was coarse and difficult to work with. Sometimes women unraveled old sweaters and hats to retrieve yarn and recycle it. Her child would begin life with new soft clothing next to tender baby skin.

Duncan and William spent many hours chopping and stacking wood from cottonwood logs they dragged from the river's edge. During autumn William finished the table and it was a fine piece. Unlike the crude, rough one left with Aspen, he smoothed the surfaces with his wood plane. There would be no splinters for little hands from this table and its benches.

These were the days of anticipation. I recorded them.

Chapter Four

CHRISTINA

"In unity, there is safety. Fear is not a healthy state of mind"

The days grew short but, I lived up to the expectations. I kept out the wind and cold, and held in the warmth. The house carried the aroma of baking bread and potatoes frying on the stove. In the evenings, the smoke streaming from William's pipe added its own allure. All these were saved in my fibers.

Helen learned quickly to manage the stove, and tirelessly prepared meals for the two couples, and any weary traveler in need of a meal. Duncan hunted often and there was never a shortage of venison, rabbit, and an occasional sage chicken. Maddie learned bread-making from Helen and in return taught Helen how to dry meat for preservation.

With howling winds outside, I held my shutters tight. Snow piled around my porch, almost burying poor Aspen. Duncan and Maddie moved in with us until the worst of it was over. I felt sad for Aspen; she must be lonely there all by herself. I tried to encourage her by passing on the memories I was recording from conversations transpiring within my walls.

On these nights everyone sat around the hearth, Helen knitting, Maddie stitching quilt blocks, William reading by candlelight, and Duncan playing the violin. As the soft melodies of Irish ballads and German hymns glided through the air currents, I felt unity. I like unity. In unity, there is safety.

It was on such a night the miracle occurred. The 1st day of December would be her birthday, six months after mine. William moved the bed to the parlor to provide Helen with the necessary warmth from my fireplace. He sat at her side as they waited for their new arrival. Sifting Helen's thoughts, I learned more of her admiration and devotion to her husband.

As she held his hand she thought, 'They have such hard calluses, and just look at these scars. He has acquired them since coming to the wilderness.'

As she thought back to the birth of Eli, I sifted her memories. 'The hands that held Eli were the soft smooth hands of a scholar, the delicate fingers of a man trained to perform surgery. They treated wounds, and brought healing. They were also the hands of a minister, hands clasped in prayer at the bedside of a dying man, or softly patting the head of his grieving child. But now these are working hands.'

She lifted his hand to her lips and kissed the palm. 'I don't care what work he chooses,' she thought, 'but I can't help but wonder if he is happy with this rugged physical work when he has such a bright mind that could be doing what it was trained to do.'

Christina was born on this night. Delivered by her father, she belted out her first wailing cry at midnight, demonstrating to us that she was a healthy determined little lady. She was named for her grandfather, Christian.

"See, Helen, my love. She is a healthy rambunctious baby girl. I would guess her weight at 7 lbs., a bit bigger than Eli." He placed the babe in his wife's arms and kissed her cheek.

That night I felt joy and celebration. It made the air flow through my rooms like a gentle breeze. I liked it, and recorded it. As my family slept I hummed the tunes I had heard Duncan play on the violin.

Days passed, and weeks turned into months. Wyoming was experiencing spring. With spring there is mud as the frozen ground melts and ice turns to water. Boots, covered with the sticky muck, remained on the porch. Coyotes and their pups yipped from the riverside in the late evening and early morning hours.

The grass on Aspen's roof turned green and geese returned to linger in the river before flying further north. Duncan spent days at the river, hunting them. The women were pleased to have down and feathers to make pillows. The aroma of baked goose filled the house, and the grease was saved to use for various lubricants. The women dried some of the meat.

As they worked, Christina was placed in her cradle, or cradle board, near the hearth to assure she escaped drafts. I hummed melodies for her down my chimney. They were my own original lullabies composed of combinations of Duncan's folk songs, hymns, and Helen's lullabies. I had to modify these to the various tones available by whistling down my flue.

Sleep now baby, little girl
May God's peace be near
I hold you in safekeeping, child.
You needn't ever fear.

Christina always calmed and smiled when I sang this to her. I always hummed it to her at night when she awoke. I chuckled when William commented how soundly their new baby slept at night, not keeping them awake as most newborns do.

With the coming of spring, supplies dwindled, but mud prevented travel to town. Duncan had preserved the hides of all the animals harvested for food. Maddie had completed a lovely quilt from scraps of cloth. They traded these items at the fort's supply store during winter, for flour, salt, sugar, tea, and lard. Now Duncan and William rationed their pipe tobacco to make it last. Maddie had discovered chokecherry trees near the river in the fall and skinned bark for tea. Helen acquired a taste for it and often preferred it to regular tea.

During the quiet evenings, the discussions often addressed the local events, both recent and past. News passed among neighbors as they stopped by on their visits to town. On rare occasions William or

Duncan went for supplies, and brought home news. Sometimes they interacted with soldiers at Fort Stambaugh and Fort Brown, providing an opportunity to gather information. These forts served to protect miners and settlers in the area.

From listening to these tales, I learned that the area had opened up partly due to the discovery of gold ten years earlier. This discovery led to the development of the town, South Pass City, and the Carissa Mine. Its name came from the name of the route where it was located; it passed over the Wind River Mountain Range. Almost immediately the population grew to over two thousand people. This was with great sacrifice, however, since Indians killed a number of miners.

The local tribe of Shoshone remained peaceful with settlers and miners. Traveling bands from other tribes passed through the area following game, and considered the area to be their hunting grounds.

After Lt. Charles Stambaugh died in such an attack in 1868, the newly-built fort completed in 1870, and located near the town, bore his name. It did not prove to be enough protection, however. In one attack, a large portion of South Pass City burned down. Duncan said Stambaugh looked more like a camp than a fort, but the men enjoyed visiting when they picked up the glass, and stove, in nearby Atlantic City.

One evening as William and Duncan sat on my front porch smoking their pipes, they discussed one of these incidents. Duncan asked, "How are the Barr, Morgan, and Mason families doing?"

"Not good," answered William, "But how could they be? After losing husbands, fathers, and friends in such a horrid massacre! The men put up a brave fight, but they were surrounded."

"Where did this happen, exactly?" asked Duncan.

"On Willow Creek, halfway between Popo Agie and the Little Popo Agie rivers, the usual route for supply wagons," explained William.

"Dr. Barr tended to the needs of the people here for years. They relied on him," replied Duncan.

"Yes, and that's why they sent for me," stated William.

"Do they know who attacked them?" asked Duncan. "I heard they think it was Arapaho, about two hundred, in fact."

"That is what I heard, but I'm not sure it's been decided for sure," answered William. "Several different tribes pass through for hunting and it may have been such a band."

Duncan gave William a sympathetic glance, "I know you don't want to practice medicine, William. I'm sure it is difficult being called in for medical services and consultation, especially with something like this. I mean, the torture; it was terrible."

"Yes, it was," William shook his head. "I've witnessed much death, Duncan, but never where it was delivered with such suffering."

"Is the gossip I heard at the Mercantile true? Did they drive the queen bolt from his wagon right through Mr. Morgan's head?" Duncan ventured to ask.

"Yes, as well as other horrid acts of torture. They also stripped the sinews from his back and limbs, probably for bow strings. I advised the sheriff to discourage the families from looking at their bodies. There is no need to burden them with such a dreadful memory; the loss is enough to manage."

"Harvey Morgan was a fine, honest man," commented Duncan, shaking his head sadly. "He had always been friendly to the tribes, and had many friends among them."

"These were outlaws, pure and simple," stated William. "They're about stealing, and killing becomes a part of it. There are good and bad among all people."

"I heard that the same band of raiders struck the Barrett ranch. That big one there in Red Canyon," continued Duncan.

"The two attacks were so close in distance, and time frames, it had to be the same band of warriors," concluded William.

"But Mr. Barrett was able to get his family into his stone front dugout and put up a good defense until they left. He did get a bullet through his beard, that was a narrow miss," he added.

"Do you think these raiding bands will be back through? Do you think they will prey on the homesteaders?" Duncan's voice revealed his concern.

"There's always a chance in the wilderness, Duncan," answered William.

Rising, he walked to the edge of the porch and emptied his pipe. Slipping it into his pocket, he added, "I think the wives should remain in the house for a while. One of us should always be here, but those men in the wagon supply party were all armed, and still unable to defend themselves."

"I guess this is the risk we take when we pioneer," mused Duncan, as he emptied his pipe. "We move in, dig gold on their hunting land, stretch fences across their open spaces, build towns on their rivers, why would they not be angry?" I knew Duncan held some sense of fairness, having married a Cherokee maid.

"I don't want our women frightened," stated William. "They must be aware, and cautious. But fear is not a healthy state of mind. This horrid massacre happened because certain things occurred at the same time. The men were taking supply wagons to Fort Augur. They had passed through the Wind River Basin many times before without incident. But on this occasion they, by chance, encountered a band of renegades."

"You know what my biggest worry is?" asked Duncan, tugging on his beard.

"Mob action?" William returned to sit in the porch rocker.

"There is some angry talk around town," added Duncan. "That band of warriors quickly moved on, probably miles from here. If some of these big-talkers get liquored up and decide to get revenge on the first Indians they see, more innocents will die."

"We can't let that happen," said William. "We are at peace with the Shoshone and they also depend on the Fort to protect them from raids, from these roaming bands. We have to keep peace. I have spoken with the clergy in town, and the sheriff. They are going to address this in sermons and conversations throughout the town. I also talked with the editor of the paper. He is going to address it in all reports; these murders were not caused by anyone from around here."

"When we hear that kind of ignorant talk, we have to stand against it," added Duncan.

Helen stepped out on the porch. "Are you two planning to stay out here all night? I've a fresh pot of tea made." The husbands followed Helen into the house, but their conversation haunted me.

The next morning Duncan came home from town and announced that the town of South Pass was raided. Two hundred horses and mules were taken from prospectors there.

"Are they forming a posse?" asked William.

"A Lieutenant from *Fort Washakie*, a man by the name of Robinson, is taking a company of the 2nd Cavalry to pursue them. They've already left," informed Duncan.

"We will just have to be on the ready," answered William. Guns were loaded, and kept near the men, but life continued through its daily routines.

I discussed it with Aspen, who had also heard the grisly tale just related on my porch. We pondered together, 'What could we do to protect our families?' Very little, we concluded. As the lamps were blown out, and the couples settled into slumber, my core was filled with fear.

This was new for me. I understood why William had said, "Fear is not a healthy state of mind."

Some days later we heard that the renegade warriors were not captured, but in fact, got away.

* The massacre described in this chapter, did occur and is part of Fremont Co. history.

Chapter Five

CONFESSION

"Guilt can't be healthy for a human, or a house"

Maddie and Duncan's baby arrived in late spring. They named him Augustus, and we called him Gus. Christina loved the new baby, and his name was one of her first words. She called him "Yus". Of course I loved him, too. I taught Aspen the lullaby, but she had difficulty singing it down her stovepipe.

Learning how to garden kept the woman challenged, the first summer in my memory. They planted in mid-May only to have late frosts wither and kill the young plants. The peas and root crops made some success, but the rabbits raided the produce nightly.

There was little produce remaining to harvest. Maddie was accustomed to the longer seasons in the southern region, and Helen did not understand the soil conditions that were very different from Maryland's rich black soil, long conditioned from rotting trees of old forests. Had it not been for Duncan's skillful hunting, and Maddie's foraging, their tables would have been empty.

Duncan dug up young cottonwood trees from the river's edge and young aspen from the higher elevation and planted them around my perimeter. Maddie insisted on planting a dead trout with each one. They bucketed water to them every day.

Maddie was delighted when, after long walks, she was able to report that many wild edible plants she had gathered in her childhood were here also; she gathered mushrooms during the wet spring. Some, they immediately prepared for food, while others they dried and stashed away. They would use them to season soups and roasts of wild game later. She showed Helen Lamb's Quarter, sometimes referred to as Pig Weed. The leaves were tasty as well as nutritious.

"This tastes just like spinach," Helen commented, the first time she prepared it.

"And we can dry the seeds for seasoning," explained Maddie.

She scouted out wild asparagus near the river, and transplanted some of the young plants into the garden plots. Streams off the river provided watercress. She gathered wild mint and dried it for tea. This, she contended, was a great tonic for illness with nausea, as well as a refreshing beverage, both hot and room temperature. When Cristina or Gus had a rash, she bathed them in warm water heavily saturated with mint tea.

"Maddie, you are so good with these herbal medicines. I should hand over my medical degree to you," William teased as he watched her hanging bundled herbs from the porch eves to dry.

Maddie smiled, "I can prepare teas and potions to relieve discomfort, but I would be lost with a scalpel in my hand."

William smiled at her and walked into the house. He was troubled; I could feel it. Helen noticed it as well. She walked up to him and put her arms around him, "What's troubling my Willie boy?"

William was silent, but he pulled her close to him. When he spoke he said, "I had to preach a funeral last week."

"What? Where? How?" His wife pulled back and looked up into his dark brown eyes.

He released his wife, walked over to one of the chairs in the parlor, and sat down. Helen sat in the other. Christina, playing on the floor with wooden blocks William had made for her, ceased her play and crawled to his feet.

"Papa," she said, raising her tiny chubby arms to him.

He picked her up and settled her onto his lap. "It was in Atlantic City. Word is out that I'm a doctor, even though I have tried to avoid anyone knowing. The day I went to pick up those supplies I ordered through the freight station, I had just gotten everything loaded in my wagon, when suddenly the Blacksmith came running to me in alarm."

Helen was focused on his face, hanging onto every word. *So was I.* Christina was trying to dislodge his pocket watch from his vest pocket. He pulled it out and allowed her to examine it with her tiny hands.

"He was screaming, 'Please hurry!! My son caught fire!' Several of us ran to his shop. And there the child lay. He was about twelve, I would presume. The father had extinguished the flames on his shirt and trousers with a bucket of water, but he was badly burned all over his body. That father cried and begged me to do something to save his son."

William stood up, took his daughter, and placed her in Helen's lap. She still had his watch. He walked over to the door, placed his right arm against the frame, and then laid his head against his arm.

Uh oh. I'm feeling something here; it isn't fear, or celebration, or unity, or . . . I don't like it.

Helen took the watch from Christina, and placed it on top of her knitting basket by her chair. She set the child down by her blocks and went to her husband. "Did the child die?" she asked softly.

William nodded his head. "I told them to fetch a doctor, but they said they have none, presently. I had nothing on hand to treat the child, not even something to ease his pain. He died before I could get him carried to his home, across the alley way."

"Willie, I know this is horribly upsetting, but surely you aren't blaming yourself?"

William straightened up, wiped tears from his face, and turned toward Helen. "I guess I am. When I practiced medicine, I went nowhere without my bag. I could have at least given him Laudanum so his last thirty minutes would be easier."

"You said there was a funeral?" Helen prompted.

William returned to his chair. "Yes, the town also does not have a minister at this time. I can't believe there is such a shortage of doctors, teachers, and clergy here."

He raised his sad eyes to his wife now kneeling before him. "They wanted to have a burial right away; it being hot summer and all. They asked me to speak at his funeral, provide an actual service as soon as his mother and his grandmother could prepare his body, as best they could."

William paused as though he needed a moment to control his shaking voice. "So, the man at the General Store said he had a wooden shipping box that would work for a casket. Then a woman, I think she's part of the Harkin woman's brothel, said she had a silk spread. They wrapped him in the shiny blue spread with long fringe all around it, and placed him in the shipping box. His father nailed it shut. Can you believe that Helen? His own father nailed his makeshift coffin shut."

Helen pulled his larger hand into her small one and gently caressed it. "He must have loved him very much."

"He felt so guilty for having him do a task so close to the forge. The boy's apron was too long and caught fire. His father said he started spinning, causing the rest of his clothing to ignite. He was able to knock him down, and pour the bucket of water on him, a large one sitting there for cooling hot metal. But, although it put out the flames, I am confident the water helped to cause the severe shock the child was in when I got to him."

Helen patiently waited for more, as did I. "Anyway, several men, including his father, grabbed shovels and went directly to the cemetery, right on the edge of town. The clerk at the freight and shipping office had heard that I am ordained. He pressed me to wait, and help them bury their boy. He said the boy's mother was raised religious, and that a real Christian funeral would mean a lot to her."

"I'm proud of you, Willie; you always do what's right," encouraged Helen.

I was sifting, listening, and meshing, trying to figure out what the funeral business was all about. I had heard this word mentioned before in regard to death, but from this event I was learning that when people cease to be, they were placed in a hole in the ground.

William continued, "I told the clerk that I had no Bible with me to read from, but I could probably remember scripture from what I have memorized. Just then the woman who brought the silk, I think her name is Lydia, said that she had a Bible. She quickly left to get it."

"Lydia is the woman from the brothel?" Helen asked.

"Can you believe it?" he asked. "I'm an ordained minister and I am miles from my Bible, yet the harlot and saloon singer has hers right handy."

"Well", Helen smiled, "I guess you never can tell where the word of God will show up."

"By the time we got to the gravesite, word had spread around town that William Yingling, from Fort Brown, was a non-practicing doctor and minister," he explained.

He took a deep cleansing breath, *and so did I.* "Once we were at the gravesite, Miss Lydia whispered to me, 'Do you want me to sing something?' I said, 'What would you like to sing?' I guess I was thinking she might belt out a dance hall tune."

Helen gasped.

William smiled at her and continued, "She turned and looked right at the weeping mother and father and begin singing Amazing Grace. She sang every verse in the most beautiful soprano I have ever heard."

Helen was silent. I think she was trying to piece it all together. "And this is why you didn't get home until long after dark? Why didn't you tell me, Willie?"

William looked back down to his hands, "I have been feeling so guilty, Helen."

Ah-ha. Guilty, or guilt, or whatever it is. That is the awful feeling that is causing my beams to shiver. Well, that's a feeling that needs to stop. I see no use in it at all. It must have to do with regretting something one has done, or didn't do. If that's the case, then one should just undo it or re-do it, or apologize, or something. This can't be healthy for a human, or a house.

"Helen, I have been so bitter. First, about not getting to go to India, and then, about losing Eli. I felt all that happened because I was a failure, at both doctoring, and preaching. But when I got back to the freight building I was walking toward my wagon, and Miss Lydia caught up with me."

She said, "Reverend, I hear that you are a doctor who doesn't doctor, and a preacher who doesn't preach. Is that right?"

I said, 'Yes, madam, I suppose that's the way it is."

Then she said, 'Shame on you! Here we are, all living around here in no-man's land without doctors or ministers, and there you set, right down there in Fort Brown, doing nothing about it. Shame on you!"

"I must tell you, Helen, my mouth was frozen shut."

"Then her voice softened a bit and she said, 'I came here from Pennsylvania. I could have gone to New York City. My singing voice is good enough for the stage. But I decided I was going where people needed music. So you see, I may not be the proper lady you think I should be, singing in a dance hall, and moonlighting at Miss Harkins, but at least I'm not hiding my light under a bushel. Now I'm thinking you need to get over whatever little grudge you have with God, and start shining your light too."

Helen's eyes were huge.

Mine would have been as well, if I had any.

"That's why I feel guilty, Helen, for blaming God, and for refusing to keep my vow to be a healer of body and spirit."

Helen stood up and then set herself on William's lap. She touched his cheek, and pulled it to face her. Looking into the deep brown depths of his eyes, she asked, "Willie, what made you first decide you should go to India?"

"I heard a missionary talk about how desperate people were there, so few doctors, ministers, very little medication . . . ." he stopped without finishing his sentence.

"And here, Willie? Is that not the same situation here? Does God love people in India more than people here? Would he call you there, and not call someone here?"

William cleared his throat. "When I prayed over that child's grave last week, that was the first prayer I have said since Eli passed. But I think I would like to pray right now. Will you pray with me, Helen?"

So there they were, both kneeling in front of the hearth. I can't remember the prayer. What I can remember is that all that guilty emotion, that ugly black cloud, evaporated.

Guilt can't be healthy for a human, or a house, I reasoned.

Chapter Six

BLACK SICKNESS

"I loved the baby's giggles, and I recorded them"

Throughout all the seasons the men kept busy providing food for our expanding families. They hunted deer, elk, moose, rabbit, ducks, and geese, as well as grouse. They fished in the river for trout. The woman worked at keeping the areas clean, and the laundry and food tended.

They dried extra meat for winter stews. The pantry was filled with dried vegetables, mushrooms, and herbs. One shelf was lined with jams made from chokecherries and huckleberries, that the women braved the local bear population to pick.

Lye soap, made from lye and rendered fat from both goose grease and pork lard, was packed in Maddie's homemade baskets. Life became a rhythm of day, weeks, months, and seasons. I did my best to keep us warm in winter and cool during the short summer months. But, regardless of routine, changes occurred.

Fort Brown, the fort and community closest to us, had been without clergy for six months. The Catholic priest returned to the east shortly after arriving, and another had not yet been sent. The Protestant pastor, elderly, and in poor health, retired and moved back to his home state. A replacement was not found for him either.

After William made peace with his vow, he commenced Sunday services at Fort Brown, Atlantic City, Minor's Delight, and South Pass, dividing the weeks among them. But funerals, weddings, and christenings, for many communities that were divided by distance, took much of his time. It was necessary for Duncan to take on more of the ranch responsibilities alone. Maddie, a strong woman, often helped him. Helen looked after the children.

William built a small, square pen-like space for them to play in. This was placed in the back parlor, and in the library. The pen kept them safe, and I kept them amused. I sang to them by blowing wind through the chimney in the back parlor. I waved the curtains and made them appear to dance. I made the pictures, and a mirror, swing back and forth, causing a rattling noise. I loved the baby giggles, and I recorded them.

In the evenings William studied the herbs that Maddie had introduced to him. He wrote down their names and what she used them for. He listed portion sizes, and preparations, in his neat handwriting. Writing fascinated me.

He dipped a tool, called a pen, into black liquid known as ink. Then he swirled and scratched lines and curves across a paper. After a while he pressed a soft pad against the marks. This was blotting I learned. I finally realized that writing, for people, was similar to recording, for me.

Soon after the funeral in Atlantic City, William began to plan his medical practice. It took most of the summer for the books he ordered from the east to reach him. These were doctor books, as well as one very large book containing pictures of various plants and information about them. He referred to it as the botany book. It was this book that held his, and Maddie's, attention by lamplight. They compared her herbs to those in the book. William took meticulous notes about them, memorizing their scientific names.

William also ordered tinctures, salves, ingredients for making medications, and a new doctor bag with needed instruments. Those arrived in early fall. It was September when he brought lumber home in his wagon, to build his treatment room.

As he unloaded the wagon, Helen watched with concern. I sifted her thoughts and knew her feelings were divided. She wanted William to return to his profession, but it required that she sacrifice a chunk of her front parlor.

"So where will the wall be, Willie?" she asked, attempting to hide her concern with a pleasant tone.

William walked to the center of the room. "I will need at least half," he answered, looking around. "I have to have room for shelves, an examining table, and a small cot, for those times someone may need care overnight. I will mostly make house calls, but there will be times when I will need a room to provide treatments. There will be surgeries, bone settings, and stitching of wounds, just like before, Helen."

Noticing her silence, he put his arm around her. "I will have one rule, darling; no contagious diseases will be brought into our house. I won't risk harm to the rest of you. I will treat all such illnesses somewhere else."

Helen placed her arms around him, "I know you will, Willie. I am being selfish, and I'm so sorry. I have a lovely home, and I should not begrudge my front parlor for your work."

"That's what you have been worried about?" he asked in surprised.

"Not anymore," she assured him. "Tell me what I can do to help; shall I make room in the back parlor for some of this furniture?"

Helen was like that. She sorted through her soul daily, rooted out wrong, and didn't allow opportunity for that awful emotion they call guilt.

In mid-September a serious illness moved rapidly through the area. Years later they would refer to it as flu, but then it was called the black sickness. With our isolation, we didn't know how it reached Fort Brown, and the surrounding communities, perhaps through stage travelers.

William was gone constantly, much of two weeks, trying to meet the needs of so many afflicted. Many were ill, and some died, in all the surrounding areas. A log house on the hill behind South Pass was set up as an infirmary, in an attempt to prevent the spread of the malady. At Fort Brown the sick were crowded into the fort's infirmary, and William visited daily.

One warm September day, William and Duncan traveled to Atlantic City and South Pass. William visited patients, and Duncan filled the wagon with wood for winter heating. As they were leaving, a woman on horseback asked if she could ride along with them down the mountain. She introduced herself as Martha Canary. The men thought her a boisterous woman, and she talked incessantly all the way down the mountain. She explained that she owned a laundry house at Fort Brown.

That evening, over a meal of fresh venison, mashed turnips, and biscuits, the men shared their experience with their wives.

"That gal has language that would make a miner blush, and she can talk a mile a minute," Duncan stated.

William chuckled, "If she has been everywhere she says she has, and done everything she says she has done, she would have to be well over a hundred years old," he added.

"If she owns a business at Fort Brown, why was she up in that area alone?" asked Maddie.

"She had been in both communities for weeks nursing the ill," explained William.

"Well then, a very kind lady she must be," decided Helen.

"Kind she is," agreed William, "and efficient. It is my understanding that she has made quite a difference in the survival of people with the sickness, in South Pass."

"Well, kind or not, I wouldn't want her for an enemy," declared Duncan.

William playfully punched his brother-in-law on the arm, "We are just not used to these rowdy western women." Then the doctor continued to relate what they had learned about Miss Canary.

"She said she had experienced days and nights of sleep deprivation as she cared for the sick in South Pass, because she didn't want wives and children to be exposed. Now, she's returning to her town to tend to her laundry business; the soldiers at the Fort are her regular customers. She also described how she had drenched the patients in cool water repeatedly, breaking the fever, rather than wrapping them up and sweating it out, as was the usual custom. I find that rather interesting."

"Her actual words were," added Duncan, "I knowd it sounds contrary, but it was the onlyist thing that worked. I jest got'em cooled off, and poured water on 'em. It brung the strongest ones through it!" Duncan mimicked her slang. "And," he added, "I am leaving out a lot of words not acceptable in this company."

William lifted his cup for Helen to pour more tea. "She also reported that in the past she has served the ill through bouts of typhoid, small pox, measles, and diphtheria, without ever catching the illness. I find that very interesting. She must have a strong constitution."

"Maybe it's the cigar she smokes," suggested Duncan. "Maybe that keeps the sickness away."

William smiled, "That was a strong cigar, and I know it made me want to keep my distance."

After the meal, William quietly checked the cupboard to assess Helen's herbals and teas. The new order for medical supplies was mailed, but it would be weeks before they arrived. The sickness had almost depleted his supply of medicine.

'I'll ask Maggie to gather more mint from the river,' he thought. 'It has proven effective for nausea.'

Maddie believed boiled bark from aspen would lower fevers when served as tea. He would get her to gather some. This would be a good time to test her theory. He was glad to see an ample supply of rose hips.

This, he knew, could enhance a person's resistance to contagious diseases. As he put water on to heat and measured hips and honey into the teapot, Helen remained aware. She knew her husband was remembering the horrible plague that had taken their son. As she stood to help him serve the tonic tea, I enveloped them in my love and protection, while Helen said her silent prayer.

Chapter Seven

CALAMITY

"I think the fear of falling helpless to her care is enough to keep one well"

Two mornings later Maddie ran up to my front door in panic. "Duncan is very sick!" she exclaimed. "May I leave Gus here with you so he won't catch it? I'm sure he's caught the black sickness!"

"Of course." answered William. "And you must stay here as well. I'll take care of him. Helen, start boiling some dried meat for broth, and make some fresh peppermint tea. I'll start him on the rose hip tea. Leave it on the porch. Do not come near the cabin!"

Helen took Gus to the kitchen and set him at the table by Christina. She gave him a slice of bread with jelly, and then started preparing the broth. I could feel her fear. Maddie wrapped up in her shawl, grabbed a pail, and went to gather fresh mint. She hoped that the early frosts had not withered it. William soon returned from checking on Duncan.

"I'm going into town to fetch Miss Canary," he told Helen. "She's been dealing with this, and she's had some success. We will need help if we all come down with it."

Several hours later he returned with Martha Jane, and Helen tended to their horses as they made their way to Aspen. This person was peculiar, I must say. She wore men's clothing, boots, held a cigar in her teeth, and packed a saddle bag with her. They disappeared into Aspen's small room. Soon William returned.

"Well," he said, "I told her I would appreciate a bit of help, but she's forcefully taken over. She ordered me out." He sat on the porch bench. "I'm not coming around the rest of you," he stated. "I was exposed to the same people as Duncan. We will see."

William worked through the day at chores, chopping wood, tending the animals, and he ate and drank only on the porch. Helen reasoned with him that he must come inside to prevent catching a chill, but he refused.

Meanwhile, next door, Martha's voice boomed. She talked as though she believed everyone was hard of hearing. Helen kept the children inside, not only to prevent exposure to the illness, (but also the language) filtering out of Aspen's stone walls.

When the broth was ready William took a pot of it, and some fresh bread, to Aspen's front door. The woman took it, and then ordered him away. He piled chopped wood near the door, and carried several buckets of water, to be within her reach. Maddie worried about her husband.

Soon a fire was burning outside, between Aspen and me. The nurse, now in charge, rigged up Helen's large laundry kettle over the fire, and was dumping in large amounts of Maddie's lye soap. Bubbles poured over the side as she hauled out bedding, and Duncan's clothing. These she put into the soapy water to boil.

She made a concoction from black tea, molasses, and whisky that she had brought in her saddlebag. She yelled to the others on the porch, "Don't know if the whisky helps," she bellowed, "but it'll surely fix his state of mind." With that, she laughed and took a swig straight from the bottle.

Maddie was concerned, "William, does she know what she's doing? She sounds like a mad woman."

William looked a bit worried, too. He hoped that her stories about her recent success in nursing were not an exaggeration. By nightfall he was feeling his temperature rise. He gave some instructions to Helen concerning the care of the animals, and then walked to Aspen's door and called, "I'm coming in. I have it, too."

For the next three days, Maddie and Helen managed the chores, the children, and kept broth and mint tea boiling on the stove. Helen made bread, and Maddie harvested fresh supplies of mint leaves and aspen bark. Martha Jane kept an outdoor fire burning so the cabin would remain cool. She pulled buckets of water from the well. Hot water was maintained for cleaning the bedding and clothes, and cold water was used for baths for the men. Maggie and Helen worried about their husbands. Was she helping them, or assuring their certain deaths?

Each morning and evening Martha yelled out of the door, "Hey little missies, ere ya'all still feelin' hardy?" Helen assured her each time that no one else was affected.

"I think the fear of falling helpless to her care is enough to keep one well." she mused.

One day, while watching from my porch, Maddie asked, "I see all of the bedding and all of the clothes worn by William, and Duncan, on the clothes line . . . every stitch of it. What are they wearing?"

Helen didn't answer. She hoped her husband's sensitive lungs would not compromise his recovery, and his state of dress did not concern her at the moment. All cups, bowls, and spoons, were boiled after each use.

At times, Martha Jane's partaking of the remedy caused her to stagger as she walked back and forth from the well. She ate her meals sitting on the ground outside of Aspen, and only went inside to tend to her patients with cold water baths, hot broth, tea, and her strange concoction. She slept in a bedroll outside on the ground. She insisted that she was used to it. She sang constantly, silly songs, some of them with language the wives found to be unacceptable.

Aspen reported that when William covered his head with his pillow to block the noise, Duncan commented, "As long as her bleating annoys us we know we're still alive."

On the fifth day, Duncan stumbled out into the sunlight. She handed him his long johns from the line, and he sat on the bench outside Aspen's door to put on his socks and shoes, all freshly boiled, and sundried. He was pale and thinner, but was able to converse. Soon Martha pushed William out and told him to dress. He attempted, but needed help from Duncan.

The wives wanted to assist, but the tyrant yelled, "Halt!" like a commander giving orders to the troops. Soon she dragged out the straw ticking and pushed it into the fire. The woman and kids watched curiously. She threw buckets of soapy boiling water on Aspen's wood floors, and then swept it out the door.

William and Duncan came into my warm inviting parlor and curled up by my fireplace, wrapped in quilts Helen brought out to them. "Oh my word!" exclaimed Maddie.

Helen walked to the front door and peered out at the scene that had startled her sister-in-law. There stood Martha Jane, without a stitch on, tossing her clothing into the boiling water. She was soaping herself all over, and rinsing off, in broad daylight. Reaching into her saddlebag, she pulled out items and started dressing, this time in a riding skirt and blouse. She slipped into the men's boots she had worn with her menswear. Fishing out her washed wet clothing, she twisted them with sticks until the water was pressed out, rolled them up, and put them in the saddlebag.

"Won't you come in and have a bite to eat?" Helen called.

"No, Missy," she answered, "I recon' the work is pilin' up back at my launder house."

"Let us pay you for your time and help," Maddie suggested.

"That's alright. I make money in town. Figure a body's gotta do some good works sometimes to make up fer the bad you've done. You just got served with some of my good doin'."

"Helen," called William, "offer her a jar of that chokecherry wine."

As Maggie carried out the jar of deep red liquid, Martha's eyes lit up. "Well now, homemade wine? Don't mind if I do." She slipped the treasure into the saddlebag with her wet clothing, and mounted her horse.

Inside, Helen questioned her husband, "Did she cure you, or did you recover in spite of her?"

William chuckled, "She scared the sickness right out of us."

Several weeks later Helen took a loaf of fresh bread to town, to give to her new acquaintance in appreciation for her aid. Martha Jane had moved on. Her brother-in-law explained that her rough language and unrefined behavior was having a bad influence on his children, and he asked her to leave his home. It had been her residence since moving into town.

"There was a bit of a row, and she decided to run on over to Deadwood," he explained.

Helen told him of the work his sister-in-law had done for her husband and brother, "She didn't even fear catching the black sickness," she marveled. "She fears nothing," he stated. "That's why we all call her Calamity Jane."

* Calamity Jane actually lived in Lander, South Pass, and Minor's Delight for a period of time during this part of history. She operated a laundry and was knows to offer services in nursing during outbreaks of disease

Chapter Eight

SETTLED

"Home needs unity, and unity needs a home"

William finished the changes in my front parlor. A wall now divided the room in half. Helen was thankful she had ordered a surplus of the rose colored wallpaper with the tiny buds on it. She had enough to paper the parlor side of my new wall. The paper already on my parlor walls was a bit yellowed from the smoke of the lamps and fireplace. But Helen was glad she had paper to cover my new wall, and didn't complain.

She used the opportunity to wash the windows. She also washed the curtains, starched, and ironed them. This put the women in a cleaning mood and they thoroughly cleaned both of my stories and the inside of Aspen as well.

Helen and William's wedding certificate, with their pictures, hung on my new wall. William brought home two used, but very nice, matching parlor chairs one day, after delivering a baby to an officer's family at Fort Brown. He had provided several services over the summer for the family, and they paid him with the two chairs.

Helen left her glass-clawed lamp-table in the room, and that completed what would be my waiting area for patients. Directly behind my parlor was my small extra room. This room was planned to be used as a summer bedroom if the weather ever became too hot to sleep upstairs.

The extra room had two large windows on the north shady side. On the west side, it had a bay window. Facing the mountains, this window could always be depended on for breezes. It was the room Duncan and Maddie used when they stayed with us during winter months.

Now it was William's apothecary room, and shelves lined one wall. Duncan replaced the table in Aspen's one room by trading mint, hips, furs, and hides. William moved the old table in to use as a work table. Here, Maddie ground dried mint leaves, rose hips, aspen bark, and chokecherry bark, with a stone mortar and pestle. She put the powder in jars, wrote the names of the herbs on paper, and pasted the labels on the jars. Anise, basil, borage, and chamomile were dried and preserved. Maddie harvested these from her herb garden, on Aspen's sunny side.

Bottles of medications were lined up on another shelf. These, ordered from back east, came in sturdy wooden boxes that both families found useful. The top shelf held the books William was collecting for his medical library.

He taught Maddie to make pills. This was done by mixing water, flour, and a bit of honey, maple syrup, or sorghum, into a dough. The precisely measured medicinal ingredients were mixed in evenly. The dough was then rolled out into a long snake like form, and carefully cut into tiny pills. These were dried on a tray by my room's sunny bay windows, before filling labeled bottles with them. When Christina was older, William made sugar pills for her to use when playing doctor with her dolls.

Family evenings were now spent in my back parlor, which Helen also called the library. Helen loved to read. Her books were shelved on the inner wall of this room. Each Christmas, birthday, and anniversary, William ordered Helen a new book which she poured over every spare minute, until she finished it.

William wrote enough letters to various mission boards until, at last, some clergy arrived. A new Catholic priest came by train. An Episcopal priest was assigned to Lander, and another sent to Atlantic City. Ladies organized groups in the large eastern churches to raise money for building and equipping churches in these western communities. William was now able to spend more time on his medical practice. He continued to assist whenever he was needed in the ministry.

Duncan made many trips up and down the mountain, snaking lodge pole logs. This was a method in which long heavy logs were transported down a mountainside. Logs were tied together in a travois fashion, and dragged by a team of horses, along trails. These logs were used to build a barn. Aspen and I were excited for this new structure to be finished. We decided he would be our brother. We named him Big Barn. Several years later, after they painted him red, we changed it to Big Red.

Big Red was never very communicative with us. He had a quiet nature, and did not initiate conversation. If we nagged him enough, he would inform us when a new colt was born, or a new litter of kittens. Mostly though, Big Red kept to himself.

A traveler passed by with a collie that followed close behind him. He visited with the Yinglings and shared a meal; Christina's fascination with the animal inspired William to find a dog for her. He reasoned that a dog would be helpful in chasing away thieving rabbits from the garden, and it could warn the family of predators.

I had no experience with pets so I was as excited as the children were when Duncan brought home the puppy. He traded for it with one of Maddie's handmade baby quilts. Having met a young Indian couple from the nearby reservation, he discovered a litter had been born to their family pet, the dog that was part wolf. There were squeals of delight when the new arrival came. I was entertained for days with his antics and the reactions of the children.

So delightful were the sounds of the laughter and play, I carefully recorded them. I would find these recordings useful in later years. Brutus, named for one of the literary stories read aloud by William during long summer evenings, became a cherished member of the family, and soon earned a reputation for protecting the property.

By the third summer, gardening had improved as the families learned the seasons and the soil. William brought home a milk cow during the third spring. He traded a nice yearling colt for the cow, and its bull calf. Now there was milk. By 1880, I had quite the reputation as the

Grand Lady of the Valley. I sported white paint with red trim. My porch had extended to wrap around my entire perimeter, and was lined with benches for summer evenings. Helen braided rugs for my floors, and a few more pieces of furniture were added. Everyone took turns at the churn, and now there was an ample supply of butter.

As the population of South Pass diminished, with the migration to greener pastures, items not sold or taken along, went for low barter. We now had a china hutch in my kitchen, containing a partial set of china. A well-worn dry sink combination, with workspace, was Helen's favorite addition. This added organization to her meal preparation. A sofa joined the rocking chair in my back parlor, and an additional lamp table. One of Helen's tatted doilies covered the top, and on it set a stained-glass lantern. Helen traded dried meat and jelly to a passing couple who were moving west, for a chest of drawers that was proving to be unworthy of the space it took in the wagon.

Maddie gathered items, also, though not as many due to the small space within Aspen's one room. When Gus was born, Maddie set about assuring that the drafts of the stone cabin would not reach her baby. Although the stones were mortared with clay and straw, pieces fell out from the force of the wind. New mortar was used to fill holes every summer. Meanwhile, the drafts found their way through.

Since Aspen was not going to be their permanent home, the couple elected to not order wallpaper to seal the inner walls. It occurred to Maddie that she could paper Aspen's walls with newspaper. The men brought newspapers and catalogs home when getting supplies from town. When travelers passed by, and stopped in, they often brought a recently-printed journal. After reading it aloud in the evenings, Maddie pasted the sheets to Aspen's walls, with a mortar she made of flour and water, and a jell derived from boiling deer hooves. One day, as she and Helen had tea in the kitchen, while waiting for bread to bake, she complained.

"In the evenings when Duncan has time to spend with Gus and me, he is drawn to the walls. He takes the lamp and stands there reading the old news."

"Whatever for?" Helen inquired. "We read the news in those papers before you pasted them to the walls."

"I can't imagine why," Maddie answered. "He just seems drawn to read it again and again. I would take it all down just to put a stop to it, but it works well in blocking the drafts."

For several days following, Maddie did not come over. When at last she visited, she was in great spirits. "I found a solution to the problem of wall-reading," she offered.

"Did you pull it all down?" Helen asked as she carried the kettle to the table to pour hot water into the teapot.

"Yes, I certainly did, very carefully so as not to rip it. But then I put it back, this time upside down," she giggled, and Helen tipped her head, a bit confused about this solution.

Aspen related to me later that it had been quite a shock to Duncan, who after dinner, took his cup of tea and lamp to the north wall, only to discover that all print was now neatly attached upside down and no longer readable. When he realized what his wife had done, he chuckled. She had complained enough times, and he realized he was out-witted. He returned the lamp to the table and reached for the violin. Maddie settled down to her knitting, happy that her cozy family evenings had returned.

On that night Duncan realized that home needs unity, and unity needs a home.

Chapter Nine

DESPAIR

"The seasons came and went in the little cemetery;
a reminder that life, like the seasons, is a cycle of change"

I couldn't remain lost in my memories following the move. I was adjusting to a new setting, and the present was, at times, a harsh reality. May turned into June.

The process melted the remaining patches of snow, transforming the moisture into mud. Jack rabbits hopped around, but did not stop to get acquainted. There were no trees to provide habitation for nesting birds; therefore, there was no windbreak that could protect me from the constant spring winds. Some days the force with which the winds pounded my walls gave my attic a terrible headache. More shingles ripped off as the wind launched them into the vast openness.

June dried the mud, and except for occasional rains, the prairie turned to desert. During one June storm, lightning struck repeatedly, within close range. I was sure that by standing there, the only upright object for miles around, lightning would strike, and fire and smoke would consume me. However, I survived June, and the hot sun of July. Its torturing heat bore down relentlessly. At least, I got a good drying out.

Mold is a house's worst enemy, and thankfully, none can develop in such intense arid temperatures.

During July, a transient man moved in. I knew he would not stay long since there was no water, but he lasted several days. He threw rubbish all around, and finally I tapped into recorded sounds of Brutus' barking, upstairs. He was frightened away. I assumed he wandered to the highway to find a ride to nowhere. I tried to read him, but he seemed to be mindless. My best efforts at sifting retrieved no information.

During the end of July, a young couple pitched a tent in my shade, on the north side. They brought water and food and stayed a week. Except for a quick tour through my first floor, they remained outside. I didn't get to know them at all. They had no sensitivity to house vibrations. They also left trash scattered around.

When I heard them discuss using my porch boards for cooking fuel, I decided they must go. I sorted through my sound collection and played a little of Duncan's violin music. That inspired them to move on. For once, I was thankful for the relentless wind that soon carried their mess away. I hate litter; even in this loathsome place, I do not appreciate it left for me to look at.

In August, a group of teens chose me for a party house. They brought portable music that blared a great racket throughout my rooms. They smoked, drank, wrestled, danced, and slept. I must admit that after being alone for such a long time, I was entertained.

They discussed their dissatisfaction with parents, society, and life in general. They ranted their youthful ideals and opinions. It reminded me of so many similar conversations over the past hundred years, watching my individuals pass from youth to adulthood, and then on to the years that demanded responsibility.

I didn't frighten them. It was obvious they didn't plan to stay long, and I hoped, if not rushed, they would clean up before leaving. This was disappointing. They departed, to seek other adventures, and their discarded trash remained in their wake.

September, October, and then November, arrived, bringing the usual hunting season that is an annual event in the northwest. Jeeps and other four-wheel-drive vehicles passed by my front porch, as hunters searched out the various prey.

During this time, a troubled young woman took up temporary residence. By sifting her thoughts, I determined she was running from something, someone, or perhaps a memory. The depression she projected put me back into my previous state of despair. I tried to project hope back to her, but could not connect through her resistance.

I sifted from her the name Megan, and assumed it was hers. Often in the night, she rattled my rafters with screams, triggered by nightmares. Sometimes I'm successful in reading dreams, if alerted quickly enough. On several occasions, her night terror sent a vision to me of a woman hanging by her neck from a rope. I realized this scene must be something she had witnessed or feared.

I could gather no more before her screams shattered my concentration. Screaming is very hard on a house. It shatters concentration and fragments vibrations. One day after crying for some time, she gathered debris from around my rooms, and paper bags she had brought with her. To my dismay, she started a fire on the floor of my first floor bedroom. This had been William's apothecary room, but later generations used it for sleeping. At first, I thought she was attempting to warm herself and I tried to project my thoughts.

Please use my fireplace. Some of my chimney is missing, but it would be better than burning my floor.

Then I realized her plan. She intended to die, and take me, in the process of her own self-destruction. I had contemplated death since my displacement, wondering if my end was near. But having it imposed upon me caused me to realize I preferred to prolong it indefinitely.

The little drifter took a bottle from her bag and dumped a large quantity of pills into her hand. With the remaining few ounces of water, she swallowed all of them. As she settled down to sleep on her ragged blanket, I became aware of the flames now rising up my wall, which separated the room from the front parlor.

They licked my ceiling, and dispersed black smoke from my windows that had long been bare of panes. I activated all the sounds in my reservoir: Brutus barking, children laughing, Duncan's violin, babies crying, but who would hear?

I settled into the resignation of dying alone, without the beloved memories around me. Then, suddenly I heard sirens. I would later learn that a hunter spotted the smoke and hurriedly reported it from his CB radio. In autumn, dry grass and wind combined with a spark, can quickly ignite a house, and inspire a massive prairie fire. Concerned citizens are constantly vigilant with observation and action.

After the firemen's showers of cold water and chemicals nearly drowned me, I peered through the steam and smoke to determine the condition of the adolescent who determined that life held no promise for either of us. Fatally overtaken by smoke and pills, they carried her away.

I didn't hear the story about her, since no one discussed it in my presence, but it left me with melancholy. A nagging curiosity of an unsolved mystery lingered. I feared it was unsolvable. We had shared something, Megan and I. We did not feel needed, wanted, or loved.

I regretted that she was incapable of sensitivity to my stored memories. Had she been able to tap into my vibrations of laughter and joy, her spirits might have lifted. If she could have drawn on my massive storage of love, she might have healed.

Death was not new to me. Many of my loved ones died in my loving embrace, but none deliberately. Hopelessness inspires self-destruction, and for the first time, this was recorded in my walls. I did not want it, but I had no choice. This anguish is tangled among my memory fibers with all the rest. The thought haunted me that some justice should be served. Justice would put Megan's spirit to rest.

Through the long cold winter looking at my charred floor, blackened wall, and smoked ceiling, in that room, sometimes caused me to wish my demise was completed along with hers. The despondency would not lighten. She had left it with me. It was like a black cloud of evil. I sought refuge from the sadness in my memories. I thought of the little family cemetery on my old home site. There, my individuals were buried by others who loved them.

Stones were carved or purchased by family. Flowers were planted around their graves. The seasons came and went in the little cemetery, a reminder that life, like seasons, is a cycle of change. I wondered where Megan would be laid to rest.

I assumed she had no safe and special place.

Chapter Ten

GREED AND SHARING

"Greed holds no compassion"

More settlers moved into the area. William's practice took most of his time now; not only did he treat the sick and injured, he was asked to work as coroner, identifying the cause of death and writing the certificate of death.

Every day something demanded his time: a birth, an illness, a broken bone caused by the risky work of ranching. There were occasional gunshot wounds. These occurred because guns were never far from any man. When an outburst of temper, misunderstandings, drunken madness, or jealous rages occurred, guns were more accessible than rational thinking.

There were still occasional incidents from marauding Indians. These crimes were committed against white settlers, and the peaceful Native Shoshone, equally. The one that drew a lot of attention happened in July, 1873. A large group of men were getting logs for construction. The women, children and elderly men made up most of those still at home in the valley.

On this Sunday my families were loading into the carriage to attend church in town. The sheriff rode into the yard at a fast speed. He called William over, a short distance away from the others.

By straining I could hear his remarks, "Doc, there's been a massacre over by the Big Popo Agie River. It was so close to town. I can't believe those blood thirsty murderers had the audacity to strike so close. They had to have been watching, and they knew that most able-bodied men were away."

I couldn't quite hear William, as he always spoke in a calm tone of voice. Duncan joined them and some discussion carried on. William returned to the carriage, and assisted Helen and Christina out. Duncan helped Maddie.

As William led them back to the porch, he explained, "Darling, we won't attend church today. There has been a tragedy. I'll be going with the sheriff, and help in whatever way I can."

"William, Duncan can accompany us," she protested. "I teach a Sunday school class. I need to be there."

"Helen, there are some killers on the loose. They may have moved on, but we can't be sure. They attacked those women at that cabin by the river: Mrs. Richardson and Mrs. Hall, Hattie Hall. You remember the little house near the Fort? That is extremely bold. They just might hit again. They may even strike at people who are traveling these roads into town. I want you to remain here."

Helen's eyes were wide, and she gasped, "The ladies who cook for the soldiers?"

Maddie was as shocked as Helen. "I sold vegetables to Hattie last summer. She said they needed them for the meals they served the men at the Fort.

"I suppose I should remain here," Duncan suggested.

William nodded, "Go get your gun and keep it in here. Pull the shutters closed, and fasten them. Bar both doors. It is still cool enough. You should do fine until I find out what danger may still exist."

"Helen, don't start a fire in the wood stove. Fix something for lunch that needs no cooking. Smoke might be spotted at a distance and draw in trouble. You all can read the Bible and pray here today. Pray for the safety of our community."

He left, and the remaining family set about doing as he requested. "I was hoping this was over," Maddie said. "It's been a long time since outside bands moved through."

"I remember how happy the ladies were getting into that cabin," remarked Helen.

"That used to belong to the Fort, didn't it?" asked Duncan.

Helen nodded, "Yes, they used it to store rifles and ammunition until they built the larger buildings inside the Fort. Miss McCarthy was homesteading, so they gave her the cabin since it was on the edge of the 160 she claimed."

"And Mrs. Cooper was staying there temporarily. She was planning to join her husband later in the summer. He had already moved farther west," added Maddie.

Late in the afternoon William returned. He explained that soldiers and Shoshone scouts spent the day circling a wide sweep around the vicinity. All tracks indicated the marauders had moved on.

"Why do they think they raided that house with two women?" Helen asked.

"They believe these warriors have been out of this area for several years. They may have thought the cabin still belonged to the Fort. It was probably an attempt to steal guns and ammunition that used to be stored there. When they kicked in the door, they may have been surprised that the house was inhabited," William explained.

"They didn't need to kill those poor women," protested Maddie.

Men, driven by greed, have no compassion," commented Duncan. "Those ladies probably started screaming, and the warriors saw no reason to let them to live."

"The funerals will be Tuesday morning, Helen. Pastor Clarke will send a telegram to Mrs. Cooper's husband tomorrow morning. Miss McCarthy has no relatives that anyone knows of. Would you and Maddie go to town tomorrow, and make some calls on the wives at the Fort? Maybe all of you can help with arrangements for the funeral. I will be going in, and I can take you." William was fervently trying to pull the thoughts away from the terror of what had just occurred. I know, because I sifted.

Later, when the men were outside, the conversation returned to this latest catastrophe. "I don't know what I would do if something like that happened to my Maddie, and my sister," stressed Duncan.

"It was horrific," said William. "It appeared the McCarthy woman was sleeping, and died in her bed, but that tiny Mrs. Cooper fought like a badger, with everything she could get her hands on. She surely retaliated with some significant blows and wounds to her attacker. The caskets won't be open. "

I pondered on Duncan's words, "Greed has no compassion. It is more joyous to give, than to receive."

Other changes surrounded us; one of them concerned the Wind River Reservation that bordered our land. It was rapidly increasing in population. The Shoshone leader, Chief Washakie, had guided his people for eight years on land designated to his tribe, by the government.

Although the land was vast, with wild animals in abundance, staples could easily run scarce and the people struggled to adjust. Settling into one place was foreign to them. They had survived hundreds of years roaming with the seasons and migration of game. They were good neighbors, and my family traded with them. Maddie made a few friends among the woman and learned more about edible plants, and natural medications of the region.

The following winter John Walking Thunder stopped by to visit. As Helen poured coffee for him he showed William his barter. A large buckskin hide processed into the softest white leather Helen had ever seen. "How did you make it so soft and pliable?" she asked.

"My grandmother makes the best buckskin," he bragged. "It is as soft as a baby rabbit."

"What would you like in exchange?" William asked, knowing Helen was already planning to make something for Christina from the leather.

"I am out of tobacco for our prayer pipe," he informed them. "We have been having lots of ceremonies lately."

"Is it a time of celebration?" asked Duncan. "Or . . . is there illness among your family members?"

"The Leaders of your people, the great ones in Washington, asked us a great favor." He stopped to take a drink of the coffee, into which he had stirred four spoons of sugar.

No one responded. They knew by now that John would take his own time to tell his story and inquiring did not probe him along any faster. "The Arapaho people are here," he finished.

William puffed on his own pipe as he measured tobacco into a small cloth bag. Helen made several of these for this purpose. Tobacco was a very important instrument of worship for our Shoshone friends. Even with William's own method of worship being vastly different, he did not begrudge them their symbols of faith, passed through many generations. In fact, while watching some of the ceremonies, he could easily compare the symbols of his own teachings to theirs, reminding him that indeed, all people served one creator.

"Yes, I noticed people pulling poles behind their horses," he stated. "I thought they were passing through," mused William.

"I heard at the Fort that they're staying," Duncan offered.

"Yes," said John, as he took the bag William offered him. "The great ones in Washington did not provide the land they promised the Arapaho people. Now it is nearly time for the snows. They must have a place to be until they can move on. No one knows where they will go, or when their land will be given."

He smiled at Duncan who pushed a plate toward him. Warm biscuits, fresh from dinner, lay waiting for the taking. He sampled one before continuing. Helen refilled the cups with more steaming coffee. Stirring more sugar into his cup, he explained, "Our chief says we must be tolerant. They are our brothers."

"Your tribes have not always been friendly with one another, isn't that right?" Duncan inquired.

William shot him a warning glance. Such questions he regarded as prying. But John did not appear to think so, and nodded. "We have had our battles, but these are serious times. Our chief tells us we must be peaceful to our brothers if we are to survive the conditions now upon us."

William looked thoughtfully at John, "Yes, Chief Washakie is a wise and fair leader. If only all people could make the choice to be tolerant," he offered. "Then maybe everyone would remember that all men are brothers."

"That is why we pray with the pipe," explained John. "With so many people moving among us, the disagreements will come. We must pray to sustain our own peace." He tapped his heart, a sign that the peace must be inside before it could be transferred to outer conflicts.

"We will also pray for your peace, and your adjustments to the changes," Helen impulsively blurted out.

John nodded as he stood and prepared to leave. "You make fine moccasins for the little ones from the skin?" He smiled as he handed Helen the leather. She smiled back, and nodded.

As he walked down the path William stood in the doorway, looking toward the mountains. He smiled at Helen's quick offer to be spiritually involved in the burdens of her neighbors. He admired her because her faith was always strong. He knew she would keep her word. The Shoshone and Arapaho neighbors would be at the top of her prayer list in her daily devotion.

He also made a mental note to buy a larger quantity of tobacco with the next trip to town. With the strain of two previously warring tribes sharing land, prayer tobacco may end up in short supply. Perhaps a large quantity of sugar should also be purchased.

I was learning a lot about sharing. The families talked about it around the table. The mothers talked about it with the children regarding their toys. William read about it from the Bible during evening devotions. And, most importantly, I watched them do the sharing. It gave me a feeling of happiness.

I understood why Duncan said, "It is more joyous to give, than to receive."

Chapter Eleven

SADIE

"Now I would say she's the Sad Lady of the Desert"

The fall of 1999 followed a summer that was the second of a seven-year drought. It caused me to spend a lot of time lost in memories. The animals clustered closer to the river, cherishing the needed moisture. It continued to decrease its life-giving waters, as each day the skies stubbornly withheld the rain.

Even the jackrabbits and field mice no longer scampered by. I had learned to regress into a state of nonexistence, but now occasional hunters aroused my interest as they slowly drove by. The grass had long ago turned to dust, and it rose above them in a brown cloud upon their passing. Looking across the crisp dead-grass fragments, I could spot their return, by the dirt clouds, long before I could hear the sounds of their engines.

Such a cloud floated toward me from the highway on a hot October afternoon. Rather than passing, the sporty convertible with top down, pulled up and parked next to my porch. A tall, graceful young woman stepped out.

She vigorously dusted off the powdered earth that had settled on her red knit top and white denim jeans during her short trek across the prairie. She then shook her long tresses, hoping to free them of the same dirt.

Silly girl, you would rather drive in high style with your car top down, than shut out the dust.'

I had to endure the stuff, since I no longer had windows, but for her, there was no reason. My guess was that she could not have been more than twenty-one or twenty-two. Remembering the tragedy of the last youthful female caused my beams to bristle.

As I was concerning myself about her intentions, another car pulled in beside her, and two women stepped out. They were the ones that had visited me before. I was still bearing a grudge. It had been their ill-fated plan that led to my displacement.

"I don't think Wiggins' Realty has any interest in this, but thought I would take a look. You know the good cause and all. So how many acres go with the house?" the younger woman inquired.

"Ten," replied one of the older women. "We wanted to assemble the historical buildings here, creating the look of Old Town Lander, but the funds are very low, and with all the effects of the drought on the ranchers, donations are just not coming in. We were only able to add a foundation, septic, and cistern, but nothing more. After that, the fire did so much damage."

"We haven't given up," rushed in the other. "If we sell this, and use the money to start again closer to town, even if it's scaled down from our original plans."

The younger woman, who I would learn is Sadie Morgan, stepped up on my porch. A board gave way just enough to suggest it might break beneath her leather hiking boot. "Hmm." she mumbled, "looks a little rotten to me."

"Well, it's over one hundred years old," encouraged historical lady number one. "Of course it will need repairs."

They pulled my creaking front door open, and stepped inside. "Ugh!" shrieked Sadie, "Look at all that smoke damage. Not sure I could sell this, nope, not sure at all."

Historical ladies one and two looked at each other as Sadie examined my first floor inch by inch; she continued offering derogatory comments, each one riling me more than the one before.

If the hinges on my cupboard doors weren't broken, I'd have taken a swing at her.

"It is a historical landmark," reminded historical lady number two.

"Not anymore," taunted Sadie. "Before you moved it, maybe, when it was on the original home site. Now it's a pile of rotting timber stuck on a patch of desert, with not even a decent road to connect it to the highway."

"Well, this house has lots of history. It was known as the Grand Lady of the Valley," defended historical lady number one.

"Now I would say she's the Sad Lady of the Desert," smirked Sadie.

Oh boy, if I could get a smack at her, I would show her the Mad Lady of Despair!

Sadie stepped gingerly back onto my porch. Pushing her hands into her back jean pockets, she squinted as her eyes scanned in all directions. "Any wells, ditches, water rights?" she inquired.

"No, just a cistern, and septic, and neither are hooked up to the house," explained historical lady two.

Shaking her head, Sadie replied, "So the buyers would have to pay to have water delivered, or haul it themselves? That would get old fast!"

"Well" . . . . started lady one, "There is talk that eventually Lander will run city water out here. Or the new owner could dig a well."

"Hmmm," grumbled Sadie. "Guess that's a lost promise since reserves are depleted and there's no prediction for drought relief. As I remember from our reports at the office, drilling wells around this area has been unsuccessful. If water is discovered, it's too oily to drink. Besides, that can cost over a thousand dollars per foot."

She stepped off my porch and started toward the car.

Just step on the loose board again, Missy, I'll drop you through, or at least trip you.

She deliberately skipped over it.

"I see there's an electric pole set, and it's not hooked up. Has the wiring been checked in the house?" she asked, glancing around. She reached in the car, taking out a camera.

"No, those are the expenses that are motivating the society to sell this lovely historical piece of architecture."

"How much did you pay for it?" Sadie pried.

"Nothing. Mr. Dickenson wanted it off the land, so he paid the society one thousand dollars to remove it and save him demolition costs. We used that money to pay the mover."

"How much did this piece of worthless land cost ya?"

The historical ladies were getting nervous, "It was donated for just paying up the back taxes".

Sadie was snapping pictures, "Owe any taxes on it now?"

"Well, just this past year."

"Well, those can't be much. It isn't worth much," remarked Sadie, still snapping shots.

"I won't be able to sell this for much on the market. Things just aren't moving now. It might take a long time, so I will make you an offer. I'll take it off your hands for five thousand dollars and you can get started on that other little project, you know . . . . get things moving. That will give me time to think of a good way to market this." Sadie placed the camera back into the car.

"We were hoping for a bit more. Five thousand isn't much."

"What were you hoping for?" Sadie opened the car door.

"At least fifteen thousand, since there's land included. That amount would purchase the land for the new project."

"Wow!" Sadie exclaimed. "I couldn't even sell this off as barn-wood, or peddle the land for anything close to that. Besides it's a lawsuit in the making. I almost fell through the porch!" She slid into the driver's seat.

"Barn-wood indeed!" Historical lady number one was turning red in the face. "We would want assurance that this old landmark would be restored, not disassembled. We would need that promise to part with it."

Sadie put on her sunglasses, "Isn't this the old house where that runaway girl died? Suicide, was it not? Ooh . . . . That is creepy! People shy away from death houses. We would have to keep that information low. A lot of folks believe in ghosts, haunts, and rubbish like that."

The ladies stepped away and mumbled together, then returned to face Sadie. "We can let it go for twelve thousand, and a promise not to demolish."

Sadie, tapping her painted fingernails on the steering wheel, appeared to be thinking. "I'll give you twelve thousand without a promise, or eight thousand with assurance it will be restored." She turned the key and started the ignition.

Lady one jumped in, fearing that Sadie was losing interest, "Eleven thousand with a promise."

Sadie shifted into reverse, "Ten thousand with a promise." That's my last offer.

"Ten thousand, it is," both women responded in chorus.

"When does the committee meet?" Sadie elevated her voice to be heard over the racy engine.

"Tomorrow night," Lady one fairly screamed.

"I'll deliver the contract to you before noon tomorrow. Thanks! Hope your project goes well."

Sadie turned around, and in the reckless fashion that people of her age often do, raced across the prairie in a puff of Wyoming top soil.

The president and vice president of the historical society stared at the cloud as if stunned, "I think we came out all right, don't you?"

"I'm not sure. It looked better to me until she started critiquing it." They got into the car and slowly drove to the highway.

Chapter Twelve

ROSELYN

"I can just picture how it will fit your needs"

She knew the additional information would follow Sadie's next breath. Sadie picked up the first cookie placed on the plate, and bounced it between her hands as it cooled.

"I found a house for ten thousand. That leaves you the other ten thousand from the life insurance to restore it, or at least make a good start." She took a bite from the cookie.

Roselyn had poured three glasses of milk and lined them up at the bar. Sadie picked up one and washed down the cookie. "There are ten acres for the kids to run, room for pets, even a pony. If you want a garden, there's great possibilities, but you will have to haul water." She gulped down another swallow of milk.

"What are you talking about?" asked Roselyn, as she dropped spoonfuls of chocolate chip cookie dough onto the baking sheet. Sadie snatched another cookie.

Garbling through her bites of a second cookie, Sadie explained. "The historical society was trying to sell the "Lady" for fifteen thousand. I got it for ten thousand, including 10 acres of prairie. It was a steal."

She reached for the third cookie. Missing lunch had caused a sugar low that was now moving in with a vengeance.

Roselyn picked up the plate and moved it to the cabinet on the other side of the kitchen. At this rate she would not be able to bake cookies fast enough to replace the ones Sadie was devouring.

Sadie reached for the second glass of milk and Roselyn playfully slapped her hand. "Are you here to tell me something, or eat me out of house and home?" Roselyn laughed as she snatched it just ahead of Sadie and placed both remaining glasses with the relocated cookie platter.

Sadie pretended to be offended and said curtly, "You can subtract it from the ten thousand you'll owe me for paying the Historical Society for your new house."

"What in heck are you talking about?" Roselyn demanded. Baby sister now had her undivided attention.

I just bought a house for you for ten thousand. It has five bedrooms, two living rooms, a big country kitchen, a pantry, an extra room suitable for a second bathroom, and a huge wraparound porch.

Roselyn sat down at the bar, looked Sadie in the eye, and asked, "What, and where?"

"Out of town, about five miles. It has been abandoned for years. It needs some work, but the ten acres are worth more than that. Land is always a good investment. Hurry, let's run out and look at it. I can just picture how it will fit your needs."

Roselyn looked at the clock, "Kids will be here any minute," she noted. She walked to the range, opened the oven, and removed the cookie sheet. She set it on the counter and started lifting the hot pastries and placing them on the platter. She poured a replacement glass of milk and turned off the oven. Just then the door opened; Maria, age twelve, and her younger brothers rushed in. They dropped jackets, lunch boxes, and backpacks, in the middle of the living room floor.

Roselyn smiled as she placed a saucer of cookies, and a glass of milk, in front of Sadie, and set up the children's snacks at the table. They rushed to their places, eager for refreshments that provided time to transition from school to home.

"So, who would I have to pay off for this *GREAT DEAL?*" she asked with a bit of sarcasm.

"Me," answered Sadie, between bites. "I bought it today, and will sign for it tomorrow. You can pay me, and I will transfer the deed. I had to move on it because I heard at the office that Mack Wilson had his eye on it. There are rumors that there's oil in the vicinity. Nothing will move in that direction until the economy picks up, but eventually the land will be worth something. In the meantime, you need a place to live, and this place needs a family."

She brushed her hands together and swept them across her lap, removing any crumbs from her hastily eaten snack.

"Is it livable?" asked her older, and more cautious, sister.

"Almost," answered Sadie standing up. "Needs a few things. Let's go look at it."

"Maria, watch the boys for a few," Roselyn instructed as she grabbed a sweater, since even warm days grow cool at sundown in Wyoming. "I'll be right back. All of you do your chores when you finish your snack."

They stepped out of the mobile home and moved to Sadie's car. Sadie put up the top, and closed the windows; she knew better than to expose her sister to that terrible dust, and after all, she wanted 'The Lady' to make a good impression on Roselyn. She, herself, had already fallen in love.

Chapter Thirteen

RECLAIMED

"What's not to love about 'The Lady'?"

"Does it have a well?" asked Roselyn, remembering that water can be a major problem for country living.

"Not yet," answered Sadie, as she turned from the street onto Highway 789, and headed toward the property.

"Meaning," Roselyn said firmly, "there is no water."

"Not yet," answered Sadie, turning on the radio and tuning in a rock and roll station. "A lot of people have cisterns, you know? It doesn't have to be a problem, just consider it part of the improvements."

"So, that means it has no plumbing?" Roselyn was beginning to lose interest.

"Not yet," answered Sadie cheerfully, "but Jeff would give you a good deal. We can shop around on deals for bathroom fixtures. I can get them wholesale."

Jeff was one of several male friends that Sadie mingled with. Roselyn knew he would probably work with Sadie's request. She was beginning to feel agitated that her younger sister would presume that she could arrange plans before she had even considered the property. She was already thinking of a way to say, "Thanks, but no thanks." to little sis, as soon as possible.

"It's hooked up with electricity, I hope," suggested Roselyn hesitantly, as Sadie pulled off, onto the dirt road.

"Not yet," said her sister, turning up the music.

The wind was flapping my shingles as they pulled into the drive, and Roselyn reluctantly got out of the car and walked to my porch. She looked at my Victorian trim that hung precariously. "Don't decide about anything until you are inside," Sadie insisted as she opened my squeaky door.

I noted her tone had changed, from the one she used with the Historical Society, while convincing them I was worthless.

Roselyn stepped into my front parlor and looked inside. "Wow! How old is this place?"

"A hundred, or so," Sadie answered. "Isn't she spectacular?"

"What? This gal said I was nothing but junk before, and now she says I'm spectacular?" She must be trying to pass me off for a profit. I had not seen such a scammer since Butch had tried his schemes years ago in my kitchen.

Well, I'm not letting her make money on me. As she and the slightly older woman walked into the first floor bedroom, I deliberately dropped my light fixture dome that had been barely attached since the fire. It crashed to the floor, and fell near Sadie's feet. Both women squealed from the startling impact. I chuckled.

"I'm not sure; my savings could make this livable," Roselyn said with what sounded like regret. "But she is an amazing old structure. Too bad someone didn't keep her up."

"I really think you have enough to rewire the house, hook up the plumbing, and repair the ceiling and walls from the fire and smoke damage. We could all do the restoration work ourselves. Mom and

Carmen would help, I'm sure. If you could just get it livable by snowfall, we could work on the inside all winter."

"Sadie, you are a realtor. Carman is a nurse. Mom is an artist-photographer, and I am a billing technician. What do we know about restoration and remodeling?"

Roselyn narrowed her gaze at her idealistic younger sister with a tone she hoped would restore her to the realm of reality."

"You can't know till you try," she answered as she started up my stairs. "If men can do it, how hard can it be?'

Roselyn followed. I sifted her thoughts and got a clear picture of three children: the first a beautiful girl, and the others, two younger boys. One, I sensed, was a rowdy, reckless child, and the youngest appeared silent as though he could not hear, or speak, or perhaps both.

As they stepped onto the landing of my second floor, they looked around. "Wouldn't Maria love this room?" asked Sadie as she opened the oak door to the first of my upstairs bedrooms.

"And that long-shaped room with the big window would be perfect for the boys. And look Roselyn, here is the perfect one for you. That area could be made into a walk-in closet, and the little room beside it, a bath."

"The last bedroom could be an office for my work." Roselyn seemed to be thinking out loud.

This wasn't going well. I clearly had not frightened them enough. I simply could not allow Sadie to use me to appease her greed. As they stood in the last room, facing the view of the Wind Rivers, I deliberately slammed the door, shutting them in.

"What caused that?" Roselyn asked sounding a bit shaky.

"Drafts, declared Sadie. "The whole place needs windows, but I can get them wholesale for you."

They returned to the first floor. Looking around the kitchen Sadie pointed out, "You will need new cabinets, but people usually like to rebuild a kitchen from scratch. Its good there isn't much to tear out. Look Roselyn, how solid the floors are. Someone really took care building this house. I wonder who it was."

The lady that I now knew to be Roselyn was thinking quietly. My sifting revealed that she was in a bit of a panic. "Well, my landlord says we have to be out in two months so the new owner can take over, so I guess this may have to do."

"I will get the deal closed tomorrow" said Sadie.

"I'll call around and get estimates about these other improvements," offered Roselyn.

"Call Mountain View Electric about all the electrical stuff and tell them I sent you. He owes me for getting him the job on the new town hall; at least he thinks I got it for him. And the plumbing, don't call anyone; I have a date with Hainsley Mills, the new plumber that just moved here. I'll talk to him for you. He's been calling me relentlessly," Sadie said as she opened the door and got into her car.

'Huh-oh,' I thought. What a little manipulator. Just like Sun Dance from so long ago, or was it Butch? No, I remember; it was Calamity Jane. That is who she reminds me of.

I would not see anyone again until ten days later when all hell broke loose. A truck arrived bringing in two toilets, a shower stall for the upstairs, and two bathroom sinks. They created noise and confusion like I had not heard, even on the day of my moving.

Roselyn stayed busy sweeping every room, brushing down cobwebs, and mopping down my walls. It felt good to be clean again. When she finished, she attached a padlock to my bedroom door, where Megan died.

She locked it up and said under her breath, "There, we just won't deal with that for a while."

I wondered if she was referring to the repairs needed in my burned room, or the dark feeling that floated out of it.

Roselyn determined the porcelain tub from my first bathroom installation should remain. She also decided to make use of my porcelain kitchen sink. She appeared to have some appreciation for me, but the workers grumbled about my state of disrepair, often commenting on the wisdom of bulldozing me over. I retaliated by making their jobs as difficult as I could manage, and causing as many mishaps as possible.

By the time the first boxes were carried from vehicles to my porch, I was in a resentful state of mind and not a bit ready for the intrusion that was about to begin.

"Sadie," replied Roselyn, "What would you have done with this place if I hadn't taken it off your hands?"

"I knew you'd want her," answered Sadie as she roughly set down a box a dishes, causing a cup to roll out and break on my kitchen floor.

"Why wouldn't you? What's not to love about *The Lady*?" Sadie replied.

Chapter Fourteen

FAMILY

"They forced me to again become involved with the living"

During those early days of moving in while the women were scrubbing, smearing white paint, sealing my cracks, and reinforcing my foundation, I was busy too. I was listening, sifting, and meshing all day and night. This family was taking over my life, and I needed to know everything I could gather about them. By the time they were settled in, I had the whole scoop.

Kate was the older woman, the mother of the three younger women. We had something in common considering I had been aging for some time, too. Age made me eccentric, I will admit, not liking new people much, but Kate amused me. I could not at first figure out why I felt I knew her. I could predict her thoughts at times before she formed them.

By meshing, I learned that she grew up, and lived, for 35 years in Seattle. She had been an art teacher in several of the local schools since moving to Wyoming fifteen years before. She recently started her own small photography business. Living frugally in the tiny flat above her studio, she was financially comfortable and free to assist with grandchildren.

She mentioned once that the brick building she rented on Main Street was one of the oldest in town. I wondered what stories the walls could tell her if she had a good rapport with the structure. I wished I could question her; we needed to be better connected for me to project to her. I once heard her tell her granddaughter, Maria, that she was adopted at birth and did not know her birth parents.

Her adopted parents raised her as an only child. Her father was a mason, and her mother a hair stylist. They moved around Seattle often. For this reason, Kate did not understand the fulfillment of bonding and communicating with a house.

In Seattle, Kate attended local colleges and trained to be an art teacher. At school she met her husband, Marty. I know little of him except from overhearing Roselyn explain to her children why they had no grandfather.

Roselyn's father was a music major, but he soon dropped out to be part of a band. He and his rock group did well for about ten years. In time, the touring took a toll on the marriage. His three daughters hardly remember him. He was seldom home long enough to become involved in their childhood.

Sadly, the availability of drugs, the life style, and the continuous flow of alcohol destroyed the group; four talented, but addicted, musicians disbanded to reassemble their lives. Marty was not successful with rehab. After three sessions of failed attempts in long term treatment, he disappeared.

Kate and the girls did not hear of him again for several years. He was discovered on a street in San Francisco, dead from a heroin overdose. I found this to be a very sad tale. Nothing like the rich memories of families I have recorded.

The same year, Kate's mother died of cancer. Soon afterwards, her father passed from a stroke. Taking her small inheritance, she moved her three daughters, Roselyn, Carmen, and Sadie, to the open spaces of Wyoming.

Her daughters were no more successful in making wise choices in husbands than Kate had been. Roselyn, the eldest of the three, married shortly after high school graduation. Her husband worked in the oil fields, and for that reason, she moved to Green River.

After ten years of marriage and three children, the rocky marriage ended with his death. He had been driving while intoxicated. She had pieced her education together between the births of her children. Once she received the insurance from her husband's death, Roselyn moved back to Lander, where she worked from her home with her computer, keeping a close watch on her family.

Carmen, four years younger, chose nursing as her profession. She married an engineer she met while attending the University of Laramie. They settled in Cheyenne, and appeared to be on the way to a happy life.

After the birth of twin sons, she discovered her husband was maintaining a relationship with his former girlfriend. She made fast work of the divorce, and moved her twin sons back to Fremont County, to be near her mother and sisters. Carmen worked as an office nurse in a local doctor's office.

Sadie, four years younger than Carmen, took a different path. She didn't wish to repeat her sisters' and mother's mistakes, and resolved to remain single. She could earn her own money and be master of her own life. She was a junior partner in local real-estate business. She fixed up a loft apartment in Lander, and decorated it in leather, glass, and chrome. This reflected her modern independent spirit.

This is the family that interrupted my fate: death by deterioration. They forced me to again become involved with the living. They finally won my devotion.

Kate, the matriarch, is a graying, witty grandmother with a relaxed casual style. Sensitive, calm, and artistic, she maintains the role of peacemaker when occasions find it useful. She is devoted to her daughters and grandchildren.

Roselyn, with her dark ebony hair, amber eyes, olive skin, and high energy, is in constant motion. She serves as mentor to her siblings in matters of the heart and spirit. She is a patient mother and has a relaxed parenting style.

Her petite sister, Carmen, is a contrast of fair skin, blue eyes, and auburn hair. Carmen has a compassionate nature. As a trained nurse, she is the women's consultant on all things medical.

Then Sadie, tall, social, and community-minded, has strong opinions. She is fearless and assertive in her approach to life. She perceives herself the family protector. With her money sense, she asserts herself in giving financial advice, even when unsolicited by her sisters. Sadie has long, thick chestnut hair, and hazel eyes that change hues depending on the color she wears She is as unpredictable as a spring storm.

Four different personalities, with vastly different appearances, but all four are alike with their slender figures, wide smiles, and almond-shaped eyes. I thought they were very attractive and amusing, but it would be some time before I would be ready to admit it.

But for now I had their personalities, intentions, strategies, and vulnerabilities carefully recorded. It would be important if I intended to keep the upper hand, and I did intend to do so.

Chapter Fifteen

CHANGES

"I had to admit that Helen would have approved of them"

Roselyn wasted no time in settling her rambunctious family in. Just days following her first visit, along with the invasion of the workers, I met the unruly band that would be my new tenants. An electrician assessed my wiring system. He was a major annoyance. An elderly "lady "does not appreciate blatant criticism about the competency of her wiring, regardless of how dysfunctional it may be.

He led Roselyn through the rooms, and pointed out the wires running up my walls, and across my ceilings. "This is not at all safe," he stressed. "I wouldn't move my family in this fire trap, no-siree-sir. The wiring here is outdated. This is an old house wired long after construction. It has rib and plaster inner walls to deal with. Doing it like this . . . . wiring on the outside is easier. This shoddy work wouldn't pass nowadays. Nope not good. Not good at all."

As they discussed the price of a complete rewiring, the boys ran amuck. The middle child, called Hunter, was trying to climb my wobbly porch pole, in an attempt to mount the roof. His younger brother, Ethan, was jumping on the creaky porch board. It appeared to me he had the intent to complete the breakthrough.

Oh, for a good skunk family when you need one!

Maria, assigned to police them, found escape in Roselyn's car. There, she played the radio full blast. I returned my attention to Roselyn, and the rude man, as they came down my stairs.

"There is no way I could come up with that kind of money," she explained, "at least not this year. I have too much to do to make this livable by winter. Could I work out some kind of arrangement to make payments?"

"Nope, I don't do that anymore. It's just too hard to get my money. If you didn't pay, what am I to do, come over and rip out my work? I don't take those kinds of risks these days."

"Isn't there another option, other than a complete rewire job?" She could not help but think that Sadie's recommendation for this man was overrated, and intended to tell her so.

"You could cover the wiring with conduit, avoid extension cords, and overloading circuits, but it's just not safe in my view. You will have to do it. No licensed electrician will cobble it up like that. His reputation would go to hell in a handbag."

"Go to hell! Go to hell!" mimicked seven-year old Hunter just as he walked in the front door. "Go to hell in a bag!"

Roselyn shot a look at Mr. Wise Guy that seemed to say, "Thanks a lot."

Just then, Maria screamed, "Snake!" Roselyn and Hunter ran to her call of distress.

As the electrician gathered up his tools of the trade, I decided to repay insult with insult. Gathering all the voice energy I could muster, I roared from my upstairs. This is a simple task really. All I must do is draw out the many words and conversations stored in my walls and run them all together in a manner that makes nothing understandable. This causes major confusion in the human brain because it can only understand single phrasing, from individual voices.

The cowardly little menace looked around in shock. He had just descended from an empty upstairs. Realizing he was alone, and without reasonable explanation, he tried to grab everything and make a hasty departure. He tripped on his own feet and fell full-bodied on my floor. All items he carried sprawled around him.

"It was only a bull snake, Maria," Roselyn reassured her as she returned to the opened door. "They won't hurt you, and they are good to keep mice away. Mr. Larson, are you OK?"

"I'm fine, just fine," he answered, scrambling to his feet, and scraping up his stuff in a single sweep. Hurrying out the door, he took a sharp left, and stepped in the hole created when Ethan succeeded in breaking through the board; he then made a second drop, this time into the loose dirt next to the porch. In a flash, he was in his pickup, disappearing in a cloud of dust.

"What's wrong with him? Is he afraid of snakes, too?" asked Maria, stepping down from the picnic table on which she had sought refuge.

"I don't know," pondered Roselyn. "Guess he was more concerned about fire than I thought."

"Go to hell! Go to hell! And go to hell in a bag!" Hunter had put the forbidden phrase to a tune and was now singing it."

Roselyn hurried inside, and Maria turned to her brother, "Not nice, Hunter."

Sticking out his tongue, and wagging his head, Hunter repeated the new melody defiantly.

"Mamma," called Maria, determined to tattle, but Roselyn's attention was consumed in deep thoughts; I knew because I could sift them. She was in panic mode; she must resolve the money issues.

The next day, the plumber came. Hensley Mills was about thirty, and walked with an arrogance that immediately soured my opinion of him. I remembered Sadie's recommendation. She stated she had accepted a date with him. The date must not have worked out to his expectation, I presumed. I sifted some resentful thoughts as he evaluated the job before him. He regretted the quote he gave Sadie. He was now locked into it, and her interest in him, since, had rapidly waned.

Time for a little more fun, I thought, and as he laid his plans, I laid mine. There would be a new toilet bowl and bathroom sink installed. The large porcelain footed tub would remain. A small bathroom would be installed in my upstairs. Finally, all must be hooked up to the cistern and septic.

He was not charging by the hour, but one flat rate. It was a good time to unhitch some of the stored-up resentment I had carried through the last long winter. A five day job turned into ten. I shut doors he opened, and opened doors he shut. I sprouted leaks repeatedly, and started and stopped faucets at will.

I soon realized the hindrance was not mine alone, when the two young lads joined forces with me with their own brand of mischief. By the third day, Hensley's self-restraint over his language depleted, and each slip was quickly adopted by Hunter. Most of them, he adapted to songs, and serenaded through the house. Maria attempted to curtail it, but the little villain ignored her. She, in turn, followed Roselyn around reporting the offenses.

As he struggled to finish this nightmare, Roselyn hauled load after load of boxes and furniture to my first floor. Carman, Kate, and Sadie, helped. As Kate and Roselyn moved things around, Carman mopped my aged floors. Sadie set about to paint my walls.

'Ha, ha!' I thought seeing her set up for the task. So excited was I to challenge this little Miss, I forgot about Hensley. My lack of focus allowed him to finish his work. The self-appointed decorator started in the front parlor, with stark white paint that I hated.

This had, at one time, been William's receiving room, and doctor's office. I remember the day he set up his practice, dividing the large room into two smaller ones. This division had long since been removed, as had the lovely rose-colored paper Helen chose for the walls.

As she poured the white liquid into a pan, Hensley approached her. Preparing to leave, he hoped she remembered the generosity of his work and the low price for doing it.

"Sadie, I've been trying to reach you," he offered. "You are a hard lady to get a hold of. The last block party of the season is on Sixth Street tomorrow night. Would you like to go with me? We could grab a bite to eat at the Brewery. They have a band; I think it's the new country one: The Mountain Men."

"Sounds like a plan, Hensley," Sadie answered, as she began sliding the first streak of the awful colorless lacquer on my wall. "I'm kind of busy though, as you can see. Would you like to help me get this painted?"

Hensley considered this for a moment as she reloaded her roller. The strife of his recent experience, fresh on his mind, led him to decline. "That's okay. I'll catch you later."

"Roselyn," Sadie called. "Come look at this."

Roselyn walked in and surveyed the half-finished north wall. "Why is it so smeary?" she asked.

"That's what I'm wondering," replied Sadie. "No matter how I spread it, the paint just globs up and make weird streaks. I told you we would need primer. I'll run and get some." With that she wiped her hands and headed for the door.

She should have asked me my preference,' I thought. 'I am too grand a Lady to be covered inside, with all white. Where's the flocked paper, the oak paneling? Where is the style?

The painting continued for the rest of the week. Primer did make my resistance more difficult, but I still managed to prevent a smooth cover. Of course between the restless renegades, and me, paint was spilled, hand-printed, and tracked, across floors.

Sadie made it her business to spread it, while the boys helped me with my responsibility to hinder her progress, and Kate and Carmen took up the task of constantly cleaning the messes made by the rest of us. Eventually, it was done, and Roselyn's attempts at hanging curtains over the newly installed window-glass met with success. I had to admit that Helen would have approved of them. They were not so very different from the first lacy ones she made, and used, to dress my first windows.

Kate and Carmen had to return to work, but Sadie took vacation days to assist, since it was her doing in the first place. The sisters worked long hours, sometimes through the night. Covering the wiring and applied sealing compound to the cracks around my windows and doors was tedious. I have to admit the attention soothed me.

They tried to be quiet, and not awaken the little terrorists, but it did not matter. While they worked, I watched the children. I watched them, as I tormented them, with noises and shadows that sent them fleeing to the women with complaints of spooky sightings.

'I'll wear the little dickens out,' I thought. 'Then they will have less energy to create havoc for me throughout the day.' At this I failed; there seemed to be no limit to their energy.

I loved making Maria scream, and challenging Hunter's plots. I avoided causing agony against Ethan; Ethan did not speak. Roselyn and the others discussed it often. He had progressed normally until about two, and then stopped talking at his father's funeral.

To communicate with him, Roselyn and the rest of the family learned sign language. He picked it up quickly. However, no amount of encouragement enticed him to speak a word. He had a special teacher's aide at school who understood his signing. He was a smart child, and Roselyn did not want him to feel different or excluded.

I could sift his thoughts and I knew he was bright. I projected my thoughts to him. He was receptive, and we started communicating. I did not want to lose his trust, so I avoided any frightful tactics with him.

When Roselyn was around, I resisted my haunting as she ignored it. Kate, also, was not easily startled. These two were practical, and paid little attention to what is unexplainable. But Carmen and Sadie were more amusing. Several times, when they were there alone, while Kate and Roselyn ran errands, I let loose.

The giggling kid sounds, accompanied by scampering feet, really shook them up. The preserved sound of Brutus howling was most effective, especially when I moved it from room to room. Once, I waited until they were taking a break, then I started the ruckus upstairs.

First, they ran to each other, and then they looked embarrassed at their girlish fear, and held hands while exploring the upstairs for a reasonable explanation. That was not a problem. I just waited until they were creeping through the upper rooms, then I administered the bouncing ball noise downstairs. This terrified them.

They had no way out of the house without passing through the sounds. They looked foolish sitting on the top step of the staircase, waiting for rescue, when Roselyn returned. They insisted they had just sat there to talk, but their cold cups of coffee, and bowls of melted ice cream on the table, gave them away. I was having such fun.

Chapter Sixteen

MISCHIEF

"Even a bratty house knows when it is time for reverence"

At Christmas time Kate stayed with Roselyn's kids, as well as with Carmen's twins, Ransom and Ridge, while the moms went Christmas shopping in Riverton. This was my first opportunity to check out the twins' fear factor; they were lively little men.

They were identical in every way. At four years old they did not speak plainly, but understood each other perfectly. Carmen explained to her family that it is called twin talk. Communicating with each other satisfied them completely, and their own dialect suited them just fine.

I pulled out my best shadow routine; pulling imagery from my memory, I converted forms into shadows while the boys played with cars or logos in my back parlor, now referred to as family room. I positioned the shadows to hover near them.

Finally one of them noticed, screamed, and pointed. Looking around and seeing nothing to cast it, they ran from the room to the front parlor piling up on a startled grandmother's lap. Maria, upstairs, hearing the commotion, ran down to investigate. There was Kate, buried under the arms and legs of four excited little boys.

"What in Heaven's name is wrong?" demanded Kate. "Why are you so frightened?"

"Shadda . . . . inna woom," cried a twin, I believed to be called Ridge.

"Ya, ya, shadda, shadda," his brother, Ransom, confirmed.

Maria shrugged at her grandmother's questioning look. "What's a shadda?" she asked, trying to calm them.

Of course I can understand them perfectly, and I might have projected the interpretation to Kate, but I was laughing too hard. In fact, I was laughing too hard to withdraw the silly thing. Suddenly, there Kate was, standing with hands on hips looking at the shadow that was being cast by nothing.

"Oops!" I thought, as I evaporated the aberration.

"Everyone, get your coats," Kate directed. "Maria, find their boots."

"Where are we going, Grams?" asked Maria, as she hurriedly obeyed.

"Just for a little ride," answered Kate, in a calm, but determined voice.

Well, what do you know? So the old girl is more jumpy than I thought.

I settled into the quiet; the Christmas tree lights were still on. They cast a festive atmosphere around the room. Moonshine, the kitten, batted a tree ornament across the floor. The aroma of gingerbread lingered from an earlier snack. The radio was playing carols.

I remembered hearing these played throughout the years with my families. I thought of Christmases past, all the way back to Christina's birth at Christmas. She and Gus had many holidays as they grew up under my protection. I reminisced about a Christmas wedding in the parlor, and other events of the season.

There were the lean holidays during the various wars. Some were less jolly than others, due to illness and loss. Many were happy, with celebration and good fortune. I had been so busy in my recent rebellion, I forgot about this special time.

I thought of the graves, by now covered in snow, with animal tracks scattered around the stones. I wondered if the pretentious new hunting lodge was built yet. Thinking of the possibility of those projects knocking down the gravestones was depressing me. I wished someone would return.

I saw lights through my front windows, and a car pulled up. It must be the shoppers; they would wonder where the children, and Grams, are. No one left a note before running away on this snowy evening. The door opened; it was Kate. She held it as four boys, and Maria, tromped in, shaking and stomping off snow. They removed their wraps; no one appeared to be fearful now. I didn't care. My memories had deterred my plans to be beasty. Then Kate took a bottle out of her coat pocket.

"Does holy water really work, Grams?" Maria asked. "Is that why they leave it available at the church, to chase off shadows?"

"Well, it certainly can't hurt," Kate replied as she walked determinedly to the back parlor where my shadow games had occurred.

'Silly woman,' I mused. 'Holy water is for combating evil, providing blessings, evoking healing, but not deterring pranksters.'

I had seen it used, and I understood its purpose. *'Well, this ceremony will provide me entertainment.'*

"Ransom and Ridge," she summoned the twins. "You will not be afraid anymore because the holy water will chase away anything that might frighten you. Here, let me pour some in your hand; sprinkle it at the place you saw the shadow and say, 'God is with me. I am not afraid."

The twins stood side by side and splashed the cold water at my wall. I shivered.

"Dod wif mi. No frid," they said in harmony. Then she armed Ethan, who silently tossed his share. Lastly, Hunter took an ample handful, threw it aggressively, and commanded, "Go to hell in a bag."

I don't know if Kate really believed she would cure my mischief, or if she simply merrily provided the children with a tool to empower them.

No discussion ever took place about it, but my mood for mischief had dissipated. I didn't feel I should act up anymore until after Christmas, so I behaved. Even a bratty house knows when it is time for reverence.

Chapter Seventeen

CARMEN

"I knew Joshua would have loved the humor of the hardy people
now in his home"

I knew I had aged through the years and that my frame was not what it once was, but as the new family shivered through the following winter months, I was disheartened. I had not really wanted strangers taking over, but it was to my shame that I could not keep out the cold. I was incapable of blocking the drafts that forced their way through the cracks around my windows, under my doors, or the cold that pushed up through the floor, from my under belly.

My chimney was declared unsafe so Roslyn installed a propane heater and had a tank delivered. I didn't like the odor of this heating source. I missed the smell of the burning wood, mingling with boiling coffee, and baking bread. I remembered how difficult it was to become accustomed to coal when it was introduced to me, so I tried to be patient with this addition. Roselyn complained of the expense of heating, and I wondered if I might actually be a useless old house, after all, no longer worthy of a family.

My new family wore layers of clothing. They sported long-johns, under flannel shirts, and several pairs of socks, inside heavy shoes. Blankets and quilts, piled high on beds, provided them warmth enough to sleep. I still wasn't sure if I liked this rowdy clan of five. To maintain my independence, I determined I must be the leader in all mischief, and the victim of none. That meant I would have to keep a step ahead of Hunter!

Mud, snow, and ice, in the driveway created havoc for Roselyn in her attempts to get to town. In spite of the inconveniences, she and the other women remained committed that I was worth their efforts, time, and expense, to restore me. Others were not so kind.

Sadie brought a young man, named Mike, over on New Year's Eve. The entire family gathered for refreshments and celebration. While Maria passed around a tray of tiny sandwiches, and Roselyn poured Irish coffee for the adults, Carmen opened cans of soda for the children. As Sadie chattered to her friend about the plans for me, he shook his head.

"I hate to dampen your spirits, Sadie, but you ladies really got taken on this one." stated Mike. "Your sister could have knocked this heap down, and built a new home for less than it will cost you to renovate."

He was walking through my rooms, looking up at my ceilings, "These need to be lowered. This is where your heat is going. And look at the walls. The paint is sliding off. You need new dry wall."

My temperature started to rise, and it wasn't the gas stove bringing it up. How do perfect strangers ever get the nerve to walk into a house, and begin insults, right from the start. We had not even been properly introduced, after all; I didn't even know his full name.

Unfortunately, for him, he was standing directly under one of the metal vents in my ceiling. These were placed in my upstairs bedrooms, during the fifties, to assist with my circulation. This one, in particular, was in the boys' room. Hunter had worked on it for several days, with a screwdriver, fancying it for use in another project.

Sadie protested the suggestion. "Why would one buy an old house because of its charm, and remove that charm by lowering the ceilings?" Her voice was testy.

"Well I wouldn't waste my time on it, or pay to heat it!" he stated, defending his position.

"I guess it's lucky that no one has asked you to." Sadie retorted.

Kate, always the mediator, rushed forward to redirect the conversation. "Hurry, let's move to the living room. They're setting up the board games."

I had been intent on shaking out the last remaining screw. Hunter left it in the vent when he became distracted. As this armchair architect turned to follow Kate, I dropped the vent, my weapon of retaliation, on his head.

'There! Of course heat goes up, dummy. That's how we heat the upstairs, see, right through this hole that's open now that this vent just fell out."

"Ouch!" he exclaimed, as he rubbed the knot on his head. Then I blinked the lights several times, just before sending the vibration of Brutus's howl through the upstairs hall.

"What was that?" he demanded, as he moved away to avoid the crumbs of plaster I was dropping in his face, and then he looked up to determine what had hit him.

"That," began Sadie, "That was . . . . a loose vent!"

"I know," he sounded impatient. "What was the noise?"

Kate took over the explanation, "The upstairs window probably flew open and let in the wind. Come into the living room and I'll get some ice for that lump. I'm so sorry that happened. I tightened the vents down myself, and I can't imagine how it could have fallen out."

The wounded guest followed, grumbling, "How could it be wind? There's no wind." Indeed, he was correct. Although usually windy, the night was calm, cold, and clear.

As the year grew to its final hour, the children packed into sleeping bags near the heater, and gradually surrendered to slumber. The adults settled around, sitting on various miss-matched pieces of furniture, the three sisters had purchased from second hand stores, and yard sales. I noticed Carmen staring at the wall opposite from her. So intently did she focus, I begin to sift her thoughts. She was envisioning a large deer head hanging from that very wall.

I was baffled at first. I had picked up from listening to conversation that these women were all animal lovers, and would never choose to hunt or collect such trophies, so why would she fantasize such a thing?

Then her thought processes cleared up the mystery. Her boyfriend, Carl, was a student taxidermist. He had presented her the massive remains of the slaughtered animal for Christmas. Reluctant to explain that it disgusted her, and did not match her frilly, fluffy feminine décor, she was seeking a new place to store the thing, out of her sight.

As the last drinks toasted the New Year, and those who planned to stay, headed for the stairs, Sadie's friend, Mike, who I would never see again, I must add, departed. Carmen carried the first sleeping twin to the car, and returned for the other one.

As she lifted him, she said, "Roselyn, that wall really needs something. It needs to make a statement. I have just the thing for it. I'll drop it by tomorrow."

True to her word, Carmen delivered the deer mount the following day. Roselyn eyed the beast curiously. "Wow, that's really going to make a statement, all right."

I sifted her thinking and chuckled. She was forming a plan to pass it on to Kate. It took both of them holding it up, and Sadie's help, to attach it to the white wall I had successfully streaked, the previous summer.

"Ugh!" commented Sadie. "Does all of Carl's work look this tacky?"

As the three stood back and examined the effect, Roselyn asked, "Is it just me, or does the poor thing have a goofy expression?"

"Tipping her head, Sadie noted, "No, it's not you. It's goofy. The eyes focusing in opposite directions cause that, I think. Can we straighten them?"

"No," Carmen replied sadly. "I tried. He glued them solid. The crooked nose does not improve it much. He must have had a serious collision with his face during his poor lifetime, or his death. "

"The only statement that will make," offered Sadie, "is, do not take any taxidermy work to Carl."

"Now, hold on!" defended Carmen. "Carl is a very nice man, the twins love him, and part of the money he'll earn when he is in business, is going to buy me presents."

"Right, like this one?" teased Roselyn. They all laughed, and entered my kitchen for coffee."

I was annoyed. There had been hunters throughout the generations who had lived within my walls, and I had supported the hangings of antlers, and bearskins. One family had a buffalo robe on their bedroom floor, as a rug. However, this was dreadful.

Throughout the years that I was alone, the animals were my only companions, and I grew to think of them as friends. Having a dead one, from his shoulders to his crooked nose, hanging in my front parlor was unacceptable. Having one desecrated by such shoddy work made it even more so. It occurred to me to chuck it to the floor. Then I remembered the plan I'd sifted from Roselyn, and decided to hold my temper for a few days.

It took longer than a few days to pass it on, but watching the family's solutions amused me. Sadie, several days later, blindfolded the critter with her knit scarf, and it hid his eyes from view for a week. Then Hunter climbed on top of the couch, removed the scarf, and placed a large cowboy hat between his antlers, and over his eyes.

Roselyn, while packing away holiday items, found an eye patch that had been part of a Halloween costume. Removing the hat, she patched one eye, and placed a pipe in his mouth. Maria provided the final remedy. With poster board and colored cellophane, she fashioned large sunglasses that fit perfectly, hid the eyes, and gave the departed deer the look of a celebrity.

They named him Roy, and he remained with us until Easter. At that time, he reappeared as a surprise in Kate's studio, decorated with colored eggs swinging from his antlers. A note attached stated, "Hello, I am your new model. Paint me, please." She painted and framed three pictures of Roy, giving one to each daughter. I honestly think these were gifts of revenge.

Roselyn quickly replaced Roy's position on my wall with a lovely tapestry she found at the antique store. "Hmmm, now that's my idea of a statement," she whispered. I whispered back my approval, but she had not yet learned to pull in my projections.

I missed old Roy a bit. I missed him because he inspired a sense of humor that lightened the chill of that very cold winter. It reminded me of a young lad from years ago. A boy named Joshua, whose pranks and laughter filled my fibers with joy.

I knew Joshua would have loved being part of the games with Roy, and the hardy people, now in his old home.

Chapter Eighteen

CHRISTINA'S SON 1892

"The last gift we can give Christina is to raise her son"

It is difficult to avoid favorites among family members. I loved all of them through the years, as generations of children grew into adults, and had children of their own. Joshua, Christina's son, was a favorite.

However, I must first catch you up on the events that preceded his birth. The seventeen years of Christina's childhood, and development into a beautiful young woman, was a delightful experience for a house. She had her father's dark hair, and her mother's light eyes. Tall, like William, she was a stately form.

Helen educated her, and taught her music from the pump organ, eventually acquired, for our pleasure. Christina, with a quick mind, accomplished all available education in this western wilderness. She had a lovely voice, as well, and at age seventeen went to Maryland to live with relatives and seek an education in music. She privately hoped for a career in performing. Her parents were not pleased with her choice.

Helen preferred she marry one of several ranchers' sons who came courting, and raise a family nearby. William hoped she would choose medicine. He taught her many things about his practice, and she accompanied him often on house calls. Neither parent approved of her traveling so far from home. Frequent stage robberies made traveling a bit worrisome. Bank robberies had increased at an alarming rate over the previous decade, as gangs raided communities and escaped into a safe fortress at 'Hole-in-the-Wall'.

Christina, and her cousin, Gus, aged sixteen, were best friends growing up. His departure left her lonely and restless. The homestead that Duncan and Maddie claimed did not work out for farming as ours did. The distance was farther from the river.

The soil, concentrated with alkali, caused difficulty with their wells. They were not productive, and the water was not usable for drinking. Duncan resorted to raising sheep. Sheep did well, even on land rejected for farming. The sheep industry thrived in Central Wyoming, shipping wool to other areas, to factories to make yarn, cloth, and garments.

A community grew up around the fort, which changed its name from Fort Brown to Fort Auger. In 1890, the community became a town. The new town was named Lander, after General Frederick W. Lander, a western explorer.

There was now more law enforcement, but crimes continued to occur. There was tension between cattle ranchers and sheep growers. This, along with the rejection by some folks, of a marriage with an American Native, eventually compromised his contentment.

As Duncan grew restless, news of gold in Alaska, and a new frontier, finally lured him to take some risks. In the spring of 1891, he said goodbye to the family: he left Maddie and Gus to manage the sheep ranch, and began his quest for fortune. He intended to return a wealthy man.

Duncan arrived safely at Birch Creek, Alaska. Maddie received a letter late in the fall describing the beauty of this wilderness, the prospects of mining, and his plans to return in a few years, wealthy enough to move the family to Oregon. There he hoped to start a farm that Gus would someday inherit.

By late winter news arrived that Duncan had died in a mining accident. His partners preserved his body, by freezing it, until his family could be notified. Maddie, heartbroken, sold their land to a neighboring rancher. She paid the expense for Duncan's partners to bring back his remains. She and Gus buried him in the aspen grove that eventually became our cemetery.

This was the first grave. Maddie used the money from the sale of land and sheep, in addition to the gains Duncan earned in Alaska, to return to Oklahoma. She hoped Gus could spend time among her Cherokee relatives.

Gus missed Wyoming, and soon returned. He lived with my family and helped with the ranch. But his leaving provided the motivation Christina needed to convince her parents she must go east. She left midsummer,1892.

The seventeen-year-old did well in her music studies for a few months. Helen, and William, read her two letters repeatedly. Eventually, a portrait arrived that had been mailed in August, but did not arrive for some months later. This encouraged her parents since they had received no word from her after the two letters. The portrait hung on the rose-colored wall.

With the package, was a hasty note stating, "I met a wonderful man and he is assisting me in meeting the right people to further my success. I hope to bring him back to meet you soon." Then there was silence.

William wrote letters to his family in Maryland; they reported to have lost track of Christina in November, several months after she left Maryland. Finally, the parents could wait in misery no longer. In the spring William traveled to his home state to begin a search for his daughter. Three months passed, and Helen and I were alone. I tried to keep happy vibrations moving through my rooms, hovering around her, but she was inconsolable.

Then the letter came, delivered by the good pastor and his wife, who remained with her for several days.

August 12, 1893

My Darling Helen,

I am writing to inform you that I located our lovely daughter. Her life's journey did not take her to the dreams she expected. She married a man that I do not find admirable. He is much older than she. He does not appear to value loyalty, or any other virtue, that I can find.

The air, food, and some of her acquaintances here in the city, are not a healthy sort for our Christina. By the time I located her, she was very ill. To my surprise, she had a baby boy. His name is Joshua, and he is a bright and lively newborn.

Friends have cared for him since his birth as Christina's frailty prevented her from providing all he needed. His father, it seems, can barely take care of himself. He drinks far too much to be of any use. I believe he spends much of his time in the opium parlors that are popular here. He has little interest in the lad, so I will be returning with him. Do you think, sweet Helen, we can raise a boy after such a long time with no children in our midst?

Now my dear I must tell you what I dreaded to report. Little Joshua and I will be the only ones coming home. Christina passed away, a few days after I found her in an infirmary, suffering from an internal infection. This was caused, I am sure, by dirty conditions around her when the midwife delivered her baby.

I believe the doctor who eventually treated her did his best, but he is of the old school, and uses strong potions, most extremely. Strong medicines were not used in our home, and she could not have acquired a tolerance for them. Perhaps they weakened her constitution. There were no homeopathic physicians available.

I fear our daughter also inherited my weak lungs, and the poor conditions of the city air overtook her. I will bring her home in a sealed coffin. We will lay her to rest in the aspen grove, near her uncle.

Since the trip is long and rugged, a wet nurse, named Hilga, will be with us to feed the babe. She lost her own child soon after birth and has been caring for Joshua. She has no husband, and desires to start a new life in the West.

I love you, sweet Helen, and I wish I could hold you now with this terrible news. Perhaps you can begin preparations for Joshua. He has nothing, and will need everything. The last gift we can give Christina is to raise her son.

Your loving husband,

Willie

P.S. Joshua is two months old, and we shall adopt him. His name is Joshua Max Yingling. He will be our son.

*   *   *

Christina's funeral was quickly completed, but the fellowship lasted until long after dark. Friends and acquaintances, from everywhere, gathered in my front yard to attend. The August day was surprisingly cool and overcast, making the outdoor service bearable.

Dr, Yingling had attended the bedside of many in the valley, and they came to share his grief. Helen had been faithful to offer comfort to others, and now they sought to comfort her. They buried Christina next to Duncan and Helen, and immediately transplanted a pink rose bush near her grave.

The men constructed a long makeshift table outside, under the shade of the cottonwoods. Food of all sorts supplied strength to those who shared its bounty. The diversity of all who attended was like no other gathering, I heard William say.

Merchants came with their wives, carrying cakes, pies, and the rare canned delicacies, brought to their stores by train. Ranchers came; their wives bringing roasts, potatoes, and brown gravies. Sheep producers came. Their families provided mutton stew and shepherd bread. The neighbors from the reservation came; the women supplied fry bread, dried meats, and chokecherry gravy.

I saw old John Walking Thunder, his white hair in long braids, walking with his children, and granddaughter, Mary. His wife died the previous year, and William officiated at her funeral and wake. In tears and grief, all were in union. No feuds, prejudices, grudges, or disagreements, were remembered on that day.

It did not slip my notice that Mary often sent shy glances toward Gus, and these were rewarded with his gentle smiles. Moreover, in the midst of it all, much attention was directed toward a small, dark-eyed babe with straight dark hair, and dimples that radiated with his smile. That baby boy sleeping soundly in his nursemaid's lap was Joshua.

Chapter Nineteen

JOSHUA

"After all, who could reminisce, and feel sad, with such racket going on?"

Christmas and New Year passed, and the time moved slowly as the cold dark days of winter dragged by. Roselyn busily worked on her computer, and the children went to school, leaving little to observe. When bored, an old lady falls back into her memories, and I found myself doing just that.

After Joshua came to our family, the joys of baby laughter, squeals, and pattering baby feet lightened my days. Gus soon married Mary Walking Thunder, and her presence added warmth.

She was young, so Helen taught her much about cooking, and sewing, in return Mary helped with the care of Joshua. Among outsiders, not everyone was open-minded toward Mary. Helen was the one to feel the hurt, caused by prejudice of the few. She loved Gus as her own, and was growing very fond of Mary. Gus seemed immune. He had grown up in the area, and was used to belittling remarks, and snobbish stares, from the few who held to the ignorance of bigotry.

But for the most part, times were happy for my expanding family. There was laughter and happenings in my kitchen, around the table, for meals, and around the hearth.

Mary felt more comfortable attending services at the mission. She had grown up under the ministry of Father Roberts. Her young husband was committed to whatever made Mary happy. Gus spent more and more time with Reverend John Roberts. The Episcopal priest had established the mission at Fort Washakie some 15 years before. Mary knew him well, having attended school at the mission.

In time, Gus announced to his aunt and uncle that he wanted to become a minister. Mary was awaiting the birth of their first child, so he went alone to study at an Episcopal seminary in Minnesota. She would join him when their child was old enough to travel.

Little Alfred Kenyon was born in February, in one of my upstairs bedrooms. One-year-old Joshua was excited about the birth of his little cousin. He was nurturing and protective. My rooms were full of the hustle and bustle of babies again. Diapers hanging on the line, and lullabies, sang to the sound of chairs rocking on my wooden floors. I continued with my own lullabies, and surrounded them with love.

In late August, when Alfred was six months old, Mary and baby left to join Gus. I was never to see them again. Joshua whimpered complaints about missing them; Helen was silent, but I knew she shed a few tears in private. William often mentioned them in evening prayers.

They wrote letters that were read around the hearth at night, and I took comfort in them. After his schooling was complete, the Reverend Augustus Kenyon, and his family, were assigned to the mission on the Warm Springs Reservation in Oregon. The letters came until both Helen and William passed, and then they stopped. I wonder even now what happened to them, especially Alfred, but I accept that I will never know.

Joshua continued to be the light of the house in 1899, when at six-years old, William, decided it was time for formal schooling. He adored his grandparents and his quick mind was always eager to learn. His mother, Christina, was taught at home by her parents, but Joshua attended the little school house operating in Lander.

Every day, he saddled his horse, a mustang William had broken and trained, and rode off to share one teacher with a group of children, who were in several levels of their education. The teacher, for the first few years, was a lovely young lady. Miss Adkins was dedicated, patient, and inspiring. Joshua advanced rapidly. But in his third years of attendance, Miss Adkins married and resigned.

It seemed another teacher would not be found, and Helen retrieved her McGuffey textbooks from storage, in my attic. Joshua must not fall behind in his studies. I loved listening to the lessons around the table in my kitchen. It reminded me of Christina's days of learning.

By August, a man moved to Lander, and was hired for the post. Mr. Barker was not liked by the students, and even the parents began to suspect his ability in the art of teaching. He was short-tempered, and did not hesitate to use the strap for the slightest offense. He gave assignments, but no instruction. Often, weeks passed before grades from those assignments were released back to the students.

During the evening meals, William and Helen conversed with Joshua about his school day. Although they never discussed the teacher in a negative way around the boy, my sifting assured me that they had great concern. Helen wanted to resume his teaching at home. William argued he should finish the year.

"If Mr. Barker is assigned again next year, we will teach him at home, "He promised.

The disinterest of Mr. Barker to educate the children, and the dislike the students had for him, developed into a volatile situation. The older boys began unruly behavior, in spite of the strap. Joshua was warned by his grandfather not to be influenced by these older lads.

A nail was driven into the seat of the school master's chair from underneath. This caused a frightening puncture when he sat down the following morning. No one confessed, so all the boys took a strapping.

"I don't think it was fair, that all of us got strapped, Papa," Joshua complained. "Tim Whitman did it, but none of us were going to snitch on him."

"Doing something deliberately to cause harm to another person is always wrong, Josh, be sure you are never a part of that sort of behavior," warned William.

William's thoughts, that I sifted, led me to believe he had talked to other parents, and something was being planned.

Another incident occurred that brought the instructor's wisdom into doubt. A first grader, Ned Smithson, was allowed to go to the outhouse, and did not return in a reasonable amount of time. His sister begged Mr. Barker to allow her to check on him.

The hateful man refused, saying, "It's below zero out there, when he gets cold enough, he'll return."

After several hours of Sally Smithson's crying, Joshua jumped up and ran out to check on the boy. He found little Ned frozen to the wooden toilet seat, with tears crusted in ice crystals on his cheeks. Joshua covered the child with a coat he had grabbed on the way out, and ran to the blacksmith shop, a short ways off, to fetch help.

Little Ned was brought to William's office, as he had experienced hypothermia. This was one of the few times I ever saw William angry. After treating the child, he came to my back parlor where Helen was sewing.

"I am going into town. I want to speak with some of the other fathers. I have reached the end of my tether with Mr. Barker. It is time to think of these young scholars."

Mr. Barker, the fathers of the students, and the clergy, had a meeting in my dining room. It was decided that Mr. Barker would be told a dismissal could be expected if one more such incident occurred. Guidelines requiring his performance as a teacher were determined, and explained.

I was very proud of William on that Saturday afternoon. He was a quiet man, a gentle soul, but he was a firm leader when the need presented itself.

The older schools boys had their own meeting, it seemed. The following morning after assigning work, Mr. Barker checked his chair carefully and sat down to fill his pipe. He observed a strange powder in his can of tobacco.

He yelled out at the class. "Who has poisoned my tobacco?" His question was met with silent stares.

"I will whip all of you, if no one confesses," he threatened. More silence.

Just at that moment, Sheriff Angus Mac Gerry opened the school house door and walked in. Everyone turned and gazed at him curiously.

"Class is dismissed," the sheriff announced. "All of you go straight home. There will be no more school until you are notified."

As the children gathered books and coats, Mr. Barker approached Sheriff Mac Gerry with his tobacco can, and held it out forcibly.

"See here, Sheriff," he demanded. "These hooligans have poisoned my tobacco. You must find out who is guilty, I want him arrested."

Angus poured some of the tobacco into his hand. He moved it around, smelled it, and then announced, "Gun powder".

He looked around the room, his gaze resting on the older boys. "This could injure someone very badly. If Mr. Barker had lit his pipe, he could have been blinded, suffered burns, and even loss of hearing. Shame on you! Now go home! I will talk to your parents later!"

"But, someone should be arrested!" protested the offended teacher.

"At the moment, Mr. Barker, my job is to arrest you." answered the lawman. He held up a wanted poster. "Bank robbery in Laramie? Does that mean anything to you?"

Sherriff Angus told this story to William and Helen in detail. They discussed it on my porch. "Can you believe it, Doc?" asked Angus, "Running from a crime like bank robbery, straight to applying for a job teaching school?"

"He was probably quite sure that no one would come looking for him in that position," reasoned William. "It is too bad there isn't a way to check on someone's past. We need to organize a board to run the school. They could check up a little more, require letters of references, and proof of education. We can't make any more mistakes like this. Our children are too important."

Mr. Barker did not teach another day, and the position was filled by volunteers until a real teacher could be found. Mrs. Jones, a widow, took the responsibility, and taught until Joshua finished 8th grade. But Joshua's lessons from the experience of having Mr. Barker, were rich. He learned to be brave against coercion, when in defiance he rescued Little Ned. But he also learned that the possible consequences of taking revenge too far, were too high a price for getting even. He was glad he had not known about the plot of the gunpowder-laced tobacco.

In 1909, the town of Lander was blessed with access to the Cowboy Line railroad, part of the *Chicago and North Western Railway*. A train station was built by the river at the edge of town. People were excited. It was believed that eventually Lander would connect with California. More products were available as merchants could ship orders directly from Chicago, and farther east, much faster than by mules and wagons.

Joshua boarded with a family in Cheyenne to attend high school. At seventeen he went to Maryland, and stayed with a great uncle. He worked at the mill, and attended medical school. The years he was away were so lonely for William and Helen. I missed him too.

A great war became the focus of my family. Later, they would call it World War I, but at that time it was, 'The War'. Helen and William discussed it often. Joshua did not go to war. He continued with medical school, and often volunteered to serve in military hospitals.

He wrote home often, and his letters were read aloud in the evenings, warming us with news and reports of his progress. It cheered us up from the dismal news of the war. Eventually, he wrote more and more about a young woman he had met, Victoria Frère. We were not surprised when he announced they planned to wed.

It was 1917. I did not remember Helen being this excited before. Joshua and Victoria were coming home to be married, and the ceremony would be within my walls. I was excited, too. How thoughtful of them to include me in this joyful event. Helen even had the front parlor repapered.

The long maintained rose-covered wall paper was replaced with a light golden brown, covered with tiny yellow daisies. Helen pulled up the rug, dragged it to the clothesline, and beat it unmercifully. Before putting it back down, she mopped the floors. The silver was polished, and the curtains were washed, starched, and ironed. William joked that he feared she would start on him next.

Finally the couple arrived by train. Victoria's mother arrived with them, as chaperone. During the two weeks she was there, the wedding was arranged. William and Joshua hand-delivered the invitations. Her wedding dress was unpacked, and carefully pressed. Then it was wrapped in a sheet, and hung in the attic, to be sure Joshua would not see it before the special day.

A cake was made, hams were baked, and a feast was laid out on the lawn. Joshua asked a childhood friend to be his attendant. Victoria wanted her mother to stand with her. It was a beautiful wedding, but of course, I had never seen a wedding so I would think so.

The photographer took pictures and soon they would be hanging on my walls. But something else now hung on the parlor's new daisy-covered paper. Joshua brought a gift home to his parents: a large mirror, set in a hand-carved oak frame. It was purchased from an artisan wood carver in New York, and Helen adored it.

The newly married couple moved in, and I was delighted. Again, there were happy sounds of women cooking, sewing, laughing, and scheming. The two doctors kept busy, seeing patients, and mixing compounds for medications, in the apothecary room.

Joshua made the house calls, so his aging grandfather could manage the patient visits at his home office. Joshua also took over supervision of the farmhands. The war ended, and life was happy and hopeful again.

The following year, Johanna was born. Blonde, like her mother, with Joshua's brown eyes; what a beautiful child she was. My walls again echoed baby's laughter, and sometimes baby's cries. I recorded them all.

Several years later, little James joined the family. He was a rowdy child, sliding down my banisters, chasing the chickens, and playing soldier. Life was wonderful, and never was any day boring.

A decade later, Joshua would bury both his grandparents in the aspen grove. They passed a few months apart from each other. It was a sad spring when I lost them, but I never felt they were really gone. At least not while I could see their graves, the orchard they planted, Helen's roses, and Christina's tulips.

The following summer, Joshua took on a new project. This was a worthy cause, started by William. During the years William was the only doctor for miles around, he thought of a plan to help spread the knowledge of safe medical practice.

He penned manuscripts of medical information that could be understood by student doctors, midwives, and trained nurses. Rather than writing one large cumbersome book, he wrote numerous small pocket-sized booklets, each addressing one particular treatment, disease, or condition. One, he wrote, was called, "Safe Methods of Childbirth and Care for New Mothers".

These were published in the East. William had a photograph taken of himself, and it was published inside the cover of each book. He explained to Joshua why he had written the information in understandable laymen terminology. By constructing information into small booklets, addressing individual's topics, he could assist pioneer doctors, mid-wives, and practical nurses, who were too far from others to seek consultation. He personally financed the project, and distributed them to western medical practitioners for reasonable prices. The money gained was used to publish more as needed.

William passed away soon after he launched the project, and for a time it was forgotten. Now after receiving requests, Joshua returned to the plan. Even several medical schools requested the booklets as reference material. Students could easily carry them in doctor bags, or a single, in a coat pocket. Receiving the newly published booklets, repacking them, and shipping them to fill orders, took a lot of time. Johanna provided the help he needed.

The memories and sadness overcame me, and I wept. Streaks of my tears formed moisture on my windows, and dripped down my panes.

But just then the door slammed. Two rowdy boys ran to the refrigerator, each elbowing the other, with the intent to be the first to emerge his head into its contents. Roselyn was clambering down the stairs from her office when Maria announced," Mama, I need some stuff for my science project."

I slipped from the past, back to the present. After all, who could reminisce and feel sad, with such racket going on?

Chapter Twenty

SPRING

"Poor Hunter," said Kate, watching from the window.
"That child really needs interaction with a dad"

By early spring the snow had melted from around the house, and much of the mud was dried. April is unpredictable in Wyoming. The family that now inhabited me was excited by the promise of longer days and more sunshine. Sadie, Kate, Carmen, and the twins, visited on one such sunny Saturday.

Ethan and the twins were playing with legos in the back parlor; Maria was sitting on my front porch, in shorts, and a sleeveless blouse, attempting to absorb the first rays of spring for a sun tan. So far all she had achieved were chills and goose bumps. Hunter, unnoticed by the others, was busy with a screwdriver, removing the knob from my bathroom door.

Carmen stirred her coffee, watching the rich cream dissipate and turn the black liquid to warm brown. "We need to do something special for Easter," she announced.

"How about an egg hunt here at Muddy Gulch?" suggested Kate, glancing out the kitchen window toward the mountains. The snow there was melting a little every day, constantly changing the view from white mountains, to purple ones.

"Now Mom," scolded Roselyn, "don't start sticking ugly names on my little paradise here." Bringing the plate of humus wraps to the table, she called Maria to come in.

Giving her a platter of cheese sandwiches, she instructed her to pass lunch out to the boys. "I think an egg hunt could be fun."

I was picking up interest. My families, in the sixties and seventies, did this on the old property. It was entertaining, watching the hunt from my lofty perspective.

Sadie, breaking off a bite size piece of her humus wrap, entered the conversation, "Let's make it a barbeque, and I could get Trey to dress up like a giant rabbit. Mom has that costume in her studio."

Trey was the new guy Sadie was dating. He was an employee of the National Outdoor Leadership School (NOLS) in Lander.

Roselyn raised her gaze, and looked at her younger sister. "How did we get from an egg hunt to such a big fuss? I swear Sadie, you make everything so dramatic."

"It's my right," Sadie argued. "I'm a Leo, and the youngest."

Her argument was cut short when Maria yelled from the back of the house, "Mom, Hunter took the doorknob off the bathroom door and won't tell me where he put it."

Roselyn rolled her eyes, "It's okay, Maria. I will deal with him later." Then, looking back at Sadie, she asked, "So, how's this romance going with Trey?"

"Don't know that I would call it a romance, but it has gotten me some free rock climbing lessons," she answered.

Kate's head turned quickly. "Rock climbing? As in crawling straight up the cliffs in Sink Canyon, like a spider? Sadie, I don't feel comfortable with that."

I'm a big girl, Mom, and Trey knows what he's doing," Sadie returned.

"Hmmm, like Ron? The dude who was going to teach you how to safely skydive, and you ended up with a broken arm?" teased Carmen.

"Or," added Roselyn," Ben, and his idea that you needed to drive his crash-up derby car in the powder puff competition?" Mom nearly had a heart attack watching Ben pull you out the car window after the car burst into flames."

"Hush," hissed Sadie. "I don't want to talk about that. But by the way, speaking of men in general, that Dennis Dickenson who bought the original land this house was on, came by our office yesterday."

"Really?" asked Kate, "Is he already trying to sell it?"

"No," explained Sadie, taking her plate to the sink. "He was asking about you, Roselyn?"

"Me?" Roselyn proclaimed. "Whatever for? I don't even know what he looks like."

"You've probably seen him," offered Carmen. "He's tall, broad, red-headed and, kind of a show-off. He's all over the place: grocery stores, bars; he even came into our office for stitches after a fight. I normally wouldn't disclose that, but since it was right across the bridge of his nose, it is no secret."

Thoughtfully, Kate stated, "When I renewed my plates, I overheard him at the court house inquiring about land that could be purchased for back taxes. Seems like a man with a plan."

"I don't know what he's up to," said Sadie. "I don't know about his plan, but he wanted to know if any land out here was listed with us. When I said it was not, he asked if you were my sister, and if you would be interested in selling."

"Really?" pondered Roselyn, "What did you tell him?"

"No how, no way, on any day," answered Sadie, using her perpetual habit of creating poetry on the spot.

The women met several times to plan the egg hunt. Carmen invited Carl's sister's family. They had three children. Sadie invited her business partner, a divorced woman, with a 10 year old son. Marie invited two of her best friends.

"Hmmm," calculated Roselyn, "so far we have eleven children, and eight adults."

"The more the merrier," announced Sadie. "I bought a really nice grill. I'll need to borrow your pickup to bring it over." She looked at Roselyn.

"Why don't we make it easy, and have hot dogs and burgers?" suggested Kate. "Kids like them better anyway."

I have the cutest pattern for turning angel food cakes into bunnies, offered Carmen. "I'll make enough for everyone."

"I'll bring a big pan of my spectacular green bean casserole," announced Sadie.

"Carl's sister makes potato salad to die for," Carmen added. "She will be happy to make it."

Kate committed to hot dogs and beef patties, and then warned, "If the guests are to bring food, we must remind them that nothing can contain peanuts, peanut oil, or peanut butter. We surely don't want to poison Roselyn, after all."

"Yes, please," agree Roselyn.

In sifting her thoughts, I could see a memory of an incident that I assumed was a reaction. It appeared she had nearly died from consuming something toxic to her. I could not remember anyone being allergic to peanuts, but I did remember an incident with a bee sting.

The Saturday before Easter, my kitchen filled with women in aprons. The counters were covered with pans of boiled eggs, and small dishes of colored dyes. Marie was assigned to occupy the younger kids; she set up a movie in the family room, my former back parlor, and sat down with a book.

She had failed to count heads. Hunter was not present. He was outside, hovered between two cars, Sadie's and Kate's. He wasn't visible from the kitchen window, but I could see him with the view of my upper story. He had snitched his mother's nail file. By pushing the sharp point into the air nozzle, he discovered he could release the air from the tire.

"This day is going to get interesting," I thought.

"Do you think four dozen will be enough?" asked Roselyn.

"Heavens, yes," answered her mother, "and most of them will go to waste. Kids fill up more on candy these days, than boiled eggs."

Sadie had left the room, but returned, and asked, "How am I supposed to use your bathroom when there is no knob on the door. How do I secure it?"

"The boot," answered Roselyn.

"Boot?" Sadie tipped her head like a cocker spaniel.

"There's a boot inside the door," explained Roselyn as she lifted a purple egg from the dye. "You go inside, shut the door, and prop the boot against it. Jeeez, Sadie, do we have to potty train you?"

"Well, what I want to know is, where's the knob?" Sadie responded, "We put in all new doorknobs when we painted."

"Don't know," her sister answered. Hunter hid it somewhere, and I haven't gotten around to buying another."

Kate suddenly looked up from painting an egg with an artist brush, "Do you still need the bunny costume, Sadie? Your friend, Trey, is he willing to be Peter Rabbit?"

"No, he's history. He was too superficial for words," answered Sadie. "But, hey, what the heck. I'll be the stupid rabbit."

The women completed their task quietly for a while, and I turned my focus to the wannabe mechanic in the driveway. I could see he accomplished his goals as both left tires on Sadie's convertible were flat, and both right tires on Kate's jeep were going down. Then, something else caught my attention. Upon the hill, where the dirt road turns onto the highway, set a red pickup truck.

"I know the truck," I told myself. I zoomed my vision to bring in detail. The driver's face was hidden behind binoculars.

At that moment Hunter trotted by, nail file in hand. Roselyn jumped from her seat, and a chase commenced from the kitchen to the yard. As she caught him, and wrestled the metal file from his hand, Hunter rewarded her with screams.

"Poor Hunter," said Kate, watching from the window. "That child really needs interaction with a dad."

The eggs were placed in the refrigerator which was filled to capacity with the foods prepared for the following day. Kate made arrangements to pick up all the kids for Mass the next morning. The sisters planned to meet here, hide eggs, and set out the meal. Goodbyes were said, and they singled out the front door. I calmly waited for the reaction. The yells of the women revealed they discovered their plight. Roselyn ran out and saw the havoc.

"Looks like Hunter struck again," she stated sadly. "Sorry."

They all pitched in and resolved the issue. Carmen's spare tire was the same size as Sadie's. She would loan it to her, and with Sadie's own spare, she could get her flat tires into town, and air them up. Roselyn's pickup spare sized with Kate's jeep, so the same plan would work for them.

Hunter was scolded soundly, and sent to his room. Only after the women completed changing out the tires, did the red pickup and binoculars turn around and drive back out onto the highway.

Later that evening, as the family settled into their beds, I entertained the idea of providing some haunting, but I declined.

Instead, I immersed into the memories of Easters past.

Chapter Twenty-One

ROBERT PARKER-1894

"My men will provide all the security you will ever need"

Thinking about Easter and the coming of spring took me back to the spring of 1894. Helen was sitting on my front porch cutting cull potatoes into small chucks for later garden planting.

The tulips were up, their bright red petals not yet opened into blooms. The climbing rose vine clung to the trellis, and displayed buds that would burst into tiny leaves in a few days. Patches of snow melted in shady areas on my north side. But the sun was bright, and Helen was comfortable with only her shawl draped over her shoulders.

Two men rode up, and stopped in front of us. Helen rose and asked if she could help them in some way. One requested to see Dr.Yingling. At that moment, William walked out of the house and joined Helen on my porch. They noticed one man appeared to be injured. The larger cowboy slid from his horse, and assisted the thinner man in dismounting. They walked toward my steps.

"My partner here had a fall," explained the heavier man. "He moaned and groaned all night. I think he broke something."

"Come on in," invited William. "I will have a look at it. My wife will pour you up some coffee."

Helen set her pot of potato pieces aside. As the doctor led his patient into my treatment room, she directed the chunkier man to have a seat in one of the two chairs in my, now tiny, front parlor.

"I will warm you some coffee, sir. What did you say your name was?"

"Robert Parker," he answered, "and I thank you for your hospitality."

I centered my attention on my treatment room where William was poking around on the man's shoulder.

"How did you bang yourself up like this?" he asked.

"I was tossed off ma hoss," he answered through a mouthful of chewing tobacco. "Landed ret on ma shoulder." He wiped his mouth on his sleeve.

"Looks like you dislocated the joint," informed William. "Remove the shirt please, and you should remove the plug that is in your mouth. When I set your shoulder, you might choke on it."

Helen brought Mr. Parker coffee, and a slice of pound cake. She sat down in the other chair and glanced into the cradle where the infant Joshua napped peacefully. Never idle, Helen picked up her embroidery.

Suddenly a scream startled both of them, waking the child, who added his howls to the alarm. Mr. Parker jumped up, reaching his right hand inside his coat. Helen moved quickly to pick up the frightened baby. William opened the door and emerged with a smiling face.

"All fixed," he announced. "Now I have to wrap it tightly."

Helen sat back down, placing Joshua on her lap. I could see Mr. Parker tucking a pistol back into an inner pocket of his light coat. I determined I did not care for this man. He had been treated with courtesy by my owners, and yet he had entered our presence with a hidden gun. Silence settled in, and soon the doctor and patient entered my front area.

William explained, "Setting a joint is painful, and he will be hurting for a few more days. I told him to keep his arm stationary for a while, letting it heal, then start moving it around gently."

Seeing his wife was comforting his grandson, William brought a chair from my dining room and said, "Sit down, young man. I will get you some of that coffee and cake your partner has. I promise you that my wife's cooking can make anyone forget their pain."

As he returned with the nourishment, Mr. Parker stood. He peeled off a number of bills from a large money-roll. He handed the bills to William. The doctor took a bill from the assortment, then handed back the rest.

"This is plenty," he said. "It only took a few minutes and no medication was needed."

"Please take it all," Mr. Parker insisted. "We really appreciate your help, and will probably come back when we need a doctor again."

William shook his head, "You can come back anytime, but you need not overpay me. Do you live near here?"

"About 75 miles north. I have a ranch outside of Dubois," he answered.

"That's a long way to come for a doctor," William suggested. "Isn't Doctor Burdick still up there?"

"He's there," answered Parker, "but our work brings us around here a lot. We do a lot of business with Herb Bassett."

As the men turned to go, I observed Mr. Parker slip the extra money into his empty coffee cup. After they left William remarked, "A suspicious sort a fellow, isn't he?"

Several week later Easter Sunday arrived. My family rose long before dawn. Helen prepared several pots of coffee, and placed them on the wood stove. She set several pans of cinnamon rolls on the kitchen table; she had made them the night before.

We were hosting a sunrise service and light breakfast. Soon a half dozen or so neighbors arrived and began gathering on the porch.

Watching the sunrise from my east porch is always beautiful, but it was especially grand as the group sang hymns through the evolving process.

Once the sunlight poured its colorful hues onto the upturned faces, William read the resurrection story from the Bible, and said a prayer. The group filed into the warm house for coffee and rolls. Jed Tanner, cup in hand, sauntered over to William.

"We were driving the buggy here this morning and when we passed the Bassett ranch, we noticed a commotion going on over there," he said. It looked like a roundup, but it's pretty early to take cattle up to the mountain pastures, and being Easter Sunday and all, I thought it odd."

William thoughtfully took a bite from his roll, "It is unusual," he replied. "Wonder what Herb's up to. Maybe he's going to drive them south to sell."

William did not make a connection, but I did. I remembered Parker referring to the local Bassett ranch, his own ranch in Dubois, and him being quick to think of his gun when his partner screamed through the bone setting. I also remember the giant roll of money with which he was so generous.

Later that spring this mystery man returned. William invited him in, and soon realized that the visit was not a medical call. Helen had set the table for supper, and of course, they invited him to stay.

Mr. Parker accepted and generously filled his plate. They discussed the recovery of the man with the dislocated shoulder, the weather in Dubois where spring arrives later, and finally, as Helen cut pie, Parker opened a new subject.

"I noticed you have a patch of good grassland between here and the mountain," he stated. "You don't seem to be using it. Do you have plans for that land?"

"I had planned to build my daughter a house there, and deed her half of my land," answered William.

Parker's eyes widened, "You have a daughter? Does she live here?" he asked with obvious interest.

"She is with the Lord," said Helen, not looking up from her task of pouring more coffee.

Robert Parker appeared confused at first, and then seemed to realize her meaning. "I'm sorry for your loss," he said quietly.

William nodded, "She was very dear to us, but we feel she is still with us in her child." He reached over and ruffled Joshua's hair. "I suppose he will inherit all this land. So you see, Sir, it's not for sale."

I was steaming mad, 'This man was up to something. I had not missed his interest in learning there might be a young lady living here. What did that suggest? Was he planning a scheme? Had he thought he could use her in his plot?'

"I wasn't looking to buy your land, Mr. Yingling," he explained. "I was hoping you would rent it to me for temporary pasture." When there was no response, Parker elaborated.

"I need a place to graze cattle while I move them to and from Dubois, a place where there is room enough to brand. I can pay you good, real good!"

William patted his napkin against his mustache, "We are not interested in renting any land, Mr. Parker," he said softly.

William looked Parker in the eye, "There is lots of rustling going on all around here lately. There is also lots of tension between cattlemen and sheep men. We have sold our cattle, and extra horses. When Joshie is older, we may do some farming, but until then, I don't want to open my land up to possible conflict."

Robert Parker's face dropped in disappointment. "You know doctor, I am able to pay you more money to rent that land for about four months, than you can make in a year of doctoring," he stressed.

Then he continued, "Your ranch is located in the perfect location for my purpose. I will even have my boys do any fencing you might need done, and provide you and your misses all the beef you can eat. If you are concerned about the range wars, and rustling that's going on, my men will provide all the security you will ever need," he added.

"My decision is final," William replied firmly.

The visitor left, and Helen pondered, "Why was he so determined? He seemed ready with a generous offer."

"Probably more generosity than he is capable of," answered William.

Late in the summer Jed Tanner made a visit. He brought eggs, a ham, and homemade sauerkraut as payment for medical services William had provided over the winter. He also brought news concerning an arrest in Lander.

"It seems," he explained, "a lot of the cattle and horse thieving was the work of one man, and his gang. He was all mixed up with the Bassett ranch, and a ranch in Dubois."

William looked up quickly, "Dubois?"

Jed nodded, "Remember last Easter I mentioned seeing something strange going on over there at the Basset place? Well, that was it; they were moving stolen cattle through. And that's not all. This bunch was also running a racket, something to do with providing security, a protection racket, that's what the sheriff called it."

William and Helen exchanged glances.

"And you know the really disgusting thing about it? That rascal seduced both Herb's daughters. Each of them thought he was in love with her, and going to marry her. It made a mess of the family. Old Herb, he's in trouble too, for letting the crooks use his ranch."

"What is this man's name, Jed?" William asked.

"Parker," Jed answered, "Robert Leroy Parker. But he goes by the name, Butch Cassidy."

* Butch Cassidy actually committed crimes in Fremont county and was arrested in Lander, though later released.

Chapter Twenty-Two

HUNTER

"The metal rattled against the smaller building.
Bees flew out in a fury"

Easter Sunday, though chilly, had promise of sunshine. Sadie and Carmen were at Roselyn's early. Kate came by for coffee, as the mothers readied the children for church. Soon, dressed in their Easter best, the woman and her grandchildren drove out the driveway, toward the highway. Carmen began loading the dishwasher.

Sadie pulled a sack from her large tote. "I brought a doorknob," she said. "We can't have people walking in on our company." Roselyn supplied her with a screwdriver, and Sadie began her project.

"What are you doing?" Carmen asked, as she passed through the hall.

"Super-gluing the screws into the wood," answered Sadie. "I'm making it Hunter-proof."

"Who's going to hide eggs?" called Roselyn.

"That would be me," answered Sadie. "Since I'm the official Easter Bunny."

"You do that," agreed Carmen. "And I will start the grill, and prepare the patties."

Sometime later Sadie returned rubbing her arm. She went to the refrigerator and retrieved some ice.

"What's wrong Sadie?" Inquired Roselyn, as she stirred the pitcher of tea she was making.

"Those darn bees," answered Sadie. I hope they don't attack the kids. They seem to be building a hive in the roof of your cistern shed, so I didn't hide any eggs near there. You need to get rid of those, Roselyn."

"Actually," explained Roselyn, "they are my helpers. Hunter is obsessed with the cistern shed, and since it is our drinking water, I don't want him to break into it. The bees keep him away."

"It very well may keep your water delivery man away," suggested Carmen. Glancing at the clock on the kitchen wall, she added, "Mom and the kids should be getting back."

"They are," Roselyn informed her sisters, as she looked out the window. The jeep was approaching down the muddy road.

"That's curtain call for me," announced Sadie, as she jumped up, grabbed her tote, and dashed into the bathroom.

By the time she came out, Kate and the grandchildren were wiping their shoes on the straw mat on my front porch.

"Eeeeee!!!" Squealed one of the twins, either Ransom or Ridge. I can never tell them apart. "Dare's da essa wabbit."

Sure enough, a large white fluffy bunny, with long ears, stepped out of my hallway. I was startled at first. I always keep a close eye on all rodents, and other pests, within my walls. Never could such a giant animal have slipped in unnoticed. Then I heard Sadie's voice. Even with her attempt to disguise it, I knew her. I remembered the discussion about the bunny costume, and chuckled.

I just may find a way to enter into this fun.

"The red truck is back up there on the entrance," stated Kate. "Do you think he could be a stalker?"

I gazed toward the highway from my second story. Yes, the truck is there, and it is the same one as yesterday.

The rabbit dug through its tote, and retrieved binoculars. Running up my stairs, it positioned itself at my south upstairs window. After a few minutes the bunny ran back down the stairs and proceeded to dig in the tote.

"You're looking for the eggs?" asked Hunter.

"No," answered the big furry hare, "my keys."

"Easter Bunnies don't have keys," protested Hunter.

"Evidently not." answered the rabbit, "Dang, I've laid them down somewhere. I'll just walk it." The rabbit stalked out my front door.

"Where are you going?" demanded Kate, hands on hips, and looking completely confused.

"To confront him," answered the bunny, "I know who that is, and he will come and introduce himself, or leave. That's just rude!"

The sisters, and their mother, stood looking out the door in bewilderment. The children were crunched against my kitchen window. Rabbit was walking with a sense of purpose down the muddy road toward the highway, hopping over puddles. The bunny arms were pumping with energy.

"I hope he's not dangerous," worried Kate.

"Well, no one is more dangerous than Sadie," mused Carmen.

"Whard da wabbit doe?" the twins asked. They sounded as though they would start crying.

"It's OK," assured Roselyn. "Want Auntie to get you an Easter cookie?"

"You know," whispered Carmen, "I think she's forgotten she's in that bunny suit."

The women rounded up the children and redirected them to my back porch, with strict orders to remain there until the guests arrived. Roselyn returned into the kitchen, and seeing her mother and sister still gazing out the window, asked, "Any sign of her?" Looking over Carmen's shoulder, she added, "You'll never get that costume clean, Mom, she can't have missed all the mud holes."

"The costume is the least of my concerns," answered Kate.

I wished I could tell them what I saw from my tower view. Easter Rabbit approached the vehicle and banged on the window with a big bunny paw. The man at the wheel opened the window. There was some conversation before the giant fluff ball walked around to the passenger side and got in.

I watched intently. What if this stranger ran off with the Easter Bunny? There would be no way I could stop him. But I wouldn't ponder long. The big red pickup started down our slushy road.

"Tell me it's not true," gasped Roselyn. "She's not bringing that stranger here! Our guests will be arriving any minute."

"Maybe he's just bringing her back," suggested Kate.

"Hmmm, I don't know that I trust someone who randomly picks up strange rabbits," added Carmen, with a chuckle.

Well, I knew I didn't trust him. This jerk took away my land, my family graves, threatened to have me torn down, and paid to move me here. I did not want him to be around me. I began to draw up all my energy, every emotion, every sound, and odor. I wasn't sure how I would use it, but I would rid my house of this pest.

My front door opened. The tall broad male, and the rabbit entered. "Mom, Roselyn, Carmen, this is Dennis Dickinson." Rabbit swished a furry arm around the circle. He has been looking over some of the surrounding properties, and is considering buying some of them."

The women nodded with courtesy to the introduction. Everyone, including Rabbit, stood awkwardly. Finally, Roselyn remembered she is the hostess on the premises.

"We're having a bit of a party, with guests. Would you like to stay?" she faltered.

I was shocked, "Not him!" I tried to convey my feelings to her . . .

Then I sifted her thoughts. She did not expect him to accept. This was her way of informing him that the family had plans. "Got it! Good girl, Rosy," I thought.

I picked up a silent protest from Carmen. She looked at her sister with dismay.

"That's very nice of you to offer," said the party crasher. "I would love to celebrate the holiday with such a fine group of lovely women."

The Rabbit offered him a chair, and Kate brought him a cup of coffee. The boys came in from the porch complaining of being chilly. Spotting Rabbit, Ethan squatted down and began rubbing Rabbit's feet, attempting to wipe off the mud.

"Essa wabbit's all mudgy," commented one of the twins.

"Ugh, mudgy," echoed the other.

"That's not the Easter Bunny," announced Hunter, "That's Aunt Sadie."

"Hush, Hunter," coached Maria.

But the debate ended as several cars pulled in and parked in the driveway. Guests began to ascend up to my porch. They carried in dishes of food and set them on the table. The intruder was introduced to everyone, and I cringed.

Outside, Rabbit was leading the gaggle of kids to the egg hunt. Carmen was flipping burgers. Her boyfriend, Carl, was standing nearby, offering annoying advice. He carefully placed two veggie burgers on the grill.

"Don't mix those up with the meat burgers," he warned. "And don't let those nasty things drip on them either."

"Hey, teased Carmen, "It's not my fault you're a vegetarian. This is ranch country, after all."

"Just watch out for my black bean patties," he pleaded.

The remaining adults meandered to the back porch. Roselyn carried her mug of coffee as she followed them. After everyone settled into the various seating arrangements, she dropped into the porch swing. Slowly, Dennis slithered in and sat beside her.

Kate stepped out of the door, camera in hand. She would be sure to turn the event into something artistic, that was a given. "Where's Hunter?" she asked no one in particular.

"I want to get pictures of everyone with the bunny."

No one answered, and she moved on to the area by the fence where Rabbit and a number of egg seekers were searching the tall grass. I scanned around my perimeter for Hunter. He would use this opportunity for mischief, and I wanted to be sure his behavior would bring me no harm.

There you are, you little rascal.

He picked up his head and looked back at me as though he heard me.

Ah-ha, I'm finally getting through to him. I will soon be able to interject thoughts to him, as I do to Ethan.

Hunter pulled a screwdriver from the pocket of his jacket. Immediately he began work on the cistern shed lock.

This can't be good, HUNTER! STOP!

He jumped, and looked around. He then returned to his project. Remembering what Roselyn said about the bees, I looked to the roof of the shed. It is a prefabricated small building that Roselyn purchased and set over the cistern. The peaked roof was not steep, but offered a small space where I could see an open gap. A few of the little yellow buzzies were climbing in and out.

The cistern shed was only a few yards from my north-side entrance. My rain gutter, on the north, was loose. I could make use of that. I focused my energy on the one area to which it was still attached. Soon, I was able to propel the metal trough toward the shed.

My plan worked. The metal rattled against the smaller building. Bees flew out in a fury. Hunter dropped his tool and ran several yards. The bees swarmed around for a while, and then retreated back into their hideout. Hunter abandoned his plot and went off to find a new adventure.

Chapter Twenty-Three

DENNIS

"She seems to generate her own wind power"

I bought my attention back to the porch where a platter was filling up with burgers and hotdogs.

I must keep my eye on Dickenson, I feel he is up to something.

"So Dennis, from where'd you come, and what brings you to Fremont County?" asked Carl, as Carmen playfully chased him away from the grill.

"I came from all over," he answered. "I was raised in Texas, and moved to Rock Springs about 12 years ago. I worked with a firm of geologists in the area for a few years, as an assistant. But I think this area is very interesting, so when I fell into a bit of money, I used it to resettle here."

"And you bought the old Yingling ranch?" asked Kate.

"Yes, the heirs were so ready to unload that property and divide up the money. I got it for a song," he bragged.

My heart felt a stab of pain. I gasped, as only a house can gasp. A muffled groan rippled through my structure. I didn't need to be reminded that the last generation of my beloved family cared nothing for me.

Dennis startled. "What's that sound?" he asked.

Roselyn shrugged, "Just the wind moving through the walls of the house."

Kate smiled. "Yes, we experience some interesting sounds, and shadows, here at times."

"There's no wind at the moment," scoffed Dennis. "Does the house manufacture its own wind?"

Roselyn was silent as if thinking for a moment. Then she stated, "You know, I have to say she does. She seems to generate her own wind power."

"She?" laughed Dennis. "You make it sound like a ship, rather than a decrepit old house."

"Whoa!" scolded Carmen, walking up just in time to hear the comment. "This house was the 'Lady of the Valley' for more than a hundred years. Show some respect."

"And now she's my 'Lady,' said Roselyn, proudly.

"Speaking of houses," begin Carmen, "Sadie told us you are planning to build a lodge on the original site of 'The Lady'. How are you coming on that project?"

Dennis drank the last of his coffee and stood up, "I changed my mind about that. I really don't think this area is ready for a full time lodge. If things work out as I hope to have a large modern log house built on that property, a luxury home, I may get started on it this summer. I'm still looking at plans."

"I did quite a bit of research at the library," said Roselyn. "A woman there who knows a lot about that property. She said there are graves there. Have you noticed them?"

Dennis leaned against one of my porch posts, "I did. A number of rustic grave stones are on a small knoll near the aspen grove, west of the apple orchard. I guess that's common on these old homesteads."

"I would hope you would not disturb them with whatever construction you are planning." Carmen suggested.

"So, what are you saying?" smirked Dennis. "That I should build a shrine to a bunch of people I never knew?"

Carmen bristled, and Carl tensed. He sensed his woman was about to start a rumble. Roselyn shot a glance at Kate. I knew, through sifting, that they were surprised at Carmen's boldness. She was the quiet gentle sister, the girly-girl.

"No one suggested a shrine," she answered tersely, "but a respectful person would never disrupt a cemetery. You could put a fence around it, and keep the grass mowed. Those graves contain the remains of individuals who pioneered this region, Mr. Dickinson. Being respectful of the history of Lander, and Fremont County, is something you should consider, if you want the citizens here to accept you into the community."

"I think it's time to gather everyone and eat," announced Kate, the perpetual peacemaker.

Roselyn flashed her mother a grateful smile. I could sense the last thing she wanted was a bad scene at her first opportunity to entertain so many guests.

Dennis reached into his pocket and removed a pack of cigarettes. "You all go ahead and get started," he said. "I think I'll walk about and have a smoke." He sauntered to the north side of the house. As he lit his cigarette, I sifted his thoughts.

'Well, that didn't go well,' he reasoned. 'I guess if I'm going to get on the good side of these fuddy-duddies, I'll have to put on the act of Mr. Goody-Goody. Heck, I figured I would only have to impress the brunette, Roselyn. She owns the place after all.'

He took a draw of his tobacco, and slowly blew it out, relishing the calm it gave him in his irritation. 'And what is it with that little redhead?' He searched his mind for the reason she seemed familiar. 'Nurse,' he said out loud. 'She was the nurse at the doctor's office. She assisted the doc in stitching me up. That's it. I told them about the fight. She's probably judging me.' He breathed in another puff.

"Hi," a small voice said. "What'cha doing back here?"

Dennis turned to see Hunter, again engaged in his attempt to pry off the padlock on the shed.

"I could ask you the same question," answered Dennis. "What are you doing?"

"None of your business," answered Hunter.

"Does your mother know you are back here trying to break into her storage shed?" inquired Dennis.

"It's not a storage shed. It's the cistern shed," corrected the little burglar.

Thoughts raced through the man's mind. 'This could get some brownie points with Roselyn.' He put out his cigarette on the bottom of his boot, dropped the butt on the ground, and then kicked it over towards the shed. Turning quietly, he made his way back into my big country kitchen.

Everyone was sitting around the table. The other children had their plates filled, and were gathered around the TV in my back parlor, err . . . family room. Dennis walked up to Roselyn.

Leaning down to whisper in her ear, he said, "There's a young boy busily prying the lock off the door of your cistern shed, as we speak."

Roselyn slowly turned, "Thank you, Dennis, for telling me. Please sit there and dish up."

She left the kitchen, and a mother/son battle soon commenced on my north side. A few minutes later, a ruffled Roselyn, and a pouting Hunter, returned. Roselyn placed the screwdriver on top of the refrigerator.

Dennis Dickenson was now on his best behavior. He complemented every dish on the table. He even offered to help clean up, but was shooed out of the kitchen. As the sisters cleared the table, Carmen approached Roselyn.

"Be careful, Sis. I don't think that man is what he appears to be," she warned.

"Well, actually, I think he's quite nice," retorted Roselyn.

"Have you forgotten that he's been parked up on the hill watching this place for several days? That's weird!" Carmen returned.

"How do you know he was watching this place?" challenged the older sister. "Maybe he was looking at all the rest of this empty land. And when did you become such a suspicious person?"

"Girls!" interrupted Kate. "Goodness sakes, am I going to have to send you to your rooms? We have guests on the porch waiting for bunny cake and ice cream. Now stop with the spat already!"

"Just be careful," said Carmen, as her last word.

"Just don't start arguments at my parties!" scolded Roselyn, determined the last word would be hers.

"Ladies!" exclaimed Kate, sternly. "How old are you? Sixteen? Fourteen? Twelve?"

Sadie walked into the kitchen to get a glass of water. She grabbed a platter of bunny cakes, Carmen picked up the ice cream, and Roselyn gathered up bowls and plates, and they walked out to my back porch.

Kate exited through the front door, stood on my front porch, and faced west. Looking at the Wind River Mountains, with the melting snow, she breathed in the cool breeze. It was comforting, but she didn't know why she needed comfort.

I sifted her thoughts as she pondered the afternoon. She was jumpy and nervous, and confused as to why. I knew why. She had picked up my anxiety. I concentrated very hard to interject assurance to her.

She sat down in the wooden rocker, and together we watched the beginning of a sunset developing over the majestic 'Winds'.

I scanned around to the back porch. Everyone was relaxed and talking. I didn't like the way Dickinson was starting to fit in. Carmen still eyed him suspiciously, but remained silent. The men discussed Carl's aspirations for taxidermy. Dennis got up and stepped away from the others. He lit a cigarette, and looked out over the prairie toward the east. He was in deep thought, but too far away for me to sift.

"Hey Mister," Hunter said, startling him from his fantasy. "Come here."

Dennis turned and followed the child. "Come here for what?" he asked.

"I wanna show you something," answered Hunter.

The man followed the boy around my outer walls to my north side. "What?" he asked.

"What kind of snake is this?" the boy asked.

"Snake?" Dennis walked closer to the gallon jar, covered with a lid.

"That's a garter snake," he answered.

"Will it bite?" asked Hunter, picking up the jar and moving closer to the shed.

"Yes, if you scare him. He's not poisonous though. Why do you want him?"

"Because," answered Hunter, moving even closer to the shed.

I now knew what he was up to. Hunter always held a grudge. Dennis was on his revenge list for tattling to Roselyn. I usually found Hunter's antics a bit disturbing, but I was pleased with this one.

"Did you notice he has red eyes?" asked Hunter, leaning against the shed.

"He doesn't have red eyes," scoffed Dickinson, taking a drag from his smoke. "Snakes' eyes are usually black or yellow."

"Not his," insisted Hunter. "Come here and see."

Tossing the cigarette, Dennis walked toward the boy for a closer look. In that second, Hunter lifted one foot, and backward kicked the side of the shed three times, then broke into a run until he was several yards away. The golden warriors swarmed out with angry intent, to retaliate against whoever had disturbed them.

The man yelled, and then screamed, waving his arms. Hunter watched amused, holding the jar, and its captive, tightly in his arms. Dennis ran in circles, seemingly confused, and crashed into my north wall. He finally oriented himself enough to stumble around to the west front porch where Kate was seated in the rocking chair.

Kate jumped up as the terrified man collapsed on the porch. "What's wrong? Are you all right?" she asked. Sadie, Roselyn, and Carmen soon arrived, having heard the commotion.

Dennis was gasping for air, "Allergic, bees, help . . ." he stammered.

I knew what was happening. I had witnessed this scene once before. He could die from this. I almost felt repentant, but, I had not angered the bees, I reminded myself.

"Mr. Dickinson, do you have an epi-pen?" demanded Carmen. Her inner nurse was already in charge.

"Truck," he whispered. "Glove box."

Sadie, the rabbit, was already sprinting to his vehicle. As she returned, she passed the device to Carmen like a gauntlet at a marathon. In one quick motion, Carmen jabbed the needle through his jeans and into his thigh.

"Sadie, take him to ER now!" she ordered.

Carl assisted Dennis into the passenger side of his truck, and Sadie, the rabbit, jumped into the driver's seat. She gunned it, and peeled out, launching a shower of mud particles over the observers.

"You think he'll be OK?" worried Roselyn.

"If Sadie doesn't kill him before he gets there," answered Carmen.

Hunter stood close to the corner of my north wall. He was puzzled. He had been stung before and it was not a big deal. Aunt Sadie was stung this morning and got over it. She didn't even cry. He had only wanted to scare the man for getting him into trouble. He wiped tears from his cheeks. He didn't want to be bad. Why was it so hard to be good?

Hunter slinked down the north wall and back to the shed. The bees had settled back into their cubby. He wondered why he was so driven to get inside. Then he noticed the cigarettes. One in front of the shed, and one next to the shed wall. Forgetting his guilty conscience, he gathered them up. He smelled one, touched his tongue to it. "Blah!" He slipped them into his jacket pocket; he would put them in his treasure box.

His treasure box was a boot box underneath his bed. It contained a butter knife, several screw drivers, a few nails, magic rocks, one half of a pair of scissors, the bathroom door knob, a mouse skull, two keys, the bottle of superglue Sadie carelessly left on the bathroom counter, a tattered disposable camera, and a red leather wallet. To these special processions he added two partly smoked cigarettes.

Roselyn gathered the adults into the front parlor, now referred to as the living room. Kate set out a deck of cards and board games, and the children congregated in the family room with their baskets of eggs and candy. As Carl began to shuffle cards, a loud scream from the family room nearly lifted my roof.

Roselyn ran to investigate, and her sisters followed. "Mercy, Maria! What's wrong with you?" she asked.

Maria, and all the children, were piled on the couch, looking in terror at her Easter basket on the floor. Hunter's garter snake slowly slithered out from under the plastic grass. Hunter was rolling on the floor in laughter.

Roselyn calmly walked over, caught the confused snake behind his head, and walked to the back door. "No!" screamed Hunter.

"I told you if you frightened anyone with Hank, you couldn't keep him," she reminded.

As Roselyn released Hank out the door to Hunter's wailing, Kate entered the room.

"Sadie called. Dennis is all right. She drove him home and walked back to her apartment. She has to show a house early in the morning, so she's calling it a day. Carl and Carmen are getting ready to leave, and one of them will drive her car back to town for her," Kate informed her.

Roselyn hardly heard this report as she wrestled a kicking screaming Hunter out of the room, to the stairs, to direct him to his room. The children slowly climbed from their perch, on the back of the couch, to carefully approach their baskets.

Later, after everyone left, and kids were in bed, Kate and Roselyn began the cleanup task that follows such events. Roselyn loaded the dishwasher a second time as Kate cleared away the scattered plastic cups, candy wrappers, and egg shells. She swept up the last of the rubble onto the dust pan, and emptied it into the trash.

Pulling the bag from the receptacle and tying the top, she remarked, "Roselyn, those bees have to go! An incident like that could cause a law suit. What if that man had died tonight? You know how scary it is when you come in contact with peanuts, many people react to bees."

"I know, I know," answered Roselyn, with an edgy tone. "I am already planning to call an exterminator tomorrow."

As my residents grew quite, I reflected on the day. I had planned to provide the entertainment, but not one opportunity provided itself. I wasn't used to being upstaged, but this family was definitely the liveliest group ever to live within my walls.

Chapter Twenty-Four

ETHAN

"I will continue playing this in your head
until you can't resist singing it"

With the progression of spring, Roselyn set her focus on repairs and improvements. She and Sadie climbed up on my roof, and nailed down shingles that had flapped loose due to winter winds. One weekend Sadie brought over a large roll of wallpaper.

"See Roselyn," she summoned, "my boss redid his kitchen, and he let me have this leftover wallpaper." She rolled it out across the dining room table. Roselyn, coming in from sweeping off my porch, walked over to see.

"Interesting. What are you going to do with it?" she asked.

"I brought it to you," answered Sadie, looking at her sister quizzically.

"For what?" asked Roselyn, looking back in confusion.

"Your downstairs bathroom," she answered.

The wall covering was light brown with huge golden sunflowers all over it.

"Sadie, I mentioned I wanted to go retro with this house, but I meant Victorian, not Height-Ashbury," Roselyn remarked.

"You don't like it?" whined Sadie, disappointed.

"Sadie, that reminds me of our last home in Seattle. Mom had green appliances, orange shag carpet, and sunflower upholstery. Ugh!"

"It has a waterproof finish," mentioned Sadie. "You know how the boys make water messes in the bathroom."

Roselyn looked a Sadie and shook her head in disbelief.

"With brown towels, curtains, and a throw rug, you could tame down the gold," Sadie suggested.

"I guess we could use it as practice, since neither of us have ever hung paper before," mused Roselyn.

"Anything's better than those blotchy walls that refuse paint," said Sadie brightly, feeling she was winning the debate.

Excuse me, ladies, I have an opinion here. I want wallpaper, but not that wallpaper. I didn't like loud colors in the seventies, and I don't like them now. Take it on out of here.

Of course no one was listening. Sadie brought in some tools and paste, and the women set about turning my bathroom into a sunflower nightmare. It was scary. I tightened the pores in my walls and tried to resist the sticky goo they slathered on me.

By afternoon they were finished, and they stood back to admire the disgrace they had made of me. "Better than I thought it would be," conceded Roselyn. "Let's run into town and get guest towels, curtains, and a rug."

I used the time while they were gone to shift my walls ever so slightly.

If I could just wiggle a bit before this dries, that's it. Boy, does this stuff itch!

The women returned just as the school bus dropped off the kids, so everyone entered together. The women scurried to my bathroom, and the kids ran to the frig. "See," said Sadie, holding up the curtains. "This tames that yellow-gold right down."

Suddenly Hunter was at the door, jumping up and down. "Hunter, go to the upstairs restroom. I'm hanging a curtain in this one."

"Can't wait! Can't wait! Gotta poop!" insisted Hunter, still jumping.

"OK, then, hurry." said Sadie. The women exited and shut the door.

I was barely paying attention. My focus remained on relieving myself of the dastardly paper. Then, I felt it give. It started at the top of each wall, and slowly rolled down, making ticking noises as it released.

"MAMA!" screamed Hunter.

Roselyn pushed opened the door, and there was my victory. Hunter sitting wide-eyed on the toilet, surrounded by rolls of wet wallpaper.

The paper was discarded, and the goop scrubbed off my walls. Life was good again.

A week later, May first to be exact, my entire surrounding area was again a sea of slushy mud. Three days of spring rains had caused a muddy moat around my borders. Roselyn referred to us as 'The Big House in the Bog', and Kate named us, 'The Soggy Bottom Family'.

The sun was warm, and my windows were slightly opened to let mountain breezes enter. Roselyn and Maria completed a week of spring cleaning. My closets were sorted out, my rough, scarred floors moped, curtains laundered and ironed, and my windows washed to a sparkly shine. *I felt quite chipper.*

As I blissfully awakened to the warm morning sun, cool breezes, and the aroma of coffee, I stretched, causing some creaking noises through my walls, and the staircase. Kate was sitting at the table with coffee, while Roselyn placed cereal bowls into the dishwasher. Maria organized her brothers in getting ready for the school bus.

Roselyn left when they did, and returned an hour later. She lugged in a contraption with a motor, and a long cord.

Eeeeek! An electric floor-sander!' I met this demon in the seventies, or one similar to it. 'No, No, my floors are over a hundred years old! They're worn thin. Don't attack them with that!

Roselyn rolled up the area rug, and dragged it into the dining room. She glanced over the instructions regarding the use of the monster. "Hold machine steady, move slowly with the grain of the wood. Cover small portions at a time. That's not hard."

Trust me, Rosy. You don't want to do this!

Plugging the cord into my west wall, she positioned the beast to face east. Standing flat-footed, she bent over, and took a firm grip on the handles on each side.

The blessing that came with electricity is that it rendered me some power to anything plugged into my outlets. As she flipped on the switch, I surged the power. I was hoping to scare her so she would discard her very bad idea. However, rather than revving up the motor, the machine jumped, causing her gripping palms to slide over the max power button.

That wasn't my doing.

The machine shot forward like Sadie's driving-takeoffs.

'Owwww! That hurts!' That was me, not Roselyn.

She was yelling, and hanging on for dear life, as the sander ripped around my room, slinging her hundred-and-ten-pound body like a dishrag. It ended when both of them crashed into my east wall. The sander flipped over, vicious grinders spinning loudly.

Crawling back to my west wall, the shaken Roselyn unplugged the cord.

She wrapped it around the machine. "So that will be enough of floor-sanding, I think," she said, as she lugged the thing back to her pickup.

That concluded my renovations for spring. I knew Roselyn was disappointed, but we have to do this right, after all. I tried to project this to her, but she didn't pick it up.

A week later Roselyn brought large pots home. She also brought potting soil, and several flats of red flowers, the color of blood. As she and Sadie planted them, I heard her say they were geraniums.

I liked the flowers. They decorated my battered porches, and made me feel cheery.

While they were working on the potting, Kate drove up, and she and Ethan got out. Ethan ran in my door, and up my stairs, to his room. *I sensed he wanted to be alone for a while. I had observed that he needed more alone time than the other children*

Kate sat down in the rocker and watched the project. "How'd it go?" asked Roselyn.

I remembered that this was the day Ethan and Kate were scheduled for a planning meeting with Ethan, and his staff. They were to plan his goals for the coming year, and summarize his achievements for the present term. Ethan requested his grandmother go with him, and Roselyn agreed, since her mother had, herself, been a teacher.

"Well, it's hard to test him on reading, since he won't speak," began Kate. But they believe he is reading some, since he does do some writing. Of course, kindergarten is still too early to be reading and writing a lot, but we can't know if he is getting the phonics since he doesn't repeat the sounds."

"I don't remember figuring out reading until second grade," said Sadie, always at-the-ready to defend Ethan.

"Right, you took off a bit slow with that," remembered Kate," but you talked. In fact, you never shut up."

"And still hasn't," teased Roselyn.

Sadie smacked her with her work glove.

Kate continued, "His teacher said he listens to all the reading being done, and answers all questions about the material with nodding and signing, so he's getting the information."

"He writes his alphabet and numbers. I've worked with him on that," stressed Roselyn.

"Well, he'll be promoted to first grade, and his aide will move with him," assured Kate.

"The school psychologist wondered if he's been tested for autism. She said that often autistic children seem to be progressing normally until around age two, and then they start pulling inward," Kate carefully suggested.

"Did you mention how he stopped using words following his father's funeral, and counseling and speech therapy hasn't helped?" asked her daughter.

"Oh, I certainly did," said Kate. "I told her that the specialist in Denver believes it's a type of Post-Traumatic-Stress, lingering anxiety, and fear. But what do you think he's afraid of? That was over three and a half years ago. He was so young. He can't possibly remember the funeral by now."

"I think he's afraid that someone else he loves will die, or disappear," answered Roselyn. "And I don't know why he thinks silence will prevent it, unless it was all the stressing we did for him to be quiet during the funeral. Maybe he connected that in some confused sort of way."

"I can' help but think he will come out of this," said Sadie. "He is one smart cookie."

I pulled my attention from my front porch, and checked on Ethan. He was lying on his bed, pushing a small matchbox car around on the spread. Very quietly he hummed the sound of a motor. I'd noticed this before. When no one was around Ethan made very soft sounds, a motor for his car, an animal sound for a stuffed toy, sometimes humming a little tune. I'd heard him call out a few words in sleep-talk more than once.

I pledged to begin my own therapy with Ethan. He would be my project. At least when I wasn't defending myself from Hunter. I could sift Ethan's thoughts easily. He, in his innocence, had no barriers. I'd been successful in projecting to him as well. My work would begin tonight.

That evening after everyone was asleep, I focused on Ethan. He looked like a cherub resting on his pillow. Using projection, I began to sing one of the tunes that was sung by children years ago, within my walls.

> *Old Dan Tucker was a fine old man*
> *He washed himself in a frying pan*
> *He combed his hair with a wagon wheel*
> *And died with a toothache in his heel.*

After several repetitions, a smile moved across his tiny lips. A muffled giggle escaped them.

I will continue playing this in your head until you can't resist singing it. That's my promise.

Chapter Twenty-Five

DISCOVERIES

"Three sisters, and a mother, bonded over tears of discovery and
I bonded, too"

Sadie and Carmen took time off, so Kate closed her studio, and all met in my living room. Kate and Carmen both brought large plastic containers.

"Surprises?" asked Sadie, as they set the boxes down on the floor near the chairs they chose.

"Yes," answered her mother.

"Sort of," answered Carmen.

"As you know, I'm offering scrapbooking classes at my studio next month. I know you are all too busy to attend, so I'm giving you a class today, compliments of The Paisley Pot." This, I knew was Kate's studio, usually referred to, by most people, as 'The Paisley'.

"So let's take all my goodies to the dining room table. I have a neat surprise for you."

"What's in your box, Carmen?" asked Roselyn.

"I'll wait until we've learned what Mom has," declined Carmen.

"Now Carmen, you know I can't keep a secret, or be kept from a secret," begged Sadie.

"OK, then," began Carmen, popping the top off the plastic bin. She slid her hand under a covering. "As you know, we are really crowded in that tiny apartment as we wait for Sadie to find us the perfect house." She looked pointedly at her youngest sister.

"Hey, it's not my fault you want three bedrooms, a garage, and a finished basement for the price of a one bedroom," retorted Sadie.

"Well, anyway. We are literally smashed together, and I need somewhere to store Carl's projects, just until we can move into something bigger. So if each of you could find a place to put one of them, I would so appreciate it," she looked at them pleadingly.

Kate sighed a heavy sigh, "What have you got?"

"Not another ghastly deer head, I hope," said Roselyn, remembering Old Roy.

"How about a Wyoming special: a Jackalope?" asked Carmen, pulling one out of her bin.

Kate reached for the fluffy bundle of fur. "I wouldn't mind putting a few of these in my window, tourists are always asking for them."

"That was his first one. He learned a lot about rabbit fur with that one. He's doing much better now, and has some orders coming in." Carmen explained.

"Oh no, he's missing an ear," moaned Kate, "and he only has one eye. What happened?"

"Well, that one was for practice," repeated Carmen. "Our neighbor, Bob, has a dog that gets loose once in a while. He brought that poor bunny home, dead of course. Bob didn't want the dog making a mess of it so he let Carl have it for practice."

"Ooo . . . yuk," said Roselyn.

"Well, it's better than going out and killing a perfectly good rabbit," defended Carmen. It's perfect in every way, except the eye. It was too mangled up to set a glass eye in it, so Carl just closed it up. And then the missing ear . . . but it looks fine from this side."

"Why doesn't Carl just throw his practice pieces away?" questioned Sadie.

"Artists don't thrown their learning projects away, do they Mom?" Carmen looked for support from Kate, a successful artist.

"Hmmm, I think Carl is a bit more attached to his than most," answered Kate gently.

"And here's the second bunny project," Carmen presented them with the second Jackalope.

Kate took it and turned it around, "OK, this is better, or it would be if it wasn't missing a hind leg."

"That one, Carl accidently hit with his car. He stopped to see if he could help it, but it was dead." Carmen shrugged, "but its face is all right."

"Carl is stuffing road-kill?" Sadie exclaimed in shock.

"Only once in a while." Carmen quickly reached in again, and pulled out a large fish.

"It's illegal to make use of animals killed by traffic Carmen," Sadie wasn't letting go of her point.

Roselyn gasped, "That's a carp! Why would he mount a carp?"

He just needed to learn the technique. Now that he's mastered it, he completed several trophy fish for customers."

Pulling out the last item, Carmen unwrapped the tissue paper, and set an owl on the table.

"This is the best," she bragged.

"I suppose you are going to tell us that owl flew in Carl's window and surrendered?" asked Sadie, with a sarcastic tone.

"Pretty much," said Carmen. It flew into his Dad's windshield one night. The windshield cracked, and the owl broke his neck."

Kate picked up the owl to examine it. "This is actually nice work, if you like that sort of thing. It's really heavy."

"Carl put a weight in its lower body so it will set solid, and not tip over," Carmen explained.

"I have an idea," suggested Roselyn. "Let's put them all back in the container, and I'll take them up to the tower so Hunter can't get them. When you move, you can come claim them."

With that problem solved, the women moved on to the scrapbooking. Kate opened her large plastic box and took out four new albums. All were different colors. "OK, girls, chose the one you want. I know your favorite colors, and got them, so it should be easy."

She then pulled out a large boot box, wrapped and tied with a long pink ribbon. "This box is full of your childhood pictures. I should have organized these already, but life was so busy, I didn't. We are going to do it now. We will sort out whose is whose."

She handed Carmen and Roselyn a pile of snapshots, but Sadie was now rummaging in the container. She lifted out a wooden box, "What's this?"

"Those are my mother's papers," answered Kate. "If we have time, we can go through them as well. I have never even looked in that box."

But Sadie wasn't waiting. She lifted the tiny golden latch, and exposed stacks of aged documents."

"Who is this Mom?" Roselyn held up a picture for her mother to see.

"That's Carmen at age three; if it wasn't black and white, you would know it by her red hair. Put that in her pile."

Sadie was working her way through the documents, "Here's Poppy's army papers", she said carefully while refolding the document.

Be careful with those, Sadie," Kate advised.

As the others divided pictures according to individuals, Sadie scoured through the wooden box.

"Mom," she tapped Kate on the arm. "Here's a birth certificate. Whose could it be?"

It must be your Granny's. Mine's at home in my business drawer," answered Kate.

"Granny wasn't born in 1950," said Sadie. She handed her mother the document.

Kate studied the paper, "I don't know whose this is," she said.

"Did you have a sister who died at birth? Maybe one you don't remember?" asked Carmen, now standing, and looking over her mother's shoulder.

"No. Your Granny Pearl and Poppy Mack couldn't have children. That's why they adopted me."

"Baby girl, born May 20, 1950. That's your birthday, Mom," exclaimed Carmen, reading aloud.

"Except this baby's name is Amanda Rose," mumbled Kate. "Father not named . . . . mother was named . . . . the print is faded." Kate tipped the paper to catch light on the writing. The mother is Alfreda Rose . . . . I can't quite make out the last name. Who writes this small?"

"Probably a doctor," snickered Carmen.

"Hey Mom, I found your adoption papers!" announced Sadie, excitedly, holding up an envelope, and a folded sheet she had slipped out of it.

"It says you were placed with Granny and Poppy on June 30th, 1950. That means they didn't get you at birth?" reasoned Sadie.

"No, I was in a Catholic children's home, Sisters of Grace. That's why my middle name is Grace," explained Kate. "Mother told me that after she and Papa were married twelve years, she finally accepted the reality that she would never have a child. She arranged for an adoption with the Sisters of Grace. A nun, Sister Kathleen, helped them through the process, so they named me Kathleen Grace."

"Did they tell you anything about your parents? I mean your birthparents?" asked Roselyn.

"Just that they died, and I was an orphan," answered Kate.

"Well, I'm thinking that old birth certificate is your actual birth," insisted Sadie. Your mother was alive long enough to name you Amanda Rose, so your birthmother must be Alfreda Rose . . . whoever."

Kate returned her attention to the certificate, and Sadie returned hers to the box. "Here are some letters. Do you think these are love letters from Poppy to Granny?"

She set a bundle of three squared envelopes, faded blue, and wrapped in a white ribbon, on the table.

Kate handled them carefully, released the bow, and looked carefully at the first envelope.

"The return address is A.R.K. I think those are initials. And then, Cragmoor #722, Colorado Springs, Colorado," read Kate aloud. "And it's addressed to my mother, adopted mother."

She carefully slid out a pale blue folded paper. A picture dropped out of the paper, and flittered to the floor. Carmen stooped, picked it up, and handed it to Kate. All four heads leaned over the wallet-sized photograph.

"Mom," whispered Roselyn, "the lady in the picture looks just like you."

The picture revealed a smiling young woman. She wore a long pageboy hairstyle, parted on the side, and long wavy bangs, partly sweeping over one eye. She had on a white sweater with a scarf tied in a jaunty knot around her neck. She smiled brightly through dark lipstick. Kate turned it over.

On the back was written, Alffie Rose, graduation day, 1944. Kate set the photo aside, and gingerly opened the letter. She handed it to Roselyn, "Please read it for me. I don't think I can."

Roselyn cleared her throat and began.

July 15, 1950

Dear Mr. and Mrs. Neilson,

I am writing you from the sanitarium, here in Colorado Springs. Sister Kathleen gave me your address. The agreement of the adoption, as you know, is that correspondence between us will be permitted, providing I do not interfere with your family, and the child.

She tells me that, by now, my little princess is settled in with you, after being observed at the foundling center for a month. She assures me that the baby is free of my disease, for which I am so grateful.

I am sending a picture of me on the day of my high school graduation. Perhaps someday, when you tell our little angel the truth, you can give her this picture. If you are honest with her, please tell her too, that her mother loved her very much. I would have kept her if I could.

After her birth, the tuberculosis that had been in remission came back with a vengeance. The Sisters of Grace, arranged for me to come here for treatment. There is a new treatment, streptomycin, which is very effective in curing this disease. I pray that it will work for me.

Sister Kathleen scolded me for not naming her father on the birth certificate. He is married, and I saw no reason to endanger his happiness, or that of his family. I suppose Mandy will be given a different certificate anyway.

I named her Amanda, after a great grandmother, and Rose, after myself and my mother. I hope you do not change the name, but I have no right to ask you to keep it.

Please love my baby, and someday find it in your hearts to tell her about me.

Sincerely, Alffie

Carmen had left the room just long enough to collect a box of tissues. Now one was at the nose of each of the participants.

I felt their emotion deeply.

"It's all up to you Mom. Shall we continue?" asked Roselyn. Kate nodded.

Carmen gently removed the second letter. She started to read through an occasional sniffle.

August 5, 1950

Dear Mr. and Mrs. Neilson,

Thank you so much for the lovely five by seven picture of the princess. I have it on my bedside table. I pray for her every day, and I ask God's blessing on both of you for loving her.

I am not responding well to the treatment. Some days I can hardly breathe for the coughing. They encourage me to eat, and try to tempt me with every kind of delicacy, but I have no appetite.

Please kiss Mandy Rose for me. Thank you again for your wonderful letter, and the beautiful picture.

Sincerely, Alfie

"Wow!" said Carmen, "That's heavy stuff."

Sadie put her arms around her mother, and said, "But see how she loved you, Mom. She did the best she could do."

"I know", said Kate, wiping her eyes.

"I wonder why Granny never told you," mused Roselyn.

"She did, in her own way," answered Kate. "She kept the letters, the picture, and the first birth certificate, for me to find."

Carmen nodded, "I think that's exactly right. Shall we read the last one?"

Kate nodded, and handed it to Sadie.

As Sadie open the folded sheet, a necklace fell out. Kate reached to pick it up. A silver heart, with a small turquoise stone inlaid, hung from a silver chain with a broken clasp.

As she turned it over, she exclaimed, "There are initials: AK and DK!"

"Read the letter, Sadie," Kate prompted.

October 29, 1950

Dear Mrs. and Mr. Neilson,

I am Rebecca Marshal, a nurse who cared for you friend, Alfreda. She made me promise some days ago, to write you and tell you of her passing. She died in her sleep last evening. When she was discovered, she was holding a picture of an infant, and this necklace. I will mail the picture to you in a separate package, but I am sending the necklace with this letter. It appears to be an heirloom.

She had no names of her nearest kin, so I am supposing you are relatives.

Yours Truly, Rebecca Marshal, RN

Scrapbooks weren't made, and pictures weren't sorted.

But *three sisters, and a mother, bonded over tears of discovery and I bonded too.*

Chapter Twenty-Six

MAY

"I believe he's a mad man. Don't give him any ideas"

The mud was drying up. By the steps of my front porch, tulips were almost ready to open their bright red blooms. I was happy that Roselyn planted them the previous fall. I knew, however, the deer that wandered through at night would munch their bright heads off. Deer love tulips.

I listened into a phone call on this May morning; it was from Dennis. Roselyn had gone out with him three times since Easter. The third time she came back, I could tell she was angry.

"I told you, Dennis, the last time we were together, that I'm not going to see you anymore."

I tried to sift the connection to pick up his response. Since Roselyn had changed to a cell phone, it was harder. Before, I could pick up conversation through the landline. This new contraption would take some figuring out.

"Because, it's obvious that your only interest in me is to talk me into selling you my property."

She put the cell on speaker phone, and laid it on the table while she checked the cake in the oven.

Yes, good going, Rosy. Make it easier for an old lady to eavesdrop.

The male voice was loud and clear, "I don't know why you say that. I bought you roses, took you to a movie you wanted to see, and even treated you to the China Dragon in Riverton. That should convince you I'm interested in you, and not your property. I own some of the best property around. Why would I want that parched gulch you live on?"

"I don't know, Dennis. Why is it that you make me offers to buy it every time we see each other? And why is it that every minute we talk, and have a chance to get acquainted, you use the time to try to convince me I'm wasting my money on my house, and should sell it to you? Why, Dennis?"

There was silence for a moment, "I was just trying to give you some good advice. God knows you need it. You told me you put all your insurance money into that place. It's a dump. That was a stupid choice. You have a kid you can't control. He's running as free as a banshee out there, playing with snakes, and bees, and whatever other lethal thing he can find. You think you can't make a decision about anything without having a hen party with your family. You need some good advice," his tone sounded testy.

"Wait, stop right there," Roselyn interrupted. "I've made a very good life, and at thirty-two, I don't need advice from you. I was willing to be a friend to you, but friends don't try to run each other's lives. And by-the-way, Bozo, what do you mean my child is out of control? So you're a child specialist now?"

"I'm older, and have more experience with business than you, Roselyn. You will be sorry someday that you didn't listen to me! Besides, you should appreciate a successful man taking an interest in you. At your age, with three kids, you'll be lucky to ever get a man's attention again."

Roselyn, having taken the cake out of the oven, slammed the oven door shut. Picking up the phone she spoke directly into it, "Listen to me, you mealy mouth worm, don't ever call me again, don't ever speak to me again, and don't even look at me again. I don't know what your racket is, but if it includes weaseling me out of my property, forget it! I plan to live and die on this property!" She hung up.

'Oooooh, I don't think that was a good idea, Rosy. Don't talk about dying. I believe he's a mad man. Don't give him any ideas.'

Later Kate came over for dinner, and showed the lovely portrait she had made by photographing the small picture of her birth mother, and enlarging it.

"I made this one for you," she handed it to Roselyn.

It did have a remarkable resemblance to Kate, or what she might have been, at eighteen.

"I also copied the birth certificate, and worked with it digitally. I was able to bring out the faded letters." She laid the copy on the coffee table.

Roselyn looked at it. "Oh yeah, I see it clearly. You enlarged that tiny writing, didn't you?"

A van pulled up, and a delivery girl stepped out. The sign on the side said 'The Chocolate Factory'. The girl, dressed in chocolate-colored pants and shirt, knocked on the door. Kate opened the door and took the package.

"Thank you," she said, "Who sent this?"

"It's a gift for Roselyn," she announced.

Kate turned around to hand the package to her daughter, "There's no card on this. Maybe it's inside."

"Could you open it, Mom?" asked Roselyn. "I want to grab a frame for this picture while I'm thinking about it."

Kate eased the pretty paper off of a large candy box, "Looks like chocolates."

"I'm sure it is," called Roselyn, from the other room. "That's what they sell at The Chocolate Factory."

"There's a card inside," announced Kate, as Roselyn walked back in holding an antique picture frame.

Roselyn took the card and opened it, "Oh brother! It's Dennis. He says he's sorry and wants to start over. Mom, you should hear what he said to me today, and what he said about Hunter. I would like to put those chocolates where . . ."

"That's OK, dear. I get your meaning." Kate popped a candy into her mouth.

As Roselyn reached for the box, Kate yanked it back. "No!", she said in alarm, through a mouthful of goo. "There's peanut butter filling in them."

"Oh my God!" exclaimed Roselyn, "I think he just tried to poison me!"

"Did he know about your allergy?" choked Kate, trying to swallow.

"Yes," answered Roselyn. "At the China Dragon I requested the waiter to explain the ingredients in the entrees. I explained to that him that I have a severe peanut allergy."

"Might he have forgotten?" asked Kate cautiously.

Roselyn shook her head, "Dennis never forgets. This was deliberate. He has some kind of obsession about this piece of land. Besides, The Chocolate Factory has over a dozen different candies. Only one is made with peanut products. It's unlikely to have been an accident."

I was worried now. I had no doubt Dennis counted on Roselyn tasting the chocolate-covered bon bons before discovering the peanut filling. Was he trying to kill her, or scare her? Was he getting even because she hung up on him?

That night, as Roselyn tucked the boys into bed, she stooped to kiss Hunter on the head. As she raised up, her eye caught a glimpse of a wallet lying on the floor, just peeking out under the fringe of his spread.

She picked it up and examined it. "Hunter, why do you have a woman's wallet?"

"I found it. Give it back. It's mine!" he reached to grab it.

"Where did you find it?" asked his mother, holding it behind her back.

"Jack gave it to me," he answered.

"We don't know anyone named Jack, Hunter. Tell me the truth."

Hunter pulled the spread up over his face.

"All right. We aren't going to argue about it tonight," she said calmly, "but I'll hang onto it until you tell me where you really got it from."

She turned out the light and quietly walked out the door.

Back in her room, she sat on her bed and opened the wallet. Inside was a windowed pocket displaying a driver license. "Megan Wells," she read aloud.

She held the wallet close, and studied the picture on the license. "You're very pretty, Megan Wells. Who are you, and why does my son have your wallet?"

I was stunned. I knew Hunter had snooped through every nook and crook of my being, but I missed seeing his discovery of the dead girl's wallet.

"Hmmm, by your birth date, I see you're seventeen years old," whispered Roselyn. "Well, when my son confesses where he snagged this, Miss Megan, I'll find you and return it." She slid the wallet between the mattress and box springs, and turned off the light.

Chapter Twenty-Seven

JUNE

"I was ready to start chewing my square-roofing nails"

The summer remained dry and hot. Wyoming, usually cool in the evenings, seized the solar fever and held onto it like a prize. The usual spring rains of April and May did not come.

Roselyn placed fans in each of my upstairs bedrooms the first week in June. All windows were opened, and quilts were replaced with light coverlets. There was a rush to the showers each morning by my parched residents, anxious to rinse away the residue of clammy night-sweats.

Carmen and the twins visited one Saturday, early in the month. Water was in the big plastic pool and the four boys were making a churn of it. Maria was sunbathing in her swimsuit. *I'm not sure I would call it a swim suit. I have seen doilies bigger than that.*

She and her mother had previously had an argument over sunscreen, and Roselyn won.

"Well . . . . ," began Carmen, pulling her legs back from the splashes of water the boys were beating out of the pool. "Boys, please don't splash the porch."

".... did you ever hear from Dennis again?" she finished her question.

"No, thank God," answered her sister. "I should have listened to you Carmen. You were sooo right about him."

"There are some great guys that come to our office, single too. You just need to get out more and meet them," encouraged Carmen.

"I'm not looking for romance. I have kids to raise, a house to restore, a job to maintain, and I have no time for romance!"

"It's not hard when it's the right man," stated Carmen. "Carl has made my life easier, not harder."

"Carl is one of the sweetest men I know," assessed Roselyn. "There aren't many men like Carl, patient, gentle, creative, funny."

"Funny?" asked Carmen, raising an eyebrow.

I chuckled. It was all true. Carl was all of those things and he was funny, too. Not only with what he did and said, but his appearance was interesting as well: tall and thin, with blond spiked hair, and a fondness for unusual hats. He was a contrast to Carmen: petite and always groomed to perfection. From the top of her red hair, to her pink-painted toenails, Carmen was perfection.

"Look!" Hunter pointed, "Grams is coming."

The Jeep pulled up into the dusty driveway, and Sadie and Kate got out. "We're bringing you an air conditioner," she announced. "My company is upgrading one in a rental unit. I had this checked out at Tuddles' Repair, and it's in tiptop shape."

Sadie and her mother lifted it from the back of the Jeep. "I even picked up a sheet of instructions from Mr. Tuddles. Let's get it hooked up for you."

By late afternoon, cool air was blowing into my living room, through my dining room, the kitchen, and almost making it to my family room.

"Maybe we should have hooked it up in the family room," said Roselyn. "We spend all our time in there."

"Just hang on. I will probably be able to get you another one. We're also upgrading the triplex on Washington Street," Sadie stated, as she washed off her hands in the kitchen sink

"My wiring is inefficient," reminded Roselyn. "This one may blow fuses, two certainly would, but thanks for thinking of us. We've been broiling."

Roselyn closed my windows, pulled the blinds on my sunny side, and brought in a pitcher of lemonade and glasses to the coffee table. The women settled into various places and absorbed the cool air that was flowing into the hot room.

"Now," said Sadie, with her business voice. "I know the last person you want to talk about is Dennis."

"Don't even mention him to me!" answered Roselyn.

"Well, I have to talk about him. There's something you need to know. That is, unless you want him in your back pocket . . . ."

"I don't want anyone in my back pocket," said Roselyn, with fervor.

"Well, he just bought the thirty-acre strip that joins your property, on your east side," her younger sister informed her.

The women stared at Sadie, expecting more information, *as did I.*

"Here's the scoop," began Sadie, as she poured herself another glass of lemonade. "In the late eighteen-hundreds, a Charles Whitman homesteaded out here. He proved his claim, but never really got a ranch going. The land's been passed down several generations, rented out to sheep men, but never lived on after the first Whitman family."

The boys opened my front door and ran through with water dripping from swim trunks, and their bare wet feet leaving prints on my wood floors.

"To the bathroom boys," ordered Roselyn, "and get dressed."

"So . . . ." continued Sadie. "The last local Whitman, Pete, is in the Pioneer Nursing Facility. He has dementia. His grandson in Oklahoma now has power of attorney, and he decided to sell the remaining thirty acres."

"How do you know all this?" questioned Carmen.

"It's my business to know when land is for sale," she answered.

"Mama, we're hungry," announced Hunter, with his shirt wrong-side-out. Ethan, wearing his shoes on the wrong feet, rubbed over his stomach with a circular motion, signing for hunger.

"Hunter, grab the Oreos from the pantry, divide them up, and eat them at the table, please," Roselyn instructed.

'Mercy,' I thought, 'will she ever get to the point of this story?'

"Well, the Oklahoma grandson called and listed it with our company," Sadie continued. "And since Dennis calls all the realtors every few days to check on listed land, he knew it before the ink was dry on this listing. He snatched it right up."

"Why?" Kate asked. "He has a lovely acreage near the river, where this house used to be. He's done nothing with that. Is he trying to become a land barren?"

Sadie giggled, "You could call it that. Mainly I think he wants this land for speculating. You know, as in 'oil'?"

"He has offered to buy me out several times," offered Roselyn. "He even says he will double what I paid for it. He must be rolling in money."

"What did you tell him?" asked Carmen.

"No, of course," she answered. "I don't know what it is about this house. I can't even entertain the thought of leaving. Besides, he kept on about it in such a pushy way. At times he even sounded angry that I wouldn't comply."

"OK, then," continued Sadie, taking a deep breath. "He's bought the back thirty. We can't stop that, but if you don't want him to surround you, we need to make a plan. I checked on the land on each side of you, and to your west. I wanted to find out if it's listed."

"Is it?" Kate asked.

"Not yet," explained Sadie. "Whitman had ninety acres. In the eighties, he sold sixty acres to Roger Burnett. Roger tried several wells, and only found bad water. He lost interest, I guess, and he left the area two years ago. It's just now been offered up for back taxes, just like these ten acres were a few years ago. There are fifty acres total. Thirty on your west, and ten on each side of you, that have been available for some time. With your ten, you would have sixty acres. You could choose your neighbors by being careful about who you sold land to."

Roselyn laughed sarcastically, "I can't even afford to get this house rewired."

"That's what family's for," said Sadie, crunching on a piece of ice.

"I'm surprised Dennis hasn't rooted out that information. It's easy to find at the courthouse," she added.

Roselyn was frowning, and attempting to rub out the crease in her forehead. "What's your suggestion, Sadie, I'm almost afraid to ask."

"We have to buy it," she shrugged. "Simple as that."

"Simple?" exclaimed Carmen. "Simple?"

"I've sold several nice properties," Sadie explained. "I stashed my commissions, and my Christmas bonus, with plans to buy a new car. But I'll fork it over, and drive Millie another year, if all of you will chip in, too."

Kate thought for a few moments. "I sold some paintings, *The Teton collection*, last month. I can add that."

"Well, I have my savings that's planned for our wedding next December," offered Carmen, "but, you all will have to help me raise a wedding from ashes."

Everyone was looking at Roselyn. "OK, I have my tax returns. I planned to paint the house, but this does seem urgent."

"Great!" said Sadie, with the excitement of an auctioneer who just spotted a high bidder. "We'll gather it all up, Monday. I'll find out how much it will cost. If it takes more than we have, we can take out a small loan. Roselyn, since you own this land, you should be the one to purchase it. That way, it'll all be in one name."

Roselyn nodded.

"Later when you're on your feet, you can buy our shares, or we can agree to sell it to someone else. You can't lose money on land if you're willing to hold onto it long enough."

As the women disbanded to leave, I sunk into worry. If Dennis bought up all this land, I would soon be a goner. I knew that. This was Saturday, and I would know nothing until Monday. That's a long time to stew. I was ready to start chewing my square-roof nails off.

The following week was successful for my girls. The land was purchased, and Roselyn was the owner of sixty acres of worthless prairie. In addition, she had a mother, and two sisters, as silent partners for a business that had no purpose.

This wasn't the kind of organizational planning I was used to, but if it kept me out of Dennis's hands, I wouldn't complain.

Chapter Twenty-Eight

REVENGE

"I sifted his thoughts, and realized he was concerned
about his snakes"

By end of June the prairie turned to dust. The continual winds from the mountains lifted it up, and blasted my outer walls. Dirt sifted through my window screens. Roselyn swept my floors several times daily, and Maria dusted constantly.

Kate made pictures of Alfie Rose for each of her daughters. She had the clasp repaired on the heirloom necklace, and wore it every day. Sharing with Roselyn, she talked about the information she gathered from Mr. Carter, the jeweler in town.

"That's really pretty, Mom," said Roselyn, looking closely at the heart-shaped pendant, hanging around Kate's neck. "Mr. Carter shined it all up for you, I see."

"Yes, and he sold me a bottle of silver polish, just for jewelry," said Kate. He said he believed the pendant is from the 1800's. We looked through his antique jewelry book and found several very similar pieces dated to the mid to late 1800's."

"So the first owner would be like your third or fourth great-grandmother?" asked Carmen.

"Probably," answered Kate. "Her initials were either AK or DK, and her husband would be the other. Mr. Carson said it was common for some couples to use a necklace as an engagement piece, rather than an engagement ring. The wedding ring came with the ceremony."

Sadie, now holding the heart in her hand, turned it over to examine the engraving. "They are more visible now that the tarnish is cleared away."

"The pictures of similar pendants appeared to have garnets inlaid in them. Mr. Carter said it seemed unusual for the piece to have turquoise. That's a stone used mostly in the Americas. He suggested the original couple may have had it made, choosing a turquoise stone," explained Kate.

"Mom, did you notice the tiny hinges on the side?" asked Sadie, closely examining the silver heart.

"No, let me take it off. You're nearly breaking my neck," complained Kate.

She reached behind her head and unclasped the chain. Then looking closely at the intricate heart, she exclaimed, "You're right, Sadie! There are two tiny hinges."

Turning it around, she added, "And here is a very tiny clasp to open it. Oh my goodness, it's a locket!"

"I can't believe Mr. Carter didn't notice," said Carmen.

"Maybe he did. We only discussed its date, origin, and condition. He may have thought I knew it was a locket," reasoned Kate.

"Let's pop it open, Mom," suggested Sadie, eagerly. "There's probably pictures in it."

"I don't want to break it," worried Kate, gently attempting to open the locket's clasp with a thumb nail. "No, it is really stuck. I'll take it back to Mr. Carter. He has tools to open it without causing damage."

"I can't believe women in those days could keep jewelry for an entire lifetime," remarked Roselyn. "I can't even keep up with a pair of earrings."

"That's because Hunter swipes them from you," giggled Carmen.

"Speaking of swiping," said Roselyn, "that reminds me of something I found in Hunter's room. I'm afraid he stole it. Hunter always lays claim to stuff lying around here, but I've never known him to actually steal someone's possession. I'll show it to you."

Running upstairs, Roselyn retrieved the wallet.

Meanwhile, Kate returned the necklace to her neck. She playfully slapped Sadie's hand that continued to reach for the locket. "Sadie, you're going to have to wait until Mr. Carter opens it. Have patience, child."

"When have you ever seen Sadie have patience?" teased Carmen.

Roselyn returned and sat on the couch by her mother. "I wanted to show you this while the kids are at day-camp. I found this wallet under Hunters bed. It belongs to a teenager." She handed it to Kate.

"It sure is grubby," commented Kate, as she turned it in her hand. She opened it, and looked at the license and ID, displayed in the plastic-covered inner pocket.

"Megan Wells. I've never heard of any Wells in town," she said thoughtfully.

"There are no patients coming to our office by that name," offered Carmen.

"She may be a tourist who passed through," suggested Sadie.

"Oh yes. You're right, I think," said Kate. "The address on the license is from Rock Springs."

"But how would Hunter get it? He's never in town without me, unless this girl was at his school at some point," wondered Roselyn.

"Did you ask him?" inquired Carmen.

"Of course," said Roselyn. "He refuses to tell me. Well, he said Jack gave it to him."

"Is he still talking about Jack?" chuckled Kate.

"Who's Jack?" asked Sadie.

"Someone he's made up," explained Roselyn. "He just started it since we moved here. He says Jack tells him stuff, and when I found this, he tried to convince me Jack gave it to him."

"I would just ignore the Jack thing," advised Kate. "It's probably just a passing fancy."

"Let's search that wallet," suggested Sadie. "There might be clues in it."

She reached for it, and Kate held it back, "Hold your horses, nosey."

Kate pulled the bill section open, "There are several ones in here, and a folded-up paper. I don't think we should disturb the contents. I say we take it to the police, or we could put a notice in the paper, maybe even have it announced on Town Talk. If she's around, she can claim it at the police station."

Looking at the clock, Roselyn announced, "I need to pick up the kids from the park. You all make yourselves at home." She jumped up and grabbed her keys.

"Come on Mom," prompted Sadie, "Let's get the locket to Mr. Carter before his shop closes. I want to find out if there are pictures inside."

"Sadie?" asked Kate, "Do you have any understanding of the concept of 'tomorrow'?"

"Nope," she replied, as they all walked out my front door.

That evening, Kate caught Hunter with her butcher knife. "Hunter, you are not allowed to have knives. What are you doing?"

"I'm cutting up a box for my snakes' house. It's too hot for them to be in their jars," whined Hunter.

"Does it ever occur to you to ask for help?" Roselyn asked wearily.

"No," answered her son honestly.

"First of all, if you care about the snakes, you will let them go. Secondly, any box you design is not going to keep them contained, and I don't want them loose in the house," Roselyn reasoned.

"I love my snakes," Hunter sounded as though he would cry.

"Well, you have a king snake, a bull snake, and a garter snake. They can't be kept together. We'll go to town tomorrow and get some used aquariums that I saw at the thrift store, OK?"

Hunter agreed.

"Good," soothed Roselyn, ruffling her son's hair. "Now, put that knife back and take those jars outside on the porch. I don't want to wake up with a snake in my bed."

While Hunter obeyed, Roselyn locked my front door, and turned off lights, making sure Moonshine, the cat, was in. Hunter returned, and she locked my backdoor. They walked up my stairs together.

After the family settled into sleep, and I sang to Ethan, I added the chorus.

> *Get out of the way of old Dan Tucker*
> *He's too late to eat his supper*
> *Supper is over, the dishes are washed*
> *Nothing is left, but a piece of squash*

I sifted his dreams, and knew he was hearing me.

Hunter didn't go to sleep; he was restless. I sifted his thoughts, and realized he was concerned about his snakes.

'They're OK, Hunter,' I assured him.

He got up quietly and slipped out. Walking softly down my stairs, he slipped out my back door. Leaning over the jars, he asked, "Are you boys hot in there?"

I sensed movement coming down the road. I could almost make out a huge form in the moonlight. As it drew near, I could tell it was a vehicle.

'It's a pickup with its lights off.' I thought.

It coasted down the hill and curve that made up part of the dirt road. The truck pulled to a stop right by the gate that entered our property. The driver carefully turned the pickup around to face out. I thought he was planning to leave. Rather, he opened his door.

As the cab light came on, I saw the red color of the exterior. I also saw Dennis Dickinson. Hunter saw him too. Peeking around from my back-wraparound porch, he watched the man creep slowly toward us.

Chapter Twenty-Nine

REDEMPTION

"I liked it when their encircling includes me"

HUNTER, RUN INSIDE!' I projected'.WAKE UP YOUR MAMA

Then, I noticed what he was doing. He had come outside to release his snakes. Two were lying in the grass: the king snake, and the baby bull snake. The garter snake was still in the jar. Hunter seemed frozen as he watched Dennis creep closer.

I focused on Dennis. He moved silently toward Roselyn's pickup; he had something in his hand. I wanted Hunter inside. I returned my attention toward Hunter, but he had left the porch.

No, Hunter! No!

He was creeping toward Dennis's truck. The cab door was open, to provide a hasty escape. Hunter leaned into the opening by the driver's seat.

What's he doing, for heaven's sakes?

I looked back at Dennis. He was stabbing the tires of Roselyn's pickup: one, two, three, and four.

I searched the darkness for Hunter. He had slithered back under the fence, curled up into a small ball, and was hiding in the shadows. As soon as Dennis climbed back into his truck, he quietly shut the door, and drove slowly away. Hunter beat it to the house; his snake jar was empty.

Hunter slipped back into my backdoor, and locked it behind him. He slinked up the stairs, and slid into his bed.

Hunter, tell your Mama!

"NO!" he said aloud, pulling his cover over his head, and blocking me out.

The following day when Roselyn discovered the condition of her only transportation, she gasped. Coming back into the house, she called Hunter. He entered my living room where his mother stood with her hands on her hips, fighting the need to cry.

"Someone slashed my tires, Hunter," she said. "All four of my tires are ruined."

Hunter hung his head like a man convicted.

No Hunter, don't act guilty. You didn't do it! No Roselyn, it wasn't him. Think this through!

"Hunter, when I told you to put the knife away, what did you do with it?"

Hunter's bottom lip was trembling. "I put it away like you said, Mama. I didn't slash your tires."

New tires will take all the extra money I have for all summer. Do you know what that means? We won't be going to summer movies now, eating at McDonalds, and I can't buy aquariums for your snakes." Tears were climbing over Roselyn's lower lids.

"Doesn't matter bout the snakes," he sobbed. "I let them go anyway, like you said."

Roselyn sat down in the wicker chair, a part of her mismatched collection of furniture, and placed her face in her hands and sobbed.

Hunter, tell her the truth, now!

Hunter walked over to Roselyn and said, "Mama, that mean ugly Dennis slashed your tires, but I fixed him. I turned Hank loose in his truck, and told him to bite him, for what he did to your pickup."

Roselyn lifted her tear-stained face and looked at her son. My sifting told me she believed his story was a cover-up.

"Hunter, are you going to tell me Jack told you to put a snake in Dennis's pickup, and told it to bite him?"

Hunter, face also tearstained, shook his head. "No, Jack told me to run inside and wake you up, but I was afraid if you came down, Dennis might use that big ole knife to hurt you."

She pulled him close to her, and for a few minutes they warmed each other's hearts.

"Sweet boy, when you want to tell me what really happened, I won't be mad at you. We will just figure out how you can help me pay for new tires, OK?"

Hunter brightened, "I could sell stuff from my treasure box."

Later Kate picked Roselyn and the kids up. She took them to get tires. Roselyn was able to finance them for six months. "It'll still be tight," she complained.

When the children were outdoors Kate suggested, "You need to call the police, and have them check this out."

Roselyn shook her head, "No, I really think Hunter did it. I think he's sorry, but I think he did it. I don't want to call the police when the problem is in my own home. Maybe I'm a bad mother. Maybe I have let him get out of control." Tears were threatening to reign terror on her very pretty face.

Kate pulled her daughter to her, "You are a wonderful mother, and I don't think Hunter did this. I don't think a boy his size has the strength to slash pickup tires. That was a man. I think Hunter told you the truth."

Roselyn pulled away to look into her mother's face, "Mom, you should hear his cockamamie story of how he put a snake in Dennis's truck, and told it to bite him. Hunter is gifted at making up stories, just like his dad was."

"Well, maybe the snake part is made up. Maybe that's what he wished he could have done. But the slashing, I think he's telling the truth," stated Kate, emphatically.

That evening the entire clan showed up, carry-in food, in hand. Carl brought vegetarian lasagna, Sadie her green bean casserole, and Kate, a salad and a cake, from the bakery. I noticed with this family, when one of them is down, the others encircle the distressed one with support, and that usually included food. *I liked it when their encircling included me.*

As they sat at the picnic table, in the shade I provided them, Carmen spoke up, "Have you heard that Dennis was in a wreck last night?"

"No, I didn't hear that," answered Kate, surprised.

"When I arrived at the office this morning, the receptionist told me she had to cancel our appointments for the morning. Our doc was called in to the ER. Dennis flipped his pickup coming into town from highway 789, from this way, actually. If another car hadn't stopped, he would have been in serious trouble. The wreck didn't hurt him much because he was wearing his seat belt, but the snakebite caused him a serious reaction, almost as bad as the bees," she concluded.

Roselyn and Kate looked at each other in disbelief.

"What?" asked Carmen.

Then they shared Hunter's story. Sadie impulsively announced, "Well, personally, I think a bit of karma occurred."

Kate shook her head, "Even if Hunter put one of his snakes in the truck, why would it bite him? Hunter handled those snakes all the time. They were docile."

Carmen said, "Oh, Doc did tell us about that. He said Dennis claimed he felt something slithering around his ankle. He reached down to swat it off, and it bit his pinkie. That's what caused him to go off the road, over-correct, and then flip. Then he said he saw a garter snake slide right out his open window."

"But," Roselyn began, "garter snakes are non-venomous. Otherwise, I would never allow him to play with them."

"Let's check it out, offered Sadie. "I'll get Roselyn's laptop."

A few minutes later, with numerous heads looking over her shoulder, Sadie read, "The garter snake inhabits most regions of the United States, and Canada. It was long-believed that they had no venom. However, recent findings indicate they have mild neurotoxin venom."

"There you go," offered Carmen. "His reaction to bees happened because of his allergy to neurotoxin poison. All biting and stinging insects, and snakes, have the same poison, just in different amounts."

"Listen," continued Sadie, "it says the reason more people don't experience bites is because the location of the garter snakes' fangs is farther back in their mouths than other poisonous snakes. It's more difficult for them to get in a position to inject the venom."

"That makes sense," reasoned Carmen. "He reached down with his hand, and the snake was able to latch onto his little finger. Most people would have had little negative response, but his allergy kicked in."

Sadie closed the laptop, "Well, he shouldn't have tried to poison my sister," she said.

Later when Roselyn tucked the boys into bed, she lingered with Hunter.

"Son, I want you to know that I do believe what you told me. I'm sorry I doubted you."

Hunter smiled, and threw his arms around her neck. She held him close.

"But, promise me this. If anything like that happens again, don't try to handle it alone. Come to me, and we will fix it together, OK?"

"Ok, like Jack said?" Roselyn rolled her eyes.

"And," she continued, "don't ever put a snake in someone's car, ok?"

"Ok," whispered Hunter, placing a slippery kiss on her cheek.

The family settled into quiet darkness, only the hums of the fans could be heard. I prepared to do my serenade to Ethan.

Chapter Thirty

JOHANNA

"His music draws me"

With the distraction of hot weather and land purchases, the continually increasing colony of bees was forgotten. They were only remembered from time to time, when Sadie noticed them. Their intimidation worked to discourage Hunter from the cistern shed.

By July the thermometer mercury hung persistently in the nineties, and above. The family spent the Fourth in town. This is, for Lander, a traditional event. They planned to attend the parade and rodeo. I wished I could tell them that Lander was the first town ever to have a paid rodeo. That was many years before it became a tradition for the July Fourth celebrations.

While settling into a long lonely day, my thoughts returned to another hot summer, long ago.

*   *   *

Joshua's Daughter

Johanna turned eighteen in midsummer, 1936. It was July, and celebrations were planned in the growing community of Lander, in remembrance of Independence Day. Ever since the war, this midsummer holiday had great importance.

I wished I could see it, and envied the houses lined up at the ends of Main Street. However, by listening to discussions, I learned there was always a parade of marching veterans, mounted sheriffs, natives dressed in ceremonial costume, and local musicians, who always formed a band for the event.

Homemade ice cream and lemonade provided cool refreshment to the citizens. A baseball game, and contests of horse-shoes, as well as a tug-of-war, added excitement. There were also pie auctions in which a single man attempted to buy a pie, baked by the charming single lady he admired most.

Pretty blond Johanna was small in stature, reminding me of young Helen, except for her coloring. She was bright, like her father and grandmother, and thrived in the educational setting of school. She completed her studies by sixteen, in the small stone high school, a block off Lander's Main Street.

Johanna was not interested in medicine, and since she was the only child, Joshua wondered if anyone in the family would carry on the tradition. With William and Helen now at rest near Duncan and Christina, by the aspen grove, Joshua and Vicky were the master and mistress of the ranch, and I loved them.

Vicky kept my floors clean, the furnishings dusted, and the garden maintained. Aromas of her cooking filled the house. Johanna learned these skills from her mother, but she dreamed of becoming a teacher.

She pursued her education in Laramie. There, the only college in the state, began in 1847, with forty-two men and women. Now it was a thriving small college, and Johanna's parents were glad she would not leave the state. The distance did not allow her to see them throughout her three years of schooling. During the summer, Johanna remained in Laramie and worked as a nanny, and tutor.

While she was away, her parents missed her dreadfully, as did I. Vicky used the time for redecorating. I must admit I am not ever pleased with change, and always do my best to resist it. With Joshua's gentle prodding, I surrendered to Vicky's modernizing.

Aspen had become a farmhand house, where various hired hands stayed to manage the farm. Much of the land was planted in hay which was sold for added income. Joshua's practice paid well, no longer relying on payments of produce, beef, or other barters, but actual payments of money.

Vicky had the big wood cook stove moved to Aspen, as well as one of the large rugs. An iron posted bed, and the table William made so long ago, went too.

I was angry for a while, and opened doors she wanted shut, and shut doors she wanted opened. I sounded out recorded noises through the night, to keep her awake.

It didn't work to prevent the progress. They blamed the noises on possible mice in the walls, and continued on with their plans.

A pharmacy began in Lander some year earlier so Joshua no longer needed to mix and make medicine. Therefore, my little apothecary room was converted into Vicky's sewing room. My large storage area in the back of the house was turned into a new kind of luxury, a bathroom.

The outhouse became the exclusive domain of the farmhand. Vicky chose a wallpaper of fern leaves, and purchased towels and washcloths of green and white. She ordered from her big Sear's catalogue, a milky white soap dish, and sink. She curtained the window with white linen, trimmed with green lace.

The odd stool was called a water closet, and it made a sloshing noise when someone pulled the string. *In time I learned to assert enough energy to make this happen, and found many useful tricks to utilize it.*

I was proud that I, the Grand Lady of the Valley, was the first family home to have electricity. Not at first, of course, but as Joshua and Vicky discussed it around the table one evening, *I began to see lots of advantages.*

Joshua explained to Vicky how much safer his procedures, and minor surgeries, would be with better lighting, and how much cleaner the air would be without the kerosene lamps and lanterns. Soon every room within my walls had a glass bulb hanging from an ornate attachment. A string dropped from the attachment with a tiny knob on the bottom for turning the light on and off.

I found it easy to circulate air, causing the string to swing mysteriously. This, I most enjoyed in my front parlor, where patients waited to see the doctor.

My kitchen got the biggest makeover. Steam and heat from cooking, had, over the years, damaged the plaster on my wall. It had been put there by William, and was just as I wanted it to be. Joshua hired a carpenter to reapply plaster over much of the area.

Vicky painted it light yellow. I had to admit it was a brighter room. Then the carpenter installed what Vicky called a kitchen sink, as well as some white metal cupboards. Moving dishes around in them caused a lot of noise; *I recorded that.*

She ordered a table and some new chairs. From Sears and Roebuck, she bought blue dishes with pictures on them. She said the scenes were of China. The new electric cook stove was placed on the spot where Helen's wood cook stove had stood. Gone were the cast iron cookware, and in were the new enameled pots and pans that Vicky proudly displayed on a rack on my wall.

If I didn't know myself so well, I would have gotten lost in my changed rooms. There was some adjustment for cooking on the new fang-dangled stove. She burned a number of meals, until she figured that out.

Plaster was repaired in the bedrooms and both parlors. My front parlor walls were papered with an ivy pattern. New lace curtains were hung, as well as blinds, that could be pulled up or down, by a string.

I soon mastered a new skill. By jiggling the windows a bit, I could make a lowered blind rapidly wind up to the top of the window, another free entertainment for patients to observe. Christina's portrait, and Helen's mirror, were hung back on my walls in their rightful place. At least that didn't change.

Helen planted roses, Christina planted tulips, and Vicky planted irises and hollyhocks. The irises, she transplanted from patches of wild iris, the hollyhocks seeds were sent to her by her mother back East. The roses continued to climb the trellises connected to my porches. The tulips lined the stone walkway to my front step. The hollyhocks hovered by my back porch, and the irises grew by the graves.

They added coal heat. Although this kept my interior warmer, with less work for the men, it smelled wretched. Sometimes it made me sneeze, causing all my inside doors to slam shut in one loud swoosh.

A new contraption came with the electricity, a radio. This provided evening entertainment. Vicky liked listening to stories, acted out, with a new episode every day. Joshua liked listening to news. They also listened to music and comedy. My world was changing and expanding. I began to learn there were other places besides just my valley: other people, other events.

During this time Joshua hired David Gregg. David and his parents came from Scotland. He explained that his family was of the Mac Greggor clan, a proud warring clan. His hair and beard were deep dark auburn, and his eyes as green as the apples in our orchard. He spoke with a lilt, and it seemed that everything he said brought laughter.

I liked him right away, as did my family.

David soon had Aspen shipshape, and she was delighted to have an energetic occupant. David was twenty-two when he moved to our farm, and he knew much about farming, for his young years. He brought with him bagpipes. Often in the evening, I could hear them playing a sad and mournful melody.

Joshua remarked that never had the land been so productive. We would find out the first summer, however, that David was allergic to bee stings. Bees were plentiful, as the alfalfa bloomed. From one sting, he nearly died, and Joshua stayed up with him all night, sponging cool water over his fevered body, forcing sips of water through his swelled lips.

After that, it was decided that additional hands would be hired for the fields during the blooming season, and David would be farm foreman.

Johanna was in for many surprises when she returned that spring of '36'. She was pleased with the house, and brought with her a device from which music played, from a large black disc. The music was about lovers, some happy, and some broken hearted.

Her beautiful blond hair was cut short and tightly waved, in what she explained was a 'bob'. Her skirts were shorter than when she had left, and she painted her lips, at which her parents remarked disapproval. But she was her own women. She was ready to celebrate her 'coming of age'.

The first evening after her arrival, she was sitting near the kitchen window, a cup of tea, and a McCall's magazine opened in front of her, when the mournful sounds of the bagpipes drifted in.

"What's that?" she asked her mother.

"That's David," Vicky answered. "He's the farm foreman. He stays in the stone cottage."

"But that sound, the music, I've heard something like that before. What is that?"

"That Scottish music comes from his bagpipes," answered her mother.

For several minutes she peppered her parent with questions about the musician, until finally Vicky asked, "Why are you so curious? You've never been this interested in knowing about any of our farmhands before."

Johanna sat quietly for a few moments, her head leaning toward the melody. "I don't know," she answered, "His music draws me."

Chapter Thirty=One

JULY

*"Each spoke in a silent voice, to the time at which they were placed
in the aspen grove. Each stands as a tribute to the living,
that marked their resting place"*

The sun setting over the mountains backlit the vehicles, spinning up dust, as they turned onto the dirt road from the highway.

I braced myself. Time to pull out of my dreamy state of mind for the day. Things were sure to liven up now.

The families unloaded, and gathered on my porch. Everyone was tired, and sunburned, but not ready to give up on the celebration. They had planned to watch fireworks from my west porch, I remembered.

They bathed the children and dressed them in pajamas. Roselyn noted she would need to call for water delivery tomorrow. Kate and Sadie pulled ice cream and root beer from the frig. They talked about making floats; this was a new treat. I was looking forward to learning what they were.

Finally they were on my porch relaxing and chatting in small groups. Roselyn appeared to be upset as she stirred the frothy mixture in her tall glass.

Kate walked over, sat down, and put her arm around Roselyn's shoulders, "It's not too late to call the police and report him," she advised.

Roselyn shook her head, "This is Wyoming," she said. "No one calls the cops every time some jerk screams obscenities."

Carmen, sitting nearby, spoke up, "I would say Dennis was not just yelling. He was behaving in a threatening manner."

"I wish I had been there. What did he say?" asked Carl.

"I had taken the boys to the restroom," answered Kate, "so I missed the ugly scene."

"Well, to summarize," started Carmen, "he approached Roselyn on the top seats of the bleachers at the rodeo grounds. He was as drunk as a skunk. The jerk got right in her face, and demanded to know if she is the one who bought the land out from under him."

"There's an example of feeling entitled," stated Kate.

"Then," began Roselyn, "I told him I bought it, and asked why he had a problem with it."

"He really started yelling," broke in Carmen. "He called Roselyn every filthy name in the book."

Roselyn took the lead again, "When Sadie returned with a cardboard tray of icy sodas for everyone, she told Dennis to back off. He then turned his caustic mouth on her, and she threw all the drinks in his face."

"Then," added Roselyn, "she smacked him on the side of the head with that big hippy tote she carries."

"Didn't anyone step up to help?" asked Kate, becoming more disturbed.

"Everyone was still scattered around," explained Carmen. "People were looking around, but no one understood what was happening."

Suddenly, Roselyn giggled. "You should have seen the surprise on his face when Sadie pushed him backwards, leaned on his chest, and yelled right back at him."

"If there's a brawl, Sadie will mix it up," said Kate, shaking her head. "Though I'm thankful she did this time."

"Now mom, she hasn't been in a rumble since high school," defended Carmen, teasingly.

Just then, cracking noises exploded and streaking lights filled the black skies. Dennis was forgotten, and oohs and ahhs were released as the light show expanded.

For now the incident appeared to be forgotten. I doubted this was over. As the family slept, I forced my thoughts back to less stressful times.

At Johanna's request, David was invited for dinner, with an invitation to play his bagpipes.

"He has always preferred to cook his own meal in the bunkhouse," explained her mother. "I'm surprised he agreed to eat with us."

Aspen was, by now, referred to as the bunk house, a title of which, she did not approve.

The early summer was filled with music. Johanna played her love songs while she helped her mother with chores. In the evenings David came to the evening meal. He was always in his best clothing. I suspected he was courting Johanna.

Johanna was especially excited that her father was now the owner of an automobile. Vicky had no desire to learn to drive, but Johanna insisted that Joshua teach her. Some afternoons were taken up with these lessons.

The open prairie provided safe space for practice driving. However, Vicky was not amused when Johanna lost control, and ran the auto through her clothesline which was supporting freshly washed sheets.

By the midsummer month of July, Joshua and Vicky were aware that David and Johanna were drawn to one another, like a pair of doves. Joshua agreed for them to take the auto to the Independence Day celebration, in Lander, on July fourth. From that day on we all knew David would become part of our family.

They were married at the church in Lander, but I was invited to the reception. It was held in my front yard, under the cottonwood trees. David moved in, and our family eventually increased. A year later, in 1938, Milton was born.

In 1940, his little sister, Miriam, joined us. The twins followed in 1942. Lydia and Leila were identical, and just as with Ridge and Ransom, I could never tell them apart.

Johanna taught school in Lander for many years, and David managed our farm, raising hay and garden produce, and being at home for the children. The following years would be filled with a busy household, and soon I was bursting at the seams.

The morning after the Fourth, Kate gave the information about the wallet to the radio station and, the wallet itself, to the police station. She came over to have coffee with Roselyn, and listen to Lander Talk, together, as they often did.

The announcer went through a list of ads: a used Maytag washing machine, a large freezer, and a Toyota pickup.

Then he interviewed a local pastor about a Vacation Bible School starting soon in a local church. Another interview followed regarding swimming lessons in the new town pool.

Then lost and found was covered. A black lab was missing, a reward offered. Car keys were found on Main Street following the parade, collect them at the police station. A lost wallet was found. The owner's name is Megan Wells. Megan, if you are within hearing distance of this broadcast, you can contact Roselyn Chalmers.

"What?" yelped startled Kate. "I didn't tell Steve to name you. I told him she could pick it up at the police station. I only mentioned you found it. Jeeez, can't he ever get anything right?"

"Well, if Miss Megan comes for it, I'll tell her where it is. Actually, I would like to meet her. Maybe she could rest my mind about how Hunter got his hands on it," Roselyn said.

Kate and Roselyn took the children to the lake for the afternoon, and I was alone again, with my thoughts.

Chapter Thirty-Two

DAISY

*"There was a deep sadness, and feeling of grief, but also,
there was love between those who shared this grief"*

The Greggs only made a few changes to my structure. David removed
the wall William had added in my front parlor. Johanna covered the
now, larger, room walls with light brown wallpaper, filled with tiny dark
brown oak leaves. Furniture from Sears and Roebuck was ordered from
Chicago, and delivered to Lander by train. It was a dark burnt mustard
color, very plump, and stuffed for comfort.

She added a new round oak table and chairs to my dining room, with
a china hutch to match. The blue willow dishes were exchanged for
heavy white crockery dishes that reminded me a bit of Helen's old
churn.

David, remembering the castles in his home country, added my tower.
He built it into my roof on the south side. It became two levels, each
with one room. They were large and round rooms, with windows on all
sides. The view was spectacular from the tower.

On many early mornings and late afternoons, David joined me, as
we watched either the sunrise or sunset. To the west, the Wind River

Mountains provided a different view every day. To the north, on a clear day, the Owl Creek Peaks were visible.

To the south, Lander, with its Popo Agie River, feeding the valley. To the northeast, the Crow's Heart Mound, where according to legend, two chiefs fought, rather that have a war. It ended with one chief removing the beating heart of the other.

My view is different now, thanks to Dennis, and the historical ladies. I could still see the Wind River Mountains, though from a farther distance, but all else was endless prairie.

Johanna's younger brother, James, the active lad who played soldier, became one. He wanted to spend his life serving his country, and joined the Navy. He left soon after his twentieth birthday and I never saw him again.

His letters were read aloud often. His picture, as he posed in uniform, sat on the piano. This would become a family heartbreak. James died in 1942, in a mishap on his ship. He was twenty-four years old. His body was returned to Lander by train.

A telegram came with the news; Vicky was distraught. She became so weak with grief, she took to her bed. While waiting for James' body, which was accompanied by a fellow sailor, Vicky would not speak, or eat.

A few days after the telegram, a letter came from James. Vicky would not allow it to be opened. She placed it with the telegram, on her sewing table, and closed the door. I didn't know what she planned to do with the letter, or what became of it, but during those days she insisted it not be disturbed.

There was a deep sadness, and feeling of grief, but also, there was love between those who shared this grief.

When James arrived, the young sailor, who came with his casket, stayed for several days. James' funeral was held in the church in Lander, and buried among our other graves. Eventually, months later, a large military stone arrived to mark his grave.

When the young sailor left, while saying goodbye, he took a few items from his pocket. "These were his. I'll leave them with you," he said.

He handed Vicky a watch, a new testament, and a sealed envelope. Vicky thanked him, and placed these articles with the previous ones, on her sewing table.

A few weeks following James' burial, the twin toddlers became very ill. The older children also experienced fever. Soon Joshua's fears proved to be true. Polio swept the county, the state, and the country. Many Native American children were affected, as well as children of families in town. The school closed down. Fear gripped the community.

Vicky pulled out of her depression to provide strength for her daughter, Johanna. Specialists from out of state visited, and provided consultation, to Wyoming doctors. Eventually the evil virus wore itself out, but not without leaving devastation in its wake.

Some children recovered, some were left maimed, and some died. Milton recovered with no ill effects. Determined to make a difference for polio survivors, he would eventually become a physical therapist.

Miriam recovered, but always had a limp. She also had her father's strong optimistic spirit. She refused to allow it to deter her plans for living life to the fullest. Miriam eventually married Thomas Carr, and would parent the next generation within my walls.

But sadly, our little twins, Lydia and Leila, did not survive the high fever. They are buried next to their Uncle James. Johanna had twin stones made for them, out of marble. Sweet-faced cherubs adorn the tops.

The little cemetery took on new character: some rugged stones, a stately military stone, and two lovely works of art, uniting one family.

Each spoke in a silent voice, to the time in which they were placed in the aspen grove. Each stands as a tribute to the living, who marked their resting place.

My thoughts were interrupted by the ringing landline phone. It was Sadie; I sifted the line, to hear.

"I just want to warn you, Roz. Dennis is still riled."

"He stopped by our office early, demanding to know if it is legal for you to buy that land."

Roselyn sat down, and put the receiver to the other ear.

"He told my boss that I steered a sale away from the office. He called it 'inside trading', Jeeez."

"What? That land was available to anyone. He's just ticked off because he didn't get there first," said Roselyn.

"Larry already knew we bought that land, and told him to buzz off. He tried to explain to Dennis that land, selling for back taxes, is available to anyone who wants to search it out."

"Wow . . ." Roselyn seemed stunned.

"Then, he shook his finger in my face and said he was going to press charges for whacking him with my tote-bag, at the rodeo."

Roselyn said nothing, just waited.

"Then Larry backed him out of the front office, and pushed him out the door. He told him if he ever came back, he would really have some assault charges to complain about. Anyway, be sure you keep doors locked."

"I have kids running in and out, Sadie. I can't keep doors locked," responded Roselyn. "He's a hothead. He'll probably cool down soon."

The next day Kate arrived with a large dog. "He's rescued from the shelter," she announced. A customer told me about her. She's three years old, and her owner passed away. She is well-trained. I think you need a watch dog."

Roselyn petted the golden head, "She almost looks like a fluffy lab."

"She's a Labradoodle, a cross between a golden lab and a standard poodle," explained Kate.

"What's her name?" asked Hunter.

"Daisy," said Kate

"Hi Daisy," cooed Maria, hugging her enormous head.

Ethan laid his head against her back. "I guess Daisy's a keeper," concluded Roselyn.

"Oh good," laughed Kate, "she wouldn't have fit in my apartment. I have dog food in the Jeep. I'll get it."

Roselyn petted Daisy, and turned around her collar. "Look, this is almost worn through. I'll have to get a new collar for you, Daisy girl."

After bedtime I approached Ethan with a new plan for my therapy. Throughout the summer I had watched Roselyn attempt to teach him to sign his address. It was a requirement for entering first grade. Ethan had showed little interest in learning it.

I had overheard him softly humming the Old Man Tucker song, and I knew he was learning it.

As I sang into his dreams, I changed the words, using the same tune, but replacing the words with his address:

> *'I'm Ethan Chalmers and my address*
> *Is Whitman's Gulch Turnoff*
> *On Highway seven-eighty nine*
> *Lander is my town.'*

'I'm determined you will say this or sing it, not sign it, to your teacher, Ethan.'

Chapter Thirty-Three

THE KEY

"The secrets, when they're painful, must remain locked away"

We were sweltering. For two nights Roselyn and the kids slept downstairs. The kids lay on sleeping bags on the floor; it was too hot to sleep inside of them. Roselyn curled up on the short wicker couch.

There were major fires in Yellowstone Park that summer. The days revealed gray smoke in the atmosphere, and the night's skies were red umber. One morning as the group sat under the air-conditioner in my living room, slurping popsicles, Maria was hit with an idea.

"Mama, rather than laying down sleeping bags every night, and picking them up again every morning, why don't we open up that locked room? We could make it a summer bedroom."

I had been drifting in and out of memories about Miriam's summer wedding in the 60's, but now I focused my attention.

"Sweetie, that room was so full of smoke and water damage, I haven't even wanted to think about cleaning it up," answered Roselyn. "It will probably be the last task, on my long bucket list, for this house."

'Good girl, Rosy. We don't need to think about that.

Maria wasn't going to let it drop, "But Mama, we don't have to fix it up. We could just sweep, mop, and wash the walls. It would just be for the rest of July, and August, probably."

NO! Roselyn, NO! Don't let her talk you into it.

"There are lots of windows in there," mused Roselyn. "If we opened them, we would have a cross breeze, whenever there is a breeze."

"And it's on the north side," reminded Maria. "It's always cooler on that side of the house."

Hunter went outside, and Ethan crawled over by my dining room door. He began standing plastic farm animals in a row, and was attempting to use the discarded popsicle sticks, for fencing. He was softly singing, 'Old Dan Tucker'.

Roselyn, look your son is singing words.

"We could drag those camp cots from the attic, and the boys and I can sleep in there. You could sleep in the family room, Mama. That futon makes out into a bed."

Oh good heavens! Rosy, we can't open that door, and besides, you're missing out on Ethan's words.

I shuddered at the thought of that part of myself. I was so relieved the day Roselyn locked it up. There was a sickening gloom held in that space, something that lingered since the fire, and that horrid death. When I looked into that part of me, I thought about those nightmares Megan had. I could still feel them, see them, and hear her screams.

Sing it louder, Ethan,' I coaxed, 'loud enough for Mama to hear.

That silenced him. He became aware of what he was doing.

So much for using him as a distraction from these frightening plans.

"Can't we just look in, and see if it would work?" begged Maria.

"I'll have to get the key," said Roselyn, standing up. She walked to my kitchen, and began feeling around on top of the refrigerator. She had disillusioned herself into believing items would be safe there, from Hunter. I held my breath.

"I can't find that key. I know I put it here the same day I put the lock on that door," she complained.

She looked into my dining room at Ethan, "Son, did you see your brother with Mama's key?"

Ethan looked up and shrugged his shoulders. He held his hands out with palms up, meaning he didn't know. Everyone knew it meant he wasn't going to lie, or tell on his brother.

"HUNTER!" she demanded, "COME HERE!"

Hunter came in from my porch, "What?"

"Do you know where my key is, the one on the chain, with the silver heart?"

Hunter shook his head side-to-side.

Good job, Hunter. Don't tell her you took it. She doesn't need that old key anyway.

"Well, I guess I'll have to put a bounty on it," reasoned Roselyn.

No, Hunter, don't let her break you. Stand strong, child.

"We're all going to look for my key, right now. If we find it in twenty minutes, we will have the Moose Tracks ice cream for dessert tonight. If we don't, then there will be no dessert at all," she declared.

Hunter was wavering. 'Moose Tracks' was his favorite ice cream.

No, Hunter! Ice cream's bad for you. It decays your teeth.

Maria picked up on her mother's plot and pretended to look under the furniture, and behind the curtains. Roselyn opened and shut drawers in the kitchen as though she was searching. Ethan returned to his farm game. He began to softly sing again. But this time he interchanged lines from the song, and parts of the address, I taught him.

Roselyn, listen to your son! He's singing his address. How can this woman have such a one track mind? She would never make it as a house.

Hunter, who had disappeared momentarily, now stood before his mother with the key.

"Why, thank you, Hunter," she cooed. "Maria, look here, your brother found my key."

"Jack doesn't want you to have it," warned Hunter.

"Oh, he doesn't, does he?" challenged Roselyn. "Well, maybe Jack needs to find out who's the boss in this house."

She walked from my kitchen, through my dining room, stepped over Ethan's farm, and headed toward *The Door.*

If houses could run away, I would have.

She turned the key in the padlock she had attached to this ancient door, and gently pushed it open.

"Jack won't like it," Hunter taunted.

Oh stop it with the Jack *already! You're making things worse.*

As the door opened inward, a swoosh of icy cold air escaped. "Holy Cats! It's cool in here", Roselyn exclaimed.

She and Maria walked inside. *I tried not to look.* "I need to buy screens. I could pick them up this afternoon. And I wouldn't think of putting you kids in here, without a coat of paint," Roselyn was thinking aloud.

"Let's paint it mint green," begged Maria, pressing for her favorite color.

I was distraught. I remembered hearing William read a story aloud. It was called 'Pandora's Box. I knew they had no idea what they were letting loose.

They went directly to town and returned with sacks of takeout food. But in addition to that, paint rollers, a can of light green paint, a bottle of Murphy's Oil Soap, and a large forest green area rug. Their project had begun.

I couldn't watch, and I also couldn't resist the paint as I usually did. I spent all my energy restraining the emotion that was in this pocket of my being. *The secrets, even though they were painful, must remain locked away.*

Roselyn opened all the windows for ventilation. After scrubbing the walls, she applied the paint. I didn't interfere, but the light spring-toned lacquer turned an ugly pea green. Perhaps it was my gray smoked walls, perhaps it was my gray mood.

With floors scrubbed, they rolled out the forest green rug. Since Roselyn had not worked in my sad space, there was no light fixture. She brought in a pole lamp, and extension cord. Roselyn decided they should not sleep in my now green room that night. It needed time to dry, and air out.

When they were back in my living room, I could contain my stress no more. I slammed the door.

"Told ya Jack wouldn't like it," bragged Hunter.

That night they enjoyed Moose Tracks, while I pouted. Then I remembered that Ethan sang the words. That was one blessing I could hold on to.

Chapter Thirty-Four

THE DOOR

*"I wanted this room to remain shut. It is held an ugly
part of my inner self that was best locked away"*

My anxiety was heightened by the commotion of the children settling
into my sad room. Three camp cots were hauled in and made up with
sheets and light blankets. All windows were opened, and mountain
breezes flowed through.

Roselyn settled into her makeshift bed in the family room. I didn't like
this changing around. I was used to the arrangement of the bedrooms
upstairs. I wanted this room to remain shut. It held an ugly part of my
inner self that was best locked away. It housed gloom, and darkness,
that I could not explain.

This room started out as an apothecary room in the late 1800's, storing
life-giving elements. It was a sewing room in the early 1900's, and a
lady's office, following that. During the seventies, it was a practice
room for a music student. Then, it was turned into a room of death. A
horrid death of someone who was too young to die. A young girl filled
thoughts of horrible scenes. That anguish caused her to nearly burn
me down.

I remembered the despondency that moved, in shadows, through that part of my space, before Roselyn moved in and locked that door. The shadows seemed to be locked in, behind it.

"Eeeeeeeeek, Mama!"

A shiver ran down the north side of my center beams. Roselyn came crashing through the dark house from the family room, stubbing her toes on chair legs. "Ouch!! Maria, what is it?"

Roselyn found a light bulb string in the kitchen. She gave it a tug, and the light beamed her way, to 'The Room'. She switched on the lamp, in my now green room, and surveyed the scene. Both boys, and Maria, were on one cot, huddled together like scared little monkeys. Their eyes were round and frightened.

"Good heavens, Maria", said Roselyn, "Did you have a nightmare? We just barely turned out the lights."

"Mama, no! It was not a dream. The moonlight was shining through the window, and in the corner I saw something." Both boys were nodding in the affirmative.

Roselyn walked to the corner, stood there, holding her hands out, palms up. "What? What did you see?"

Ethan placed his hands around his neck and stuck out his tongue, the sign for hanging, no doubt.

"A person hanging from a rope," choked Maria.

"Probably Jack," offered Hunter.

Roselyn sat on the cot and looked at her children, "There is no Jack! There are no ghosts! It's just a different room. It has more windows. You'll get used to more moonlight shining through."

She straightened the covers on the cots, "Now, everyone, back to bed."

No one budged.

"Kids! I have a full day of computer billing tomorrow. I have to get some sleep, now back to your cots, boys!"

No movement.

"Mama, can't you please sleep in here with us, just for tonight?" Maria pleaded.

Roselyn rolled her eyes, "Let me get my pillow."

As she padded back to the family room, three pairs of feet followed. Maria, holding to the back of her pajama top, and both boys holding onto Maria's sleeves.

Roselyn grabbed her pillow and herded them back, "Now, see here kids. I spent money I did not plan to spend to freshen up this room. I'm committed to payments for new tires. I have also spent my savings to buy land I didn't need, and we are not going to make our lives harder by being scared in this house! Do you understand?"

There was no answer, but the boys climbed onto one cot, Marie into hers, and Roselyn tried to settle down on the remaining one. By morning, she was buried under the bodies of three children.

I thought of this throughout the rest of the night. A person hanging from a rope? That was the nightmare I sifted from Megan, the young girl who died in that room. Could she have left her memories? Was it memories that sent the gloom through my space? I thought it was her death, the fire, the fear I felt at the time, but maybe it was more.

During the next few days the news reported that the fires in Yellowstone were spreading.

Reports of the 'Sho-Raps', a Native American firefighting crew, made up of members of both the Shoshoni, and Arapaho tribes, were continually transported to hot spots. Tourist trade was down, and Yellowstone and Teton National parks were allowing no campfires. The Native Americans, preparing for their religious Sundance ceremony, prayed for rain.

But we had our own hotspot, my *'Green Room'*. I knew there were problems looming there, but I could not convey it to Roselyn. I tried to communicate to Hunter since he had the most open mind to me. Hunter had his own interpretation of those communications, however, and continued to talk about what Jack said. The kids made attempts to sleep in 'The Den of Gloom' for three nights, always leaving in a panic, before sunup.

During these days Ethan became withdrawn, and ceased his singing, and Maria appeared to be depressed. Kate and her daughters sat on the porch, with margaritas, and discussed these changes. Carmen's twins, and the boys, splashed in the plastic pool. Maria slinked off to the shade of my north porch, lost in her own grim thoughts.

Carmen cleared her throat, and prepared to address it with Roselyn. "Sis, I really think that we should have Hunter visit Doctor Reese. He's the new child psychologist. I'm hearing great reports from parents who come into our office. We should arrange it now, before school starts up again. I can quickly get a referral for you."

Roselyn bristled, "My son doesn't need a shrink," she snapped.

Carmen maintained her calm gentle voice. "Roselyn, it is not a disgrace to see a doctor for mental, or emotional, issues, any more than it is to see a medical doctor for physical problems. Hunter is seeing things, and talking to someone named Jack."

"Hunter has a vivid imagination," defended Roselyn. "Jack is probably an imaginary friend. I had one, remember, Mom? Jon-Jon was my buddy til I started kindergarten.'

"Yes, you had an imaginary friend until you were five, but Jon-Jon played with you. He didn't try to scare you to death. Besides, Hunter is much older, too old for imaginary friends. I think he's using Jack to blame things on, or to tease you," Kate advised.

"However, I'm more concerned about Maria. Depression is a real illness. Her grandfather suffered from it. A predisposition can be inherited. If anyone should see Doctor Reese, it should be Maria," Kate concluded.

Sadie returned from checking on Maria. "Roselyn, the bees there, I thought you got rid of them."

"I did," answered her sister. "I got a beekeeper to move them to his hives. These are new ones. I don't think they are a real swarm, just some stragglers. I keep meaning to buy some spray, and wipe them out after dark, when they can't fight back."

"That's what you said last time I brought it up," reminded Sadie.

"Sadie, we were discussing the kids," Kate informed her youngest. "Haven't you noticed a difference in them the last few days?"

"Ethan refuses to communicate with me in sign language," Sadie informed her mother. "He's always loved to communicate with me."

"Probably the only one who needs to see Doctor Reese is me, for buying this house in the first place," concluded Roselyn, as frown lines creased her forehead.

"Or, Sadie, for convincing you two," teased Carmen.

"Hey, this house rocks. Don't insult her," scolded Sadie.

"Then you come and sleep in the green room," challenged Roselyn. "All three of the kids have had horrid nightmares in there. And, yesterday, when I was cleaning it, I swear I heard weeping. When I stepped out, it stopped. I stepped back in, and there it was, very quiet weeping."

"Sure, I'll take a nightshift in the green room," boasted Sadie. "I bet I will figure it out. It's probably refraction from the moonlight, the noises in the walls are water pipes, maybe? Heck, I'll stay there tonight. It's Friday, and I don't have to get up tomorrow. Bring it on!"

Chapter Thirty-Five

THE ROOM

"If I tried harder to work with Roselyn, maybe together,
we would find a cure for this very ill part of me"

That evening Sadie settled in, book in hand, and a 16 oz sippie cup full of Diet Coke. Maria climbed under the light coverlet on her cot. Roselyn turned on a rotating fan; she had one in every room now, to boost circulation, and assist the small air-conditioner. Ethan cuddled close to his aunt. Hunter stood hesitantly at the door.

"Auntie Sadie, did you come to talk to Jack?"

"If there is a Jack here, I plan to kick his butt out," bragged Sadie.

Ethan giggled as Hunter entered the room and climbed onto his cot.

"Auntie Sadie, there are really scary things in this room," Hunter whispered.

"There is nothing in this valley scarier than me, Hunter," she answered.

Hunter seemed to consider this for a moment, accept it, and then turn over to fall asleep.

Several hours later, Sadie closed her book and slipped quietly off the cot. She carefully lifted Ethan's relaxed body and placed him beside his brother. Flipping off the lamp, she darkened the room, and slipped through the door to visit the bathroom.

"Darn Coke will keep me awake all night," she thought.

As she returned, she felt her way to the cot. The moonlight cast a glow into the room, and the breeze rippled through the sheer curtains. Together, they cast wiggly shadows against the walls. Sadie lay on her back, watching the shadows dance. Her eyes grew heavy. She closed them, and then began sinking, sinking.

Daisy curled up next to the cot, resting her fluffy head on her golden paws.

Suddenly, Sadie's eyes popped open. Why? She had not heard anything. She tried to close them again, but again they popped open. Daisy raised her head. In the far corner, the darkest corner, what appeared to be a limp body swung to and fro, its head twisted in an unnatural position.

A low growl escaped from Daisy's throat.

I saw the scene as well, and froze in fright.

Sadie sat straight up, and blinked. It was still there. Daisy stood up, facing the shadow. Her growl was repeated with emphasis. Sadie slipped out of bed, and flipped on the lamp. The swinging body was no longer there. She turned the light off. Nope, whatever it was disappeared. Daisy wagged her tail, and seemed embarrassed for growling at nothing. Sadie settled back onto her cot. Daisy nuzzled her, before laying back down.

"That was weird," Sadie whispered.

I thought so, too.

While falling asleep, she explored her mind, and I sifted. Her young mind was racing, trying to solve the mystery. Was it just a shadow cast by the moon? Was she dreaming? Had she been in the hazy place between sleep and wakefulness, where dreams are muted? What had Daisy seen? Finally, she drifted off, and I settled into my own form of restfulness.

The clock in the living room struck four. I became conscious of movement. Sadie walked out of my green room, and found her way through the dark to the kitchen. She turned on the light, went to the sink, and splashed water on her face. She filled a mug and put it in the microwave. Rummaging through the pantry, she located a package of instant hot chocolate.

"Need something, Sadie?" Roselyn asked, from the doorway.

Startled, Sadie jumped. She tossed the chocolate, and screamed. This surprised Roselyn, who then responded with her own scream.

My shingles quivered, and my eves creaked, which is my way of screaming. I wish they wouldn't do that! I'm getting too old for shocks!

They settled down at the table and calmed themselves.

I tried to do the same.

"Why are you up, Sadie? Was the cot uncomfortable?" inquired her older sister.

Sadie shook her head and pushed her long hair back. "I had a horrible nightmare!"

"You want to talk about it?" asked Roselyn, softly.

"I dreamed I was being carried by a man. In the dream, I felt like I knew him. I was dazed, like drugged, or drunk, or something. I was helpless. I couldn't move, to fight back."

Sadie rubbed her hands over her face, and again pushed her thick locks back.

"He took me to a building, like a garage, warehouse, or something. I knew he was going to kill me. Then I saw a girl standing in the shadows, by the door. I wanted her to run away. I wanted to yell to run away, but I couldn't speak. Then I woke up."

"Hmmm," said Roselyn. "In my study of dreams and their meanings, things are often symbolic of the situations in our lives. We aren't supposed to take them literally."

"How is being murdered a symbol?" asked Sadie, shaking her head.

"I don't know. Think about your job, is anyone trying to double-cross you there? Is a co-worker attempting to sabotage something you're working on, kill a deal, so to speak? Do you feel paralyzed concerning one of your goals? Murder, and killing, can symbolize some other difficult issue in your life."

Sadie took a sip of the hot chocolate. "No," she said thoughtfully, "Everything at work is peachy. It's never been better."

"Were you reading a murder mystery before going to sleep? What was the book you brought over?" asked Roselyn.

"It was a steamy romance novel, and there was nothing violent in it, whatsoever."

Both women were quiet for a few moments. Sadie broke the silence, "I hate to say it Roselyn. There is something about that room, something dark and foreboding. Before I went to sleep, I saw it, the thing the kids thought they had seen. I was ready to chalk it up to a semi-conscious dream, but after this nightmare, I say it's the room".

"Well, I don't know what to do about a dysfunctional room," moaned Roselyn. "I can't send the room away, or cut it off, and discard it." She shrugged her shoulders, helplessly.

"Do you think a murder happened in that room?" asked Sadie.

Roselyn shook her head. "I've researched this house thoroughly. I've read every news story about murder in the area, in the library archives. I even talked to the historian there. She had a special interest in this house, and I now know the names of everyone who lived in it."

Roselyn stood up, walked to the refrigerator, and took a notebook from the top. Holding it out to Sadie, she continued, "The first couple, the builders, were William and Helen Yingling. Here are the following generations. There were no murders. All deaths were natural.

Well, there were two children who died of polio, but no murders, or suicides."

I was stunned. Roselyn knew all about me? My loved ones? She cared enough to find that out? Suddenly, Roselyn was very dear to me. I felt a new bond with her. I decided that I would try harder to work with Roselyn. Maybe together, we would find a cure for this very ill part of me.

Chapter Thirty-Six

DREAM WEAVING

"You will not be afraid of the terror by night,
or of the arrow that flies by day"

The morning after Sadie's nightmare, everyone's nerves were on edge, including mine.

It was Saturday, and all the women had breakfast with Roselyn. The kids finished their French toast, and wandered off to occupy themselves. The women lingered over coffee, and studied a crayon drawing Roselyn found on the coffee table.

I pulled myself from my thoughts to hear what Kate was saying.

"So, this is Ethan's work?" asked Kate.

"Yes," answered Roselyn, "Hunter never draws, and Maria is much more sophisticated in her art".

"It's definitely a picture of a hanging," confirmed Carmen.

"He deliberately drew long hair and a skirt. Whatever he saw, he concluded it was a woman," pointed out Roselyn.

"Well, I think the children should not spend another night in there," Kate advised, firmly.

"I'm going over to the storage unit today and pick up that other air conditioner. Larry said I could have it. We'll set it up in that window, in the upstairs hall. We won't know if your circuits will handle it until we try," determined Sadie. "Then all of you can sleep up there in your own rooms."

"I've decided to spend tonight in the room," announced Kate. "Sometimes I feel like something in this house speaks to me. I can't explain it. It's like thought that I didn't think up by myself. Maybe I'll be able to pick up on something."

"Better watch out, Mom," teased Sadie. "Jack might start talking to you, too."

The women laughed. I was glad they were able to have a sense of humor.

Mine had recently left the premises.

By evening, Sadie and Roselyn had the air conditioning cooling my upstairs. It felt good to my fevered mind. The kids were excited to have their spaces back, and tolerable for occupancy. They spent the entire evening amusing themselves in their rooms.

Kate arrived around 9:00 PM. She carried a bottle of holy water, a Bible, a rosary, and a picture of a guardian angel. She also brought a portable CD player, with a CD of 'The Singing Monks'.

Roselyn laughed at seeing her mother's arsenal. "Maybe you should have invited the archangel, Michael, as well," she teased.

Kate hung the rosary in the corner, where the shadow was seen. The guardian angel was placed over the head of her cot.

She opened the Bible to Psalm 91:5-6.

"You will not be afraid of the terror by night, or of the arrow that flies by day; of the pestilence that stalks in darkness, or of the destruction that lays waste at noon."

She repeated it several times as she sprinkled holy water around the inner perimeters of my distressed room. She then started the soft chanting of The Singing Monks, and settled down on the cot, and went to sleep.

I felt calmer than the previous four nights. Not that I thought my illness was cured, but rather, that its origin might be determined in this holy atmosphere.

Several times through the night, Kate sat up, repeated the scripture, and started the music, before falling back to sleep.

I have to hand it to her. She lasted until 6:00 AM, before leaving her post, and then only to answer a bladder call.

The next morning, with children safely delivered to swimming lessons, the women gathered on my porch.

"Let's put what we know together," Kate said. "Roselyn, write all this down so we can go over it. That's sometimes helpful." She handed over a pen and a small tablet.

Kate continued, "The kids, while in the room, saw an image of someone hanging by a rope, dead, right?"

The women nodded. Roselyn wrote, #1 Hanging dead woman.

"Sadie, when you spent a night in the room, you dreamed of being dragged and carried by a man. In that nightmare, he took you to a building, like a warehouse, something like that, right?" she asked, looking at Sadie.

Sadie nodded, and added, "I couldn't move, like I was paralyzed. I saw a girl, and I wanted to tell her to run for her life".

Roselyn added this to her list:

#1 Hanging, dead woman
#2 Paralyzed, and carried to warehouse
#3 Girl watching

Kate continued, "Last night I didn't see anything. I think the apparition develops from the energy of fear. But three times through the night, I dreamt of being a witness to the hanging of a woman. In the dream, I felt like a child. I saw myself running away in fright".

To the list, Roselyn added:

#1 Hanging, dead woman
#2 Paralyzed, carried to warehouse
#3 Girl watching
#4 Girl runs away in fear

"So, Roselyn," Kate looked at her daughter, "you're the dream wizard. Can these incidents be woven into something reasonable?"

Roselyn walked over to the bookcase, and pulled out her dream book dictionary. "Many things are symbolic," she warned. "Death, hanging, and running away, can represent things that are not what they seem to be."

"But, can't they also mean the obvious?" asked Sadie. "What if that girl's ghost is hovering in the green room, causing these dreams? Maybe she wants us to solve this for her."

Ghost? No! No! No! I admit Megan's death left a horrible feeling in that room. It is contagious, even creepy, but a ghost? No, I have lived well over one hundred years. Deaths have happened in my rooms. Not one has ever resulted in a ghost. I have watched those silly haunted house movies with the family, and laughed my roof off. Houses make things happen, not ghosts.

Roselyn thumbed through the book, jotting more things down on paper. "I think you're right, Sadie," she said. "Different people dreams include different symbols, depending on what certain things mean to them. But three people dreaming the same, or similar dream, is probably a case for the obvious."

"So, we can all agree that from what we either saw, or dreamed, someone was hung, correct?" asked Kate.

They agreed, and so did I.

"And," began Roselyn, "I think you, and Sadie, each had one-half of the dream."

I was hanging onto every word.

"Sadie, your dream was of the victim that was hung. Your dream tells us that she was either a paralyzed woman, or she was drugged in some way to prevent her from fighting back. Before her death, she saw a child, and wanted to warn her to run away."

Chills were climbing up my inner, and outer, walls.

"And in my dream, I was that child," Kate said thoughtfully. "I must have been the girl that died here."

By now Roselyn's list had developed into a hypothesis.

    #1 Hanging, dead woman—murdered
    #2 Paralyzed, drugged—to prevent struggle, carried to a warehouse by a man
    #3 Girl watching—maybe her child?
    #4 Girl runs away—could this be the girl who died here?

Questions to search out:

Was this the girl's mother?

If so, who would murder her mother?

Why?

Was the girl afraid of the murderer?

Did she have something to do with it, and she felt guilty?

Did the murderer get away with it?

Where is he now?

"There's no way the police would take this seriously," stated Sadie.

"No, our haunted experiences wouldn't work as evidence," agreed Kate.

"The wallet!" remembered Roselyn, covering her mouth, as her eyes grew wide. "Of course, I feel so stupid. Hunter didn't steal it. He found ᴏly in that room, before I got the windows replaced. He could ᴄ been climbing in and out, even though I had the room locked up. You know how he snoops through everything."

"See, Mom," scolded Sadie. "I told you we should have gone through the wallet. There may have been something that could have been used, for concrete evidence."

"The police should have gone through it," defended Kate. "It's their job to search."

"Not if they think it's just a lost wallet," said Carmen. "They probably just looked at the license. If no one comes to pick it up, it could sit in a lost and found box for years."

"Well," began Sadie, thoughtfully, "I'm going to get on the net tomorrow at work. We have a program for background checks. I'll run Megan's name through. If she comes up as a missing person, it might give us a lead to follow, like who her mother is, or was."

"We already know she was from Rock Springs, because of her driver's license. That gives you a place to start in your search," suggested Carmen.

Roselyn glanced at her watch. "Yikes!" she squealed. "Look at the time. I have to pick up the kids."

She jumped up and ran through my front door. Tossing the tablet on the coffee table, she grabbed her purse.

The other women also stood up, "Let's meet at the Taco Hut, suggested Carmen. "I'll pick up Carl, and the twins, and bring them there."

"Good plan," agreed Roselyn. "I'll be there soon, with Maria and the boys."

As they all left, I noticed that in her haste, Roselyn did not lock the door, or put Daisy in the house.

Chapter Thirty=Seven

TRESPASS

"The wallet . . . 'No! Dennis, it's not here"

I felt relief. Kate's suggestion that there would be no additional use of my greenroom was reassuring. I was certain that the door would be locked when Roselyn returned. For the moment, Kate's Bible still lay open to Psalm 91.

"You will not be afraid of the terror by night, or of the arrow that flies by day; of the pestilence that stalks in darkness, or of the destruction that lays waste at noon."

I took comfort in that Psalm during the past evening. I repeated it over and over now. I must commit this to memory. The assurance might be useful at a later time.

The rosary, holy water, and guardian angel, appeared to have the restless angry energy subdued. I slammed the door shut; that should hold things down until my family returned.

I looked out from my towers. What I saw startled me. Dennis's red truck was parked up at the highway entrance. He stood outside of his pickup, and looked in my direction with field glasses. Daisy walked around the front yard, sniffing for rabbit trails.

Maybe the dog will discourage him from coming around, I hoped.

Dennis returned to his truck. He pulled back onto the highway, but rather than turning right, the direction to Lander, he turned left. I watched him drive down the highway slowly.

He must be planning a turn', I thought.

His truck became a small red dot, in my view, as he made a left turn.

I released a sigh. He has a right to visit his land. Daisy wandered around to my backyard. A rabbit darted out of the brush, and she chased it to the fence. As I watched the rabbit hop through the fence, I saw the red dot grow larger. The pickup was moving across the prairie in my direction.

Maybe he's driving the perimeter, and checking his fences.

Too soon he was next to the back of our property. I was becoming concerned. This was Roselyn's fence. I wondered if he planned to cut the wire. Daisy barked, raised her neck hair, and growled.

Dennis opened his window and talked to her in a friendly voice. She slowly and hesitantly wagged her tail.

'No, girl. He's a bad man. Don't let him sweet-talk you. She was too far away to pick up my projections.'

Dennis tossed something toward Daisy. She walked over, sniffed it, and quickly gobbled it down. He got out of his truck, and walked toward the fence. He handed her more of the treat and she took it from his hand.

I could feel the panic climb from the base of my foundation. I won't fear the arrow by day or the destruction at noon, I quoted my newly learned promise.

Dennis climbed over the fence and petted Daisy. Daisy had been orphaned when her master died, then kept in a shelter before coming to us. I understood that she was still confused as to where her loyalties lie.

As she responded to his voice and touch, Dennis slipped a long leash on her collar and tethered her to the fence post. He dumped the contents of treats from the box in front of her. Daisy lay down, unconcerned with the tether, and began munching on biscuits.

Dennis returned to his pickup and retrieved an item. As he turned I saw him slip it under his denim jacket. I wondered why he would wear a jacket on such a hot day. I suddenly had a memory of Butch Cassidy slipping a handgun in and out of his light jacket. I had no doubt Dennis had a gun.

Then another alarming thought occurred to me. His pickup, although visible to me from my tower outlook, couldn't be seen at ground level. The rise of the land would block it from Roselyn's view when she returned.

Even as I pondered this, Dennis climbed the fence and started walking toward me. He checked the back door. It had been locked this morning when Roselyn took the kids to their swim class. He circled around me, taking the route of my wrap-around-porch.

My very core was trembling. I began the barking of many different dogs whose voices I had recorded. Dennis stopped, tipped his head, and listened. He removed his gun and tried my front door. It was unlocked, and opened easily.

I attempted to rush him with a swoosh of air, but the air-conditioning offered interference to my usual dynamics. He stepped inside, and I began to sift his thoughts.

'I know it's here,' he thought. 'The radio announcer said you have it, Roz.'

The wallet . . . No, Dennis, it's not here!

Dennis was looking on bookshelf surfaces, and he glanced through the china closet's glass door. As he turned around, his view met the coffee table. I tried to shift air space, and move the tablet, perhaps to the floor, and under the couch. If it had been simply a piece of paper, I could have. The tablet was too heavy.

I tried to distract him with children's giggles from my upstairs. He paused for a moment, looked up at my ceiling, "Stupid old house. He cursed. You, and your sounds, will burn to the ground today, after I get what I want."

My structure grew cold with fear. I must repeat the verse. I tried to remember it, but I was trembling.

Dennis walked over to the coffee table and picked up the tablet that had all Roselyn's notes from the women's dream-weaving session.

- #1 Hanging, dead woman—murdered
- #2 Paralyzed, drugged—to prevent struggle? Carried to warehouse by a man
- #3 Girl watching—maybe her child?
- #4 Girl runs away—could this be the girl who died here?

Questions to search out:

Was this the girl's mother?

If so, who would murder her mother?

Why?

Was the girl afraid of the murderer?

Did she have something to do with it, and felt guilty?

Did the murderer get away with it?

Where is he now?

"You damn bitch! You're on to it. There must have been something in Megan's wallet. I should've killed that little brat first. I would've, if I'd had known she'd run. I thought I'd persuaded her to leave with me."

Dennis shook his head at his own thoughts, "Silly girl, we could've had a good life here with your mother's money. You had to ruin everything, running away, and killing yourself. And why here? Why didn't you run somewhere else? You and your mom were really stupid, Megan!"

As I processed all that I had sifted from his mind, Roselyn's pickup pulled into the driveway.

Dennis slid the tablet under his jacket and slipped out of sight, into my hallway. My family walked up onto my front porch. I tried to project my thoughts.

Don't come in, Rosy, get back in the pickup and drive away!

No one was tuned in. Daisy, aware that the family was home, began barking from her tethered place at the fence.

"Mama, where's Daisy?" asked Hunter.

"She's probably chasing rabbits off the property," answered Roselyn, jovially.

They stepped in and closed my door. "Can we play with the Xbox?" asked Hunter.

"Yes, you may," answered his mother. "Please play quietly, and give me a couple of undisturbed hours to work."

Roselyn walked over to the frig, and placed a new carton of milk inside. She laid her cell phone on the kitchen cart next to my family room door. Glancing in at the boys, now engaged in a game, she smiled and closed their door.

She turned and started back toward my living room. As she passed through my dining room, she stopped. Standing there with a sneer on his face, was Dennis.

"What are you doing in my house?" she demanded.

"What are you doing messing around in my life?" he hissed, holding up the tablet with the list written clearly on the front.

"Excuse me?" she asked. My sifting could read her fear. She knew he had read the information on the paper. She had not connected Dennis to Megan's death. Her thoughts were scrambling in an attempt to make sense of his anger.

"I have no desire to have anything to do with your life, Dennis," she said firmly.

Shaking the tablet, he snarled, "And this, you are checking up on me! You called the cops on me, didn't you?"

"No," I haven't called the police," she answered truthfully.

He ripped the paper from the tablet, and wadded it up into a ball. "I should make you eat this, you nosey bitch!"

Chapter Thirty-Eight

MADNESS

"Women never get the credit they deserve!"

Roselyn stepped back, but Dennis was moving forward. His eyes were wide and wild. His teeth clenched; his hands were balled up into tight fists.

"I did not call the police," Roselyn said, calmly, as she continued to move backwards.

"Where is the wallet?" he demanded. "Give it to me, and I just might let you live."

"I don't have the wallet. It's in the Lost and Found at the police station," she tried to reason with the enraged man.

She had been slowly moving toward my living room. I sensed she was trying to move the danger as far from the boys as possible. Her tone was calm and quiet. I knew she didn't want them to hear the conflict, and come out of my family room.

The man drew back his arm full length and slapped her hard, sending her flying across the room. She landed in a heap on my floor. With nose bleeding, still on her bottom, she inched her way closer to my living room entrance. I wondered if she was thinking of a weapon.

What to do? I surveyed the area for something I could bring down on his head, but Roselyn had everything tightly secured. Everything was Hunter-proof, which made it immovable for me, as well.

"They have no evidence on me," he yelled. "That's why they aren't looking for me. But you do, right? You found something in this house, didn't you? Something that brat left behind. You'd better hand it over because I'm tired of everyone messing up my plans."

Roselyn had gotten back onto her feet. I pulled myself out of my momentary state of shock. I started Brutus's barking, music from the pipe organ, piano, violin, and bag pipes, all at the same time. The enraged man was undaunted.

Roselyn had worked her way to the small ornate table by my front door. I saw the letter opener laying there. I hoped Dennis didn't see it. He hadn't drawn his gun, and as long as he didn't, we had a chance.

Just then Hunter opened the door, "Mom, who is yelling?"

"Run, Hunter!! You boys run away!" screamed Roselyn.

Ethan, who had now stepped out, was standing by the cart.

ETHAN, GRAB THE CELL PHONE, NOW! Without hesitating, the small boy seized the phone.

RUN TO THE TOWER BOYS!!' 'USE THE BACK STAIRCASE!

The boys scrambled up my back stairs, and headed for the stairs to the tower.

I could see Daisy jumping, and yanking, trying to free herself from the tether.

Roselyn, looking past Dennis, saw Ethan take the phone. She attempted to stall Dennis, speaking calmly. I knew she was buying time.

"I didn't even know that you were acquainted with Megan, Dennis," she tried a friendly tone.

"She was my step-daughter. I've been in love with her since she was twelve," he offered.

Roselyn was sickened by this confession, as was I, but she managed to compose herself.

The boys were at the top landing, eyeing the door at the top of the second landing. Roselyn had locked the tower to prevent Hunter's expeditions. The padlock keys were now safely hidden from him.

"I'll get my tools," he stated, turning to run to his room.

ETHAN, CALL 911, NOW!

To my amazement he obeyed. Hunter ran back, armed with two screwdrivers and a hammer.

Roselyn always kept her cell on speaker phone, "Hello, this is 911. What is your emergency?" asked the operator.

SING YOUR ADDRESS, ETHAN, SING! I sang the tune and words into his mind.

I was aware of Daisy barking on my back porch, digging at my backdoor.

She must have broken that worn-out collar.

The operator repeated her request. *'SING!' I ordered the stammering child.*

To my amazement, Ethan began singing his address. "Do you need help, little boy?" she asked when he finished.

"Yes," answered Ethan, "My mama."

Hunter, who had been busily hammering the screwdriver's flat edge under the padlock latch, popped it off.

BOYS!' 'RUN UP TO THE TOWER! NOW!

Downstairs, Roselyn had inched her way out of the corner. She held tightly to the letter opener, hiding it, by holding it flat against the side of her leg. She navigated to the center of the room, trying to keep distance between them.

Dennis lunged, and as she turned to run, he grabbed the back of her hair and pulled her backwards. She fell onto her back. Dennis pulled his foot back to kick her. As his leg came forward, and his boot made contact with her head, she drove the letter opener into his inner thigh. He screamed in pain, and she lay limp.

Daisy was digging through my wooden backdoor with fury, barking incisively. I feared if she got in, Dennis would pull out his gun and shoot her. I was surprised he hadn't already used the gun to intimidate Roselyn.

He fell back on the couch and examined his leg. Making a twisted face, he yanked out the letter opener, and blood began to gush.

Where are the police? They should be here by now!

Dennis attempted to get up. The globe lamp was now directly above his head. As he straightened up to his full height, I gathered momentum and slammed it into the back of his head.

"Damn!" he yelled, as the glass shattered around his head and shoulders. He staggered forward, and I saw a gash, now bleeding, through his curly red hair.

Sifting his thoughts, I realized that Dennis now remembered the boys.

He limped to the stairs. "Boys?" he called, trying to soften his tone. "Hunter, come here, buddy."

He proceeded up my front stairs, leaving a bloody trail. He reached the landing of my second floor, and limping down my hall, he peered into each bedroom. I looked for anything I could slam, or drop. Everything was fastened down solid.

"Hunter," he called, playfully, "I've got something for you."

He paused at the bottom of the attic staircase, and then slowly he started to climb the stairs.

I realized the boys could not lock the attic door from the inside.

HE'S COMING, BOYS! THROW THINGS AT HIM, ANYTHING!

Suddenly the attic door swung open, and out came a barrage of critters. First, the one-eared Jackalope, and then the three-legged Jackalope. Following those, a large raven, and the carp. Each missile hit his face, and he batted them away, or tried to dodge them. Finally, the ten-pound owl bolted out like a cannonball. I couldn't believe Hunter was capable of launching it with such force, but it met its mark: Dennis's face, or more accurately, his nose. Blood spewed down his face, and onto his chest.

Dennis, off-balance, fell backwards, and rolled, heels overhead, to the first landing.

I heard sirens. Daisy was now at my front door continuing to attempt her own break-in. If only the boys could hold him off with the taxidermy arsenal a bit longer, we would have help.

Dennis heard the sirens, too. He pulled himself along the floor, and rolled down the stairs to my ground floor. Hoisting himself up with the help of my banister, he lunged toward the backdoor.

As he pushed through the screen, I remembered the bees.

Oh, no you don't, you'll not get away.

During her spring fix-up, Roselyn secured my rain gutters. Now, I couldn't rattle anything to stir them up. As Dennis hung on to the side of the cistern shed, he looked in the direction of his truck. Clearly he intended to make a get-away.

Daisy ran around my north side. As she rounded the corner, her barking elevated to an angry pitch. Dennis pulled the gun from a holster under his jacket. Sirens squealed to a stop. The sheriffs got out and entered my front door.

Don't let him kill Daisy!

Then I saw it. Rather, I saw her. A filmy stream of white vapor poured out of the open window in my green room, and sped down my outer north wall, like a streak. The vapor zoomed into the tiny opening under the cistern shed's gable.

Out swarmed the bees. Seeing no one to blame but the wounded intruder being wallowed by an angry dog, they waged their revenge. Daisy retreated. Dennis shot wildly into the air. I was aware of the boys watching from my tower window.

A deputy burst out my backdoor. Kate, Sadie, and Carmen pulled up in their separate cars. I realized Hunter must have called them.

It's safe to go down, boys, Gram's here now.

Carmen tended to Roselyn. She packed couch pillows around her neck to prevent movement until the ambulance arrived. I was relieved when she said her heart and breathing were strong.

The deputy managed to rescue Dennis by pulling him away from the swarm and into my backdoor. He took his gun.

"Help me!! I'm allergic," Dennis begged. "There's medicine in my truck."

Looking around, the deputy said truthfully, "I don't see a truck."

Soon both victim, and attacker, were on their way to the hospital. Carmen rode along with Roselyn.

The couch was bloody, so Sadie and Kate sat in the wicker chairs. Each had a boy on her lap.

The deputy began asking questions. Hunter was able to explain enough for the officer to understand a major part of the crime, though more would need to be discovered.

Then the deputy asked, "Which one of you brave boys called 911?"

"He did," answered Hunter, pointing to his brother.

"What?" exclaimed Kate.

Ethan nodded his head, and pointed to his chest, "Yep, I did!" he proclaimed.

Both women were dumbstruck.

Then Hunter, wanting some of the praise, spoke up, "But I broke the lock on the attic door, and clocked him with the owl."

"Wow!" praised the officer. "How did you boys know what to do?"

"Jack told us," answered Hunter.

Ethan nodded affirmatively, "Jack," he said.

The deputy threw a questioning look at Kate who shrugged.

"And then, Jack flew out of the window and told the bees to sting him," Hunter added.

Ethan nodded affirmatively again, "Jack flew," he agreed.

Jack? Are you kidding me? There's no Jack. I instructed the boys, and Megan rallied the bees. Women never seem to get the credit they deserve!

Chapter Thirty-Nine

AFTERMATH

"It's unity," I thought, and love.
"That's what's needed to heal painful memories"

The next few days following Dennis's attack, the family attempted to regain a sense of calm. Kate made plans to stay with us, and care for the children, while Roselyn spent three days in the hospital. Roselyn had a mild concussion, and whiplash.

When she did come home I was overcome with distress; she was in a neck brace. One side of her face was horribly bruised from Dennis's brutal kick. Her lip was split by his slap. She had a ten day prescription for her nerves, and she spent a lot of time in a dazed condition.

I was so distraught at the sight of her. I wished they made tranquilizers for houses.

But before Roselyn's arrival home, Kate, Carmen, and Sadie set about to clean up the mess. As soon as the investigating officers were finished taking pictures and gathering whatever possible evidence they could find, the purge began. The area rug, with its trail of Dennis's bloody boot tracks, was rolled up and hauled away. The door to my *green room* was now locked.

I was glad for that. I knew that area of me was ill, but I hadn't realized there was a ghost there too, one that had been with me for over three years. Frankly, after what I saw her do to Dennis, she frightened me more than just a little. My only hope was that she stayed behind that locked door.

As the women stood looking at the worn furniture, bloody couch, and my scarred floor, from Roselyn's wild ride on the sanding machine, Sadie remarked, "I wish we could just completely fix up this room so that the memories of what happened here wouldn't be so intense for her".

Kate thoughtfully agreed, "You're right, Sadie. If we could even get new furniture, that would help change the whole look of the room".

Carmen shook her head, "With these streaked walls, and the messed up floor, I don't think furniture would be enough to make a difference".

Sadie pulled her cell phone out of her jeans pocket, "I have an idea".

In a few minutes she was talking to her boss, Larry. "Larry, do you think you could get some volunteers together to help renovate my sister's living room?"

She listened to his response for a few moments, and then continued, "The attack happened in that part of the house. The rug is ruined, and so is the couch. We really wish we could change it completely, and make it cheerful".

There was more listening, and then she closed her phone. "Larry's on it. He's going to call some of the business owners and craftsmen. He thinks there will be some willing volunteers and donations."

Her mother and sisters looked stunned. She continued, "Lander has always been a great community when there's a need to back up one of its own. Don't look so surprised".

Her words turned out to be true. As they continued to mop up blood and tracks from my stairs, and upstairs hall, calls began coming in. Robinson's Furniture Store offered to donate a new sofa, coffee table, and three chairs.

"With the Queen Anne chair and two antique tables Roselyn picked up at the antique store, this room will be set up nicely", said Carmen.

The Winsome Walls store manager called and asked someone to come and pick out wall covering. She informed Sadie that the paper hanger she usually contracted was eager to hang wallpaper for no charge, and she would donate paper and supplies.

I was excited. I love wallpaper. That's the way my walls began. As long as it wasn't a pattern with giant sunflowers, I would be pleased. Hopefully they wouldn't allow Sadie to choose the design.

No sooner did that call end when the owner of the House of Lights called, offering a chandelier.

While Kate and Carmen prepared dinner, and Carl wrestled with the twins on the floor, Sadie explained Larry's last call. "Larry is sending a man over to refurbish the floor."

"Anyone we know?" asked Carl.

"He's some kind of old-house expert from Montana. He came here to take classes from National Outdoor Leadership School. Larry's renting the sander, and buying the supplies. He's the best boss I ever had."

"He's the only boss you ever had," reminded Carmen.

"Oh yeah," Sadie agreed with a smile.

I loved the mood; it was getting light and hopeful again. So much fear, pain, and negativity were within my walls, only a day ago.

It's unity and love. That's what's needed to heal painful memories.

The women decided to keep the makeover a surprise from Roselyn. Carmen took the kids home with her so they wouldn't find out, and let it slip, while talking to their mother on the phone.

Carl hauled the blood-soaked couch and, two wicker chairs, away the following morning. Kate picked out the paper. She brought home three different samples to decide on. I projected intensely, and honestly believe I was successful in my influence. She picked the soft peach-colored flocked paper over the one with light blue stripes, and the other with the palm leaf design. But then again, maybe we have the same taste.

A few hours later the paperhanger arrived. I had no intention to resist this improvement. He had my complete cooperation. After all, we were doing this for my mistress.

When he finished by early evening, I was elated. I just wanted to stare at my beautiful walls. I thought of Helen, Vicky, Johanna, Christina, and Miriam. All of them would have approved.

That evening, the floor sander arrived. He planned to work all night so that it would be dry for furniture delivery before Roselyn came home.

Kate left while the workmen were there. She left the key to my front door at Sadie's office, with instructions that they leave it, or pick it up there, as needed.

I heard very little about Dennis. Apparently, no one wished to acknowledge his existence for a while, but finally I heard Carmen do some explaining.

"He lost a lot of blood", she began.

"Right. We spent a day mopping it up, remember?" Sadie remarked sarcastically.

"Well, with less blood, and so many stings from the bees, he is quite overloaded with toxins," she completed her thought.

"He's in a coma," said Carmen, "which means there can be no arrest until he wakes up. One of my clinic's doctors took his case, but he's in bad shape."

"Not as bad a shape as the women he murdered, or that poor girl who killed herself because of what he's done," Sadie said bitterly.

I sensed there was no sympathy for Dennis, and I could understand why.

I was surprised at the outcome of my living room floor. The workman was gentle, almost loving, and only lightly sanded its surface. Using a filling compound, he repaired the gouges Roselyn had made. He stained it with a rich oak color, and some hours later, applied a thick protective finish.

He was finished by mid-morning when Kate arrived. They introduced themselves out of earshot from me, but when they stepped upon my porch and looked in, Kate gasped.

"That's beautiful!" she exclaimed. "Roselyn will love it."

"This is a nice old house," he commented. "I love working with places like this."

"I hear you're an expert," said Kate.

He laughed, "Well, I don't claim to be an expert, but I've worked the last three years as foreman for a project up in Billings. The city restored three square blocks of Victorian houses in the old part of town. They got grants so we had a fair amount of money to work with. That always makes it easier."

"From the looks of this floor, I would consider you an expert. You've no idea how little success we've had with anything we've tried," she stressed.

"You have to be very sensitive," he stated. "These old beauties have a mind of their own. You learn to work with them, not on them."

"So, when can we move in the furniture?" asked Kate.

"Should be fine by early tomorrow morning," he answered. Then he loaded up tools and machinery and drove slowly away.

Chapter Forty

ASHER WILKES

"It's too pretty to be called a living room.
From now on it's the front parlor"

The next morning at 8:00 AM furniture arrived. I then realized that Kate's choice of wallpaper had more to do with the color of the furniture, as my projecting.

As the women looked around and basked in the beauty of my first completely restored room, a black car pulled up in my drive. A man in a suit walked across my front porch, and up to my open door. He knocked on the side of my door and offered an introduction.

"Hello, I'm Detective Wilkes," he said holding out a leather wallet, containing a badge. "I'm here to ask some questions about Megan Wells."

He was invited in. Kate closed my door, and turned on the air-conditioner to keep the room from heating up, as the outdoor air began its temperature climb.

Everyone took seats in my lovely new room.

"We've already told the police, and the other detective, everything we know," stated Kate.

"Yes, I understand," he answered. "I've read their reports. I'm from Rock Springs, and I'm here to follow up on a missing person report regarding Megan Wells, and to inquire about what you might know about the death of her mother. I have to conduct my own investigation."

"Roselyn will be home this evening, late afternoon," offered Carmen. "She's the one who was attacked by a man we believe killed Megan's mother. However, my sister had a very traumatic experience. I hope you won't upset her."

The detective was a handsome man in my opinion. He was average height with a broad, muscular build. I fancied he would be more comfortable in hiking gear, than a suit. He had light brown well-groomed hair and a square jaw. He looked intently into people's faces when he spoke to them, his hazel eyes not wavering, and yet, his voice was calm with authority. I imagined he would not be one to be easily deceived, and would be a match for the worst of villains.

Sadie, in her usual manner, took the initiative to unload the secret, "Detective Wilkes, may I ask you a question? Then we will answer any question you ask if we can."

"Certainly," he answered, looking directly at Sadie.

Sadie couldn't hold the gaze, and glanced down at her hands, fiddling with her ring.

That's unusual. This is Calamity the Second, after all.

"Do you believe in ghosts, or psychic stuff?" she asked.

"I believe in facts," he answered. "But I'm not closed to any information that's helpful, regardless of how it's obtained. In the end, I can do nothing with it without facts."

"But," continued Sadie, "if that information leads you into the direction to find the facts?"

"I know what you're getting at," he said. "When I was in L.A., before Rock Springs, the department secretly consulted a psychic concerning several unsolved murders. She didn't tell us who the guilty person was, but her information led to finding clues. Is that what you mean?"

"Yes, exactly," said Sadie. "Then what we are about to tell you won't shock you, or make you think we're nuts."

She got up and stepped into my dining room, returning with the paper Dennis had wadded up. She straightened it out on the coffee table and then handed it to the detective.

"We found a wallet. The one that's at the police station," she began.

Wilkes nodded, "I saw it."

"There was always something creepy about that room," she pointed at the locked door. "Megan died in there from smoke inhalation, and probably would have died from an overdose of depression medications, if the smoke hadn't gotten to her first."

The man nodded, "I'm familiar with her autopsy report."

Sadie took a breath and continued. "Mom and I each had a dream, rather, we each had a nightmare while sleeping in that room. I dreamed I was paralyzed, or drugged. A man carried me to a large building, like a warehouse. I assume he hanged me, but I woke up as he put a rope around my neck."

Sadie rubbed her neck with her right hand as though relating to the stress of her dream.

"Before he put the rope around my neck, I saw a young girl, fifteen or sixteen, watching from the open back door. She was hiding in the shadows. I sensed, and accepted, I was going to die, but I feared for her."

Wilkes listened intently, "Go on, please," he said without so much as a change in his expression.

"Mom also had a dream," continued Sadie, glancing toward Kate. Kate nodded. "She dreamt she was the girl that was hiding, and she felt terror."

"In my dream," Kate interrupted, "I was torn between trying to stop him, and running away. In my dream, I ran."

"And this?" he asked, holding the paper.

"That's what Roselyn wrote down the day Dennis attacked her," explained Carmen. "That morning we tried to make sense of the dreams. We believe they pertained to the girl who left her wallet here, but we made no connection to Dennis. We just thought he was a regular ordinary jerk."

Wilkes almost smiled but controlled his sober expression.

Sadie continued, "We left the dream summary on the coffee table. Roselyn told us that when she returned home, Dennis was in the house. He demanded that she give him the wallet. When she questioned him, he stated that Megan was his step-daughter. He also said things that indicated he had been molesting her, possibly since she was twelve."

"He wadded up the paper," finished Kate. "Everything after that is in the police report."

"Do you mind if I keep this?" he asked, folding it gently and putting it in the breast pocket of his suit jacket before anyone had time to answer.

Looking intently at Sadie, he began to talk as though directly to her. "I'm very sorry about your sister and her encounter with this man. If he was when he should have been, this wouldn't have happened.

"Your local prosecutor," he continued, "will deal with what happened here. I met him and I'm confident he will be successful with assault charges. But my job now is to find out if Dennis Dickinson was connected to a women's death, in Rock Springs, four years ago. I am also looking into the possibility he may have abducted Megan, whom I understand committed suicide in this house?"

"Is this a cold case that you're just now getting back to?" asked Sadie.

"Not exactly," he explained. "They ruled Mrs. Dickenson's death a suicide. She was very close to her father, who had been murdered a year before. That happened in Utah. It was never solved, and it appeared to be a home invasion with the intent to rob. He was a wealthy man. Stella Dickinson suffered so much depression from all of that, she was under a doctor's care. She even spent several months in a mental institution."

Detective Wilkes continued, "This was all common knowledge in Rock Springs. It wasn't a secret. Her husband talked enough about it that the poor woman probably thought everyone considered her crazy. It wasn't a surprise when she was found hanging in warehouse. She was into restoring antique automobiles, old classics. I understand she did all the work herself."

The women were listening intently.

I strained to hear every word.

"There were no bruises, or marks, on her body to suggest anything but suicide," he explained. "She was on a cocktail of prescription drugs, from her psychiatrist. The autopsy tests concluded that the medications, not any poisons, were in her body.

"But wasn't anyone looking for Megan?" asked Kate.

"Megan had a history of running away. It started when she was around twelve and it was so habitual no one thought anything about it. She got as far as New York City once," explained the detective.

"She was trying to get away from that monster," said Kate, sadly.

"But I heard him say he came into some money and that's what led him here," mused Carmen. "He was hell bent for leather to buy up all the land around here. He thought he was going to strike oil, I guess."

"He did have money," answered Wilkes, standing up to leave. "His wife's inheritance was settled three months before her death. She was willed several million from her father's estate."

"Didn't that cause suspicion?" asked Sadie in astonishment.

"In hindsight, yes," admitted the detective. "But at the time she was viewed as a very troubled woman, consumed with grief. Dennis had been legally given the power of attorney over her affairs because of her fragile state of mind."

As he walked to my door, he turned, "You have given me a lot to think about and I'll do some research. However, I haven't a shred of actual evidence against him in Stella's, or Megan's, death."

Pausing to think for a moment, he added. "Even if Roselyn testified that he made those comments to her, it would be hearsay. I'm convinced he killed his wife, and because of his abuse, his step-daughter killed herself. Proving it will be hard. Thank you, ladies."

A few hours later my little bruised mistress came home. Her surprise was worth all the work that went into my new room. Of course, she called it her new room. She said, "it's too pretty to be called a living room. From now on, it's the parlor."

Chapter Forty-One

BANYAN TAYLOR

" It sounds like one of those made up names, like Sundance,
or Cassidy, or Calamity"

September brought rains that ended the drought. The children
started back to school. A sheep grower offered my family a fair price
for the west thirty acres. They accepted. Each was reimbursed for her
contribution to the purchase. They agreed that the profit would be
used to continue my restoration.

The new owner was an elderly man that was immediately liked by the
family. He fenced the area for sheep pasture and graveled the road
to his property. This improvement benefited us, as well. There would
be less mud to drive through from now on. Mr. Gilbert built lambing
sheds, and buildings for shearing. These were located close enough
that the events could be watched from my west porch.

Once the flock was settled in, we were as excited as if the animals were
our own. A beautiful white Pyrenees sheep dog lived with the sheep.
She and Daisy communicated through the fence. Frankie was her
name, and her constant patrolling the fence line offered additional
protection for us.

On one warm Sunday afternoon, in early September, the family lounged on my east shady porch. Kate made a suggestion, "We need to do some special fun activities before winter comes around again."

Carmen presented the next idea. "This month, we should all go to Thermopolis and enjoy the hot springs. We could make it a family picnic."

Roselyn was quiet. Her contract work with billing didn't allow for time off. I could sift her thoughts, and she preferred to stay close to home.

"Well," offered Sadie, "Yellowstone is a must this fall. The autumn leaves will be glorious. We haven't been there for several years."

"It would be disheartening this year," reminded Carl. "The fires burned so much on this side of the park. Let's wait until spring."

"I think my fun activity is going to be deciding what I'll do with that money to improve this place before winter," sighed Roselyn.

"But I think the rest of you should get away. Maybe I'll send the kids with you," continued Roselyn. "I have so much to do to fix up "The Lady." I think I may have found someone who'll do some of the work for me."

"Really?" Sadie was all ears. She couldn't imagine something being organized without her initiation.

"The same man who fixed my floor," answered Roselyn.

"Oh, you mean the one Larry contracts. His name is Taylor, Ben Taylor," offered Sadie. "Larry mentioned he has lots of experience with restoration of old houses."

"No," corrected Roselyn, "Taylor is his last name, but you have the first name wrong."

I was paying close attention.

Kate sat down in the swing and pulled one of the twins onto her lap, "I met him for a few minutes when he completed the floor. He seemed like a very nice and knowledgeable young man. I found myself liking him immediately."

I smiled to myself. I had been practicing projection with Kate, and my success was showing. My thought of liking the floor finisher had popped into her mind.

"Have you talked to him?" asked Carmen.

"I met him at the library. I was there talking about 'The Lady' with Mrs. Biggs, the town historian. He was there checking out some books and he overheard our conversation," Roselyn explained.

Her mother and sisters were leaning in, waiting for the story.

"He mentioned he loved old houses and worked on a lot of them in Montana. We were shushed several times when our voices got a bit loud in our excitement about restoration. He invited me to coffee where we could further discuss it."

Kate straightened up in the swing as Ransom wiggled off her lap. Looking at her daughter, she asked, "You picked up a stranger at the library and went for coffee?"

"I'm a big girl, Mother," scolded Roselyn. "Anyway, we discussed what I've done, and want to do."

"Why is this new guy here, in Wyoming?" Carmen questioned.

"He moved here from Montana where he worked on a project in Billings. The city restored several square blocks of historic buildings. He explained a little to me about the difficulty in fixing up old houses. And, by-the-way, his name is Banyan Taylor, not Ben, and not the new guy."

Banyan? What kind of name is that for a man? It sounds like one of those made-up names, like Sundance, or Cassidy, or Calamity,

"Banyan is an odd name," commented Kate. It sounds like an alias." Kate picked up my thoughts. *I chuckled.*

"Well, it is a real name," defended Roselyn. "I saw his driver's license when he opened up his wallet to pay for the coffee and pie."

"I asked him about his name," continued Roselyn. "He said his father met his mother while in the Peace Corp in India. After his time in the Corp was completed, he married her. She was studying medicine so they continued to live there for ten years. Banyan and his sister were born there. They named him Banyan after India's national tree, and his sister, Lotus, after the national flower. Sort of weird, isn't it?"

"Well, at least unusual," agreed Kate.

They're nice names," said Carmen. "I like them."

"That's coming from a woman who names her twins Ridge and Ransom," teased Sadie.

"Not to worry, Mom. He seems really nice. I'm sure he's on the up and up," assured Roselyn.

Dennis fooled Roselyn. This man might be a regular cad, as well.

"Just be careful," warned Kate. Dennis seemed to be a decent man, and he turned out a regular cad."

"Cad?" Roselyn stared at her mother in disbelief. Have you been watching the Turner Classic Movie Channel again? No one says 'cad' these days," she giggled.

Kate looked a bit confused. She didn't know I slipped that one in on her. If she was to be my voice, I would need to be careful of my wording, and keep it up-to-date. Good Golly Gee, every generation, changes the English language. How's an old lady supposed to keep up?

Several days later it was raining when Banyan came to have a second look at my condition, and give advice.

I dreaded this. I remembered the insults of past workmen.

Kate was there as a black Ford crew-cab turned onto our road. "He's just here to look and give me an estimate on how much it would take to do some things. If he doesn't seem legit I won't hire him," Roselyn reassured her mother.

Roselyn invited Banyan Taylor into my new parlor. He slipped out of his hiking boots on my porch. He was average height and build and looked like a man conditioned by labor, not a weight room.

His sculptured features and olive complexion did encourage a second glance, even from an old lady.

"Don't worry about the mud," Roselyn said. "We're very used to it."

'Yes, worry about it, You just varnished these floors, and mud grinds the dickens out of a varnished floor.'

"Actually, you just varnished this floor and mud grinds the dickens out of a varnished floor." Kate piped.

Roselyn shot her mother a quizzical look. Kate, herself, appeared surprised at what had fallen out of her mouth.

She is completely tuned in to me.

"I've learned from experience," began Banyan. "These treasures deserve and expect reverence." His wide smile brightened his entire face; his eyes appeared to be laughing.

Treasures? Hmm. That could mean a lot of things. I remembered some of my children reading 'Treasure Island.' A treasure can be something someone steals and hides, or something someone finds and keeps, even though it isn't the finder's in the first place. Or it could be something like Hunter's treasure box, a container full of trashy things that gets him into trouble.

"Would you like some coffee, Mr. Treasure?" Kate offered.

Poor Kate, she and I are so mentally connected today.

"Taylor, Mom, Banyan Taylor," Roselyn corrected.

Banyan smiled good-naturedly, "I'd love some shortly, but may I walk through and look first? Last we talked you said she is called 'The Grand Lady?'"

Chapter Forty-Two

PROGRESS

"Your house, my dear, just threw a tantrum"

Roselyn led Banyan though my rooms, and Kate slipped off to the family room. She sat in a recliner. I knew I had overwhelmed her with projections; it showed on her face. I wanted to comfort her. I appreciated that she was finally able to pick up on my vibes, but for now, I needed to keep up with this stranger who happens to be named after a tree.

They paused in my living room. Banyan ran a callused hand over my plaster, "What do you plan for her walls?"

"I haven't thought that far," answered Roselyn. "Other, more pressing things, are higher on my to-do list. We tried to paint, but the walls were so dingy and damaged with smoke and water, that the paint won't adhere to this plaster. I love the way the parlor turned out. Maybe I'll wallpaper all of it."

"I see . . . that would be a good choice," mumbled Banyan.

They walked through my dining room, and into my kitchen. Banyan glanced all around, and up and down. "Have you thought about what you want in here?"

"Well, as you can see, I kept the old sink. It isn't in the most convenient location for a modern kitchen, but I love the look of it."

"That can be moved," Banyan assured her.

"Cabinets? What do you want for workspace?"

"I haven't made up my mind. As you can see, the few I have are portable, and temporary. We had to rip the old ones out. But I have the money stashed for a new range and frig. I'm waiting until I know what will fit. A new kitchen, with an old look, would be wonderful."

They peeked into my family room; Kate had drifted off to sleep in the recliner, bless her. They passed her by.

Upstairs they went into each room as Roselyn explained how she and Sadie had covered the electrical wires, tried to paint, and even hung wallpaper, without success.

"These old houses can be a challenge," said Banyan. "But with the right methods, it can be done."

Downstairs they settled into my new parlor, with coffee, discussing how far Roselyn's money would go to restore me. Banyan glanced at the door to the 'Green Room'.

"I didn't see in there," he commented.

"Oh that," answered Roselyn. "We keep it locked. A fire occurred in there before we bought 'The Lady'. It really messed it up."

I was getting nervous. My underbelly was shaky. I wished Kate was awake so I could use her voice to discourage them from opening that door.

"Can I look it over? Surely, you don't want to have a trashed out room taking up space in a restored house, do you?"

NO! NO! NO! Banyan looked around. For a minute, I thought I got through to him.

Kate staggered in from the family room, "Who's yelling?" she asked.

"Yelling?" inquired Roselyn.

"Yes," insisted Kate. "I heard someone yelling, No! No! No!"

"Mom, you must have been dreaming," laughed Roselyn. "No one in here yelled."

Banyan smiled at Kate, "No one we can see, anyway."

Roselyn went to retrieve the key. Kate sat down on the couch and rubbed her temples.

"If I were younger and going to college parties, I would swear that someone slipped wacky weed into the brownies," she muttered.

"What's the scoop on that room?" he nodded his head toward the door.

"Oh, a bad thing occurred in there," answered Kate. "You'll need to get Roselyn to tell you about it."

Roselyn returned with the key and opened the door. Cold chilled air rolled out like a cloud. Roselyn stood back as Banyan walked in, and turned around slowly, facing each wall for a few moments, listening, but to what?

Banyan's dark hair was not unkempt, but longer than I was accustomed to. It reached below the collar of his chambray work shirt. Combed back, it revealed a slight widows' peak. The light from the window highlighted dark auburn undertones.

"If you decide you want my help, this room is where we'll start," he said firmly.

That does it! He just lost my vote. After all that horror, and the memories in that space, not to mention a killer-ghost. We finally got all that negativity locked back up, and 'The Ban Ban Tree' comes in and wants to stir it up again. I don't think so.

With all my might, I slammed the door on Mr. Taylor, nearly whacking Roselyn in the process.

That part was an accident.

"Ohhh!" Roselyn quickly opened the door.

"Are you OK? We have crazy drafts that rush through sometimes," she explained.

Banyan stood there, facing the door, thumbs hooked into his jeans' front pockets.

He had a knowing smile that I wanted to slap off his face.

"I am so sorry, Banyan," stressed Roselyn. "Like I said, this house has a thing about slamming doors."

Mr. Know-It-All stepped out of my Green Room and gently pushed the door shut behind him. He took the key from Roselyn, secured the lock, and then handed it back to her.

"We could start here, and then again," he said smiling, "with old houses, everything's negotiable."

They sat down again, and began to list all planned renovations. After that they sorted them in order of importance.

"I know it's tempting to start with the cosmetic issues," he reasoned, "but it's more important to take care of safety issues first, and those needed for comfort next. Beautification can wait until last."

They concluded that rewiring would be the first task on the list. Next, would be insulation in my attic, and under my frame, where cold air had seeped in during the past few winters. When these plans were made, and a schedule drawn up to begin work, they sat back and began the small talk.

Banyan informed Roselyn that his parents still lived in Bozeman, Montana. There, his mother practiced medicine, and his father taught Eastern Culture classes at the University. He attended the university for a while, but left to do the work he enjoyed most.

Roselyn shared a bit about her family, but soon Banyan brought up a new subject.

"Now tell me everything you know about the history of this house," he requested.

Roselyn brightened. She loved talking about my history, "Just a second."

She scurried to the kitchen and grabbed the notebook from the top of the frig.

"Here are all the names of the families that have lived in 'The Lady' beginning with the Yinglings, who built her."

Banyan studied the graph she had drawn. "This looks like a family tree," he stated.

"It is, actually," she confirmed. "Direct descendants lived here until the Carrs, in the eighties. After that she stood vacant, except for a few times relatives passed through the area during the early nineties."

"Do you know anything about them?" he asked.

Only about their occupations, whom they married, and how they died," she answered. "Look, here are copies of pictures I found at the library. Mrs. Biggs helped me locate them."

They spread out the old photos, and of course I looked over their shoulders. "This is William Yingling right in front of the house. Notice the tower isn't added on yet," she pointed out.

"And who is this?" Banyan pointed to a man standing by William.

"We finally found that out. It's Duncan Kenyan, Helen's brother," Roselyn explained. "Mrs. Biggs found an old newspaper article that reported his death, in Alaska."

"Is this his wife beside him?" questioned Banyan.

"I believe so," answered Roselyn. "And on William's other side is Helen."

"Duncan's wife appears to be ethnic," commented Banyan.

"She was Native American, but not from here, from Oklahoma, I think," explained Roselyn.

"Being half East Indian, I notice such things," he smiled. "It hasn't always been easy for couples to cross racial lines in marriage. In India, some people didn't accept my father. Then, when we came to America, others didn't accept my mother. I can just imagine what it must have been like for a couple back then."

After looking at all the old photos, newspaper clippings, and copies of yellowed deeds and certificates, he put them down gently. "Now, what is the history of that room?"

Roselyn told him everything. She explained about the wallet, the dreams, the investigation regarding Dennis, what Dennis had said about Megan during his attack, his panic to find out if she had evidence, and finally, Hunter's mystery man, Jack.

Banyan listened intently. "I can't solve a murder mystery, but I can solve house issues," he began. "And this lovely lady has been through trauma. She has it locked up in that room. It's like you or me. If we have a horrible secret we couldn't deal with, what do we do? We would lock it up, and refuse to face it."

"What do you think it is," asked Roselyn, "the suicide of Megan Wells?"

"Probably," he answered, measuring his words, "and perhaps anything she talked about, dreamed about, or thought about. I think 'The Lady' absorbed the grief and terror that embodied that girl."

"But, Megan died. Wouldn't that die with her?" Roselyn almost whispered.

"Negative energy survives as long as someone fears it," he answered. "In this case, it is the house that fears it."

Roselyn chuckled nervously, "You are talking like she's alive, the house, I mean."

"She is, in a sense," he answered gently. "She exists because of the energy of those who built her. She absorbed that, as well as energy of all who've lived within this space, and cared for her. Even your energy is now imbedded in these walls."

Roselyn just stared at him.

Ok, Ban-Ban, I'm with you. This makes sense.

"You're used to a culture that believes only humans have spirits," he began. "Other cultures accept that everything God created has a spark of the creator. When you gave birth to your children, you passed that spark. When you give of yourself to others, you also pass a bit of the eternal energies. God is in us, but he's also in the animals, the plants, the trees, and even in the buildings, temples, churches, and houses we build. We put him there."

Roselyn opened her mouth to speak, but seemed to forget what she wanted to say.

I was speechless, as well.

"Now, taking all that into consideration, let's contemplate all this house has been through. From what you've told me, she was moved from her original location. Then she was abandoned for several years. A teen stayed here for an unknown length of time, then died at her own hand. The house survived a fire, set to destroy her by that teen. If she were human, they would call it Post Traumatic Stress, don't you think?" Banyan finished.

"OK, this is pretty weird, but I'll play along," agreed Roselyn, "How do we cure a house with Post Traumatic Stress?"

Banyan nodded toward the Green Room, "We have to clear that out."

NO!' I opened and shut the greenroom door. Then I swung the new chandelier, frantically. I opened and slammed my backdoor, then opened and slammed my front door. I started barking dogs, and bagpipes. I played 1940's music, and ended by flushing the toilet.

Daisy whimpered, and tried to crawl under the couch.

Roselyn was positively pale. She had experienced all these things one or two at a time, but never all together in such fury, "What just happened?" she asked weakly.

"Your house, my dear, just threw a tantrum," Banyan answered calmly.

Chapter Forty-Three

ANSWERS

"Fear is an unhealthy state . . . Who said that? Now I remember,
William said that"

The next weekend Banyan was to begin rewiring. Roselyn invited him to come to breakfast Friday morning at 7:00. I was still annoyed about his plans for my dark space, but I also was impressed that he understood about my feelings.

Roselyn got up earlier on that eventful morning. It occurred to me that she made a special effort to impress him. On weekday mornings, the children always sat down to cereal, toast and juice. Today, she had a platter of bacon, and another of hotcakes. She opened a jar of her new chokecherry syrup. She and Kate picked chokecherries a few weeks before and made jelly and syrups, setting them back for winter.

'Don't be getting any ideas Rosy Girl, he's a good fixer-upper, but he's not a keeper.'

"Why are we having hotcakes?" asked Hunter. "Hotcakes are for Saturdays."

"Yep, Saturdays," parroted Ethan.

"No reason," answered their mother "Aren't you glad for a change?"

"But hotcakes are supposed to be on Saturday," he persisted.

"Just eat, Hunter," coached Maria, "we have to catch the school bus."

Banyan pulled up in my drive and shuffled his feet on the door mat before knocking. Maria went to the door as Roselyn prepared another place setting. Maria led to my kitchen where the family always had breakfast.

"Hello, Banyan," smiled Roselyn, "Kids, this is Banyan Taylor. And these are my sons, Hunter and Ethan and my daughter Maria."

Banyan nodded at each of them and smiled. Maria sat back down and Roselyn directed Banyan to the chair at the end of the table and opposite of her. Maria continued with her breakfast, Ethan grew shy but Hunter looked like a greyhound warming up for a race.

"Are you having breakfast with us?" he began his interrogation.

"Yes, your mother was kind enough to invite me," he answered. "And I never turn down a meal."

"Oh," continued Hunter, "that must be why Mama made hotcakes. We usually have cereal for breakfast except for weekends."

"Banyan has a long day of work ahead of him, Hunter, I wanted to have him fed and fueled for all that energy he'll be using," explained Roselyn. She looked like she would like to stuff her oven mitt in his mouth.

Maria passed the platter of hot cakes to Banyan. Roselyn poured him a cup of fresh, hot coffee.

"Well, Mama said the chokecherry syrup is for special occasions, "added Hunter, "and since she got it out today, I guess you're special, Mister"

"Hunter," prompted Roselyn, "Please eat so you will be ready for the bus." She sat back down in her place and passed Banyan the plate of bacon.

"No, thanks," he said. "This will be plenty." He poured the syrup on his hotcakes and stirred some sugar in his coffee.

Hunter eyed him curiously, "You don't like bacon?"

"You can have my share," answered Banyan.

Hunter prepared to pounce, but Roselyn picked up the plate. "You will share it with your brother, Hunter."

She forked each boy two pieces of the meat and sat the plate down.

"So, why don't you like bacon?" pursued Hunter, with a mouthful of pork.

"Ooooh, Hunter," scolded Maria, "Don't talk with your mouth full!"

"And stop asking our company so many questions," advised Roselyn, "Allow the poor man to eat."

"Uncle Carl doesn't eat meat at all," informed Hunter, pushing the last piece into his mouth.

"Actually, neither do I," explained Banyan.

"Is it because of religious belief?" asked Maria, gaining interest in his food preference.

"Not so much that," explained Banyan," my mother never ate meat or prepared it for the family so I just never became accustomed to it.

"What did she feed you?" Hunter pressed for more information. "Don't you get hungry just eating vegetables?"

"No, I'm never hungry," answered Banyan cheerfully. "She's a great cook and her Indian cuisine provides lots of choices."

"Like what?" questioned Hunter.

"Enough!" intervened Roselyn." Get your jacket and backpack. You have five minutes until that bus gets here."

As the children clambered to connect with their ride to school, Roselyn shot Banyan an apologetic glance. "I'm sorry about the inquisition. I don't know what got into him."

Banyan smiled "No problem, he feels he's the man in your house. A stranger just dropped in for breakfast. There's nothing wrong with him wanting to find out all he can."

Roselyn refilled both of their cups as the bus stopped in front of my drive and Maria hustled her brother in its direction. Roselyn's cell phone rang.

She picked it up and looked at the screen, "Hello, Carmen, what's up? You never call me this early." She listened as her sister imparted information and then asked, "When did he gain consciousness?"

More listening and then a reply, "Yesterday? Are they going to question him? I wonder if Detective Wilkes knows."

Carmen explained something else and Roselyn questioned," So is he all right? Will he be arrested and charged now? I guess you wouldn't know that. You're only informed on the medical stuff. But if you hear he's about to be discharged, let me know. I'd like to receive warning."

Banyan had been politely ignoring her conversation with her sister, but her final question caused him to take an interest.

No more interested than I, I might add.

Roselyn flipped her phone shut and looked at Banyan. "That's a call from my sister, Carmen. The doctor she works for is treating Dennis, the man that attacked me. He's been unconscious as I explained last time you were here. He's awake, talking and taking in some food by mouth now.

She came back and paced across the room. Then she got up and began to gather up the dishes. Her movements were quick and tense. Banyan reached across the table and gently touched the top of her hand, bringing the clattering to a stop.

"Don't allow him to bring fear to you Roselyn. Men like that have power because of the fear they cause to others."

Roselyn sat down and placed her face in her hands "This man killed his wife, abused his step daughter and would have killed me and my boys, if he could have." There were tears in her voice.

"Just because he's awake, doesn't mean he's moving around," he assured her. "Now they can question him, and they will. Now they can press charges."

Roselyn grabbed a napkin from the table and wiped her eyes and nose. "But he has so much money; he can get a good lawyer. What if he beats this? "

"I can't see how, offered Banyan, "they know what he did to you. The town is behind you. Look at the way they rallied around to help." Anytime you feel that someone should be here with you until they get him locked up, any number of people are willing, including me."

"Thanks," Roselyn offered a weak smile. "I'm just having some of the Post Traumatic Stress you were talking about."

"And you have every right to experience it, but don't surrender to fear. There are times we need fear. It's part of survival. But, most of the time it's just plain unhealthy. Now, shall we get your wiring done?"

I was in deep ponder. 'Fear is an unhealthy state . . . Who said that?' Now I remember William said that.

Roselyn called Kate and requested she take care of the boys after school for a while. She knew Hunter would be underfoot during this project. Kate agreed to keep them over night. Maria went to dance class after school and then to a friend's house.

Roselyn ran into Lander and picked up Vegetarian pizza from the Pizza Palace, and the two had dinner by candlelight. Not as an attempt for romance but because my electricity was still turned off and would be until tomorrow afternoon.

They sat in my parlor and it reminded me of the first night Helen and William ate their first meal within my walls. Roselyn has two too many sisters, however, to expect a quiet candlelight dinner with a handsome house whisperer. And his cell phone soon interrupted.

"Hello Sadie. What's up? I've got the phone on speaker, and Banyan is here, so talk nice."

"Well, I'm probably not supposed to tell anyone this but it's too good to keep," she said excitedly.

"It's never stopped you from telling everything before," laughed Roselyn.

"Can your friend be trusted, it really isn't supposed to be out," she wavered.

Banyan made a cross over his chest.

"He's promised," assured Roselyn.

"Ok, here's the scoop. Asher got a search order from Judge Barrows. He and the police are going to search Dennis' apartment."

"Asher? You're on a first-name basis with Detective Wilkes?" inquired her older sister.

"So?" sassed Sadie, "Anyway, since he leased his apartment from us, Larry is sending me over with a key to let them in tomorrow at eight sharp."

"Great, I hope they find some kind of evidence to solve that murder," stressed Roselyn.

"Me too," agreed Sadie.

"And what is going on with you and that detective?" asked Roselyn, in her bossy sister voice.

"Don't be so nosy!" scolded Sadie.

"Nosy? You're calling me nosey?" Roselyn demanded in pretended shock.

Sadie giggled and hung up.

Chapter Forty-Four

HOUSE WHISPERER

"Banyan would become known as the House Whisperer,
but I always thought of him as the Kid Whisperer as well"

On Sunday morning Roselyn, not having been able to sleep, was up early. Banyan arrived at seven-o-clock with large coffees and hot oatmeal from Mac Donald's. They talked over breakfast and he explained that he would be adding more outlets to each room.

"When they first wired The Lady, there were fewer electrical appliances. They only put one outlet in each room. Using these extension cords isn't safe. Now you won't have to do that. You'll also have a breaker system so no more fuses to worry about," he said.

That will be a real improvement," agreed Roselyn.

"You are going to have to make some final decisions about your kitchen," he urged, "I have to know where your electrical outlets need to be. Why don't you draw a basic kitchen plan for me? Sketch in the fridge, range and where your counters are going to be. I'll get back to looking at your design is a little while, but now I'm going to have to work in that room." He nodded his head at the Greenroom.

I had settled into the idea that wiring would require him working in there, but I hoped the restless spirit wouldn't do harm to anyone.

He opened the door gently and stood looking in for a while. "Ok, all I'm going to do is improve things here. So let's all keep cool."

He preceded and to my amazement all remained calm. Roselyn busily sketched out my new kitchen as a soft mountain breeze flowed through my open windows. At eleven-o-clock, her cell phone rang. She saw it was Sadie.

"Hello," she answered, "what's up, little sis?"

"The search is over. I wasn't allowed to go into the apartment, but I hung near the door. They found child pornography, and additional snapshots of a nude girl. I can't say for sure, but I'm betting it was Megan."

"That's not a surprise, anything else?" asked Roselyn.

"Yes, actually, the drug, Rohypnol. There was no prescription label on the bottle to indicate Dennis had a medical need for it."

"What's it usually prescribed for?" questioned Roselyn.

"I called Carman about that," Sadie continued. "She told me it's used for anxiety and to treat patients with seizures. It has side effects of sedation and extreme muscle relaxation."

"Oh my goodness, the dream you had of feeling drugged, Sadie!" Roselyn exclaimed. Do you think he used that to drug Megan's mother?"

"That's what I'm thinking," answered Sadie, "and Carman says it is one of the drugs that's used as a rape drug. A large amount, mixed with alcohol, would have put Megan's mother in a state of helplessness, though possibly enough awake to realize she was being murdered."

"That horrid man, and all for money," moaned Roselyn.

"And he was smart," added Sadie. "Remember, Asher told us the woman was a mechanic and restored old cars. She was strong and healthy. He had to drug her so he could manage to set up the hanging scenario without a struggle. In a fight, she would have held her own or at least ended up badly bruised."

"But wait, wouldn't the autopsy have picked up on a rape drug?" asked Roselyn.

"I dropped into the clinic. Carmen and I researched it on a special medication program in her office." Sadie explained. "It's easy to miss. General benzodiazepine-detection testing doesn't pick it up. They wouldn't do the special testing if they didn't suspect a rape drug. To find it, they would have to use gas chromatography-mass spectrometry analysis"

"That's so sad," Roselyn lamented. "With her depression, it was easier for authorities to accept suicide than drug-assisted murder."

"Exactly," agreed Sadie.

"What does Asher say about it?" asked Roselyn.

"He won't talk to me about it," answered Sadie, "but he listens to what I have to say. I've told him what I've learned about Rohypnol. I'm sure he'll check with a specialist. I know if Dennis can't prove he has a medical reason for having the drug, it's going to work against his defense. Also, that combined with the child pornography and nude snapshots of a very young step daughter sets him up for big trouble."

"Are they releasing him?" asked Roselyn.

"That, I do know," assured Sadie. "Asher told me he is under guard at the hospital until he can be held in jail. As soon as he's well enough to travel, he'll be transported to Rock Springs. Asher doesn't believe he will be granted bail. He's a flight risk"

"That's a relief!" exclaimed Roselyn. "Thanks so much Sadie, for all that work you did on this."

"No problem, I'm finding that I like this detective stuff. I think I might start a new career."

Roselyn laughed, "Sadie, you always like whatever interest your boyfriend has. So, don't quit your day job."

"Hold on a minute, Miss Presumptuous, who says Asher's my boyfriend?"

"Well?" prompted Roselyn.

"Let's just say, I'm open to the idea. He's the first man I've ever met who actually makes sense."

"And maybe the first one you can't manipulate?" teased Roselyn.

"Hush!" retorted her sister, "I've gotta go. Talk to you later.""

In the late afternoon, Kate brought the kids home with take-out from The China Moon. She was pleased with my updated electrical system.

"I'm so relieved, she said to Banyan, "I always worried something would cause a fire here."

Hunter was excited too and as full of questions as he had been the day before.

"What are you fixing next?" he asked, "I can help, you know."

I'll just bet you can," answered Banyan "Tomorrow, I'm starting on insulation and I'm sure I can use a couple of assistants."

You have no idea what you're in for!

"I have tools," offered Hunter. "If you need to borrow any I can lend them to you. Do you want to see?"

"Sure, said Banyan, do you have them in a tool box?"

"Nope, in a treasure box. Come and see." He started toward my stairs.

"Banyan is resting Hunter," Roselyn attempted to intervene.

"It's ok," Banyan reassured her, "I never pass up an opportunity to see inside a treasure box."

A few minutes later, Banyan and both boys sat on my floor as Hunter spread out his collection.

"Wow, you do have a lot of err . . . tools." commented Banyan. "Do you really need all this stuff?"

"Not really," agreed Hunter, "I use the screwdrivers a lot, and the hammer. I was thinking of selling the other stuff, to pay for Mom's new tires."

"Mom's tires," echoed Ethan.

"Well, I might just be in the market for a few treasures," ventured Banyan "What will you take for those cigarette butts?"

"Do you smoke?" asked Hunter.

"No, cigarettes are nasty," replied Banyan. "They're harmful to people and to the environment."

Ethan giggled, "Nasty."

"I'll buy them from you so I can throw them away," he offered. "How about twenty-five cents for the both of them?"

"OK," accepted Hunter, pushing them toward Banyan and holding out his hand for payment.

"Hold on, Hot Shot," Banyan said, "I'm not through shopping yet. Get a piece of paper and pencil and add up my charges."

Hunter dug a piece of paper and a pencil from his backpack. "What else do you want?"

"These broken scissors, where did they come from?" Dennis inquired.

"I found them in this house when we first came," answered Hunter. "You want them?"

"Sure, I'll give you fifty cents," offered Banyan.

"Sold," responded Hunter, writing the numbers on his paper. "Anything else I can sell you?"

"I'm kind of interested in the camera. Are you sure that's not your mom's or sister's? I don't buy hot merchandise. "

"Hot dice," copied Ethan.

"I didn't steal any of this," retorted Hunter, "I found all of it."

Banyan turned the camera over in his hands. "Did you find this here in this house like the broken scissors?" he questioned.

Hunter nodded, "In that scary room, after we first came. I climbed into the window and I found a wallet and this camera. Mama took the wallet though. They were on the floor, right inside the closet."

"I'll give you a dollar for the camera, now what do I owe you?" he asked.

After a bit of math on paper, head tipping and head scratching, Hunter announced, "Two dollars."

"What?" protested Banyan, looking at the paper.

"Tax," explained Hunter.

"You've been hanging around with your Aunt Sadie too long," teased Banyan.

Ethan's bottom lip was pushing out when Banyan looked at him. "Hey, Little Buddy, what's wrong?"

"No treasures," answered Ethan, holding out his hands, palms up.

"Oh, you are so wrong," responded Banyan. "You have many treasures, and I'm willing to buy some from you."

Both boys looked at him with questioning faces.

"Your words, Ethan," explained Banyan. "Your words are your treasures. If you tell me a story this evening after dinner, I'll pay you a dollar."

Banyan would become known as the House Whisperer, but I always thought of him as the Kid Whisperer, as well.

Chapter Forty=Five

THE CAMERA

"Their proximity was closing in, I noticed"

Banyan, Kate, Roselyn and children sat around the dining room table eating fried rice, spring rolls, and a salad that Roselyn made to go with The China Moon's take-out. Hot tea added to the theme.

Hunter and Ethan fought over the opportunity to sit by Banyan. Roselyn rearranged seating so one sat on either side of him.

"Is this the kind of food your mama made for you?" asked Hunter.

"No, it's different, but this is really good. Don't you agree?" responded Banyan.

Hunter nodded his head in agreement. "I like these rollie-pollie things" he said, forking himself another spring roll.

"Rollie-Pollie," repeated Ethan.

"I will cook dinner tomorrow night," offered Banyan, "If it's agreeable with your mother."

"Like what your Mama cooks?" asked Hunter.

"Yes," replied Banyan, "like my mother cooks."

He glanced at Roselyn for approval. She nodded, "I would love that," she said. "I've never tasted eastern cooking."

Later, the children left the table and the adults enjoyed another round of hot tea.

"Roselyn, do you have a teapot?" Banyan asked.

She shook her head, "No, it's tea bags, and a microwave here."

"Tomorrow, I'll expose you to a wonderful treat," he said, smiling.

"Mama," Hunter exclaimed, running back into the room. "I forgot to give this to you." He laid the money on the table. "It's to pay off the new tires."

"Where did you get this, son?" she asked.

"I sold stuff from my treasure box," he answered, looking at Banyan.

Banyan nodded agreement. Roselyn looked down at the bill and four quarters.

"He drove a hard bargain," explained Banyan, sensing that Roselyn might consider refusing Hunter's gift. "He was very clear that he wants his profit to go to your tires."

Roselyn pulled her son to her and gave him a big kiss on his cheek. "Thank you Hunter, would you like to go with me to pay this on the bill?" He nodded.

After Hunter left the room, Banyan pulled the camera from his cargo pants pocket. "I almost forgot. This is one of the items I bought from Hunter, it concerns me. He said he found it in that room you keep locked."

Kate leaned over to get a better look. "That's one of those disposable cameras everyone was using some years ago," she commented.

"I'm thinking this may have some photos that were taken by the teen who died here," he said.

"Mom, you can develop those in your darkroom, can't you?" asked Roselyn.

"I use all digital now," answered Kate, "but I still have a darkroom. It wouldn't take long to set it up. I think I still have developer and paper stored in the studio closet."

I was excited. I believed there were important images on it. Why would Megan have hung onto it even while running away? I projected these thoughts to Kate.

"I'll bet there are important photos on it. Why else would Megan hang onto it even while running away?" Kate repeated, as I knew she would.

"Let me run this to The Paisley and work on it this evening, if anything looks important, I'll call you."

Roselyn began to clear the table. Banyan stood up to help, but Roselyn shooed him out of the room. "You've worked hard all day," she said. "This won't take me long."

Banyan walked into my family room. Hunter was flipping through channels with the remote and Ethan sat on the floor, building with Legos. Banyan dropped to the floor beside him.

"So, Ethan, are you ready to sell me your story?" he asked.

Ethan shrugged his shoulders.

Banyan looked at the Lego structure. "What's this?" he asked.

"It's a house," answered the child.

"Tell me a story about this house you built," he suggested.

"Slowly Ethan began "This is Jack's house. He needs a house. Jack looks after us."

As Banyan pulled conversation from a child not use to talking in full paragraphs, Roselyn's cell phone rang in my kitchen. My attention was drawn there. As usual the cell was set on speaker.

"Hey Roz, it's me Sadie," the caller began.

"What's up, Sis?" responded Roselyn.

"The police and Asher both questioned Dennis today, at the hospital."

"And . . . . ?" prompted Roselyn, putting the mop back in the broom closet.

"He confessed to the assault . . . sort of," she continued. "He says it was self-defense and that you attacked him first with the letter opener."

"That's such a lie," angrily exclaimed Roselyn.

"He also says you invited him in and then turned on him," continued Sadie, "but, of course he pursued the boys upstairs after kicking you unconscious. His blood trail proved that, so the cops were able to back him down. He's willing to plead guilty on trespassing, and aggravated assault. He refused to acknowledge any connection to Megan's running away, or her mother's death."

"Of course he does," snarled Roselyn. "And the child pornography?"

"He says that was there when he moved in and he just didn't bother to discard it," answered her sister, "but I know better. I personally helped clean that apartment before he leased it. I would have found that rubbish."

"I guess that's why the detective said he needs facts to prove guilt," said Roselyn with a sigh, before saying goodbye.

Banyan, having paid Ethan for his story, entered my kitchen. Seeing Roselyn's trouble expression, he asked, "bad news?"

"Let's go in the parlor," she suggested, "I'll tell you what I just heard."

They both settled down on the couch. Their proximity was closing in I noticed.

Roselyn relayed all that Sadie had told her and they discussed the possibilities of how things might turn out for Dennis. Banyan continued to assure Roselyn that he would receive the punishment he deserved.

Roselyn asked him what he thought she should do about the bees. He questioned the need to exterminate them.

"The days are getting cooler," he reasoned, "they will hibernate soon. I must tell you, I don't like killing them. Bees are threatened enough already and they benefit the environment. After all, the only person ever bothered by them was Dennis."

Roselyn went upstairs to put the boys to bed. Her cell rang and she called down my staircase,

"will you answer that for me, Banyan?"

Banyan greeted the caller and jumped when Kate's voice came loudly across the connection. The cell was still set on speaker. He moved it farther from his ear. "This is Banyan, he informed her, "Roselyn's with the boys."

"I'm looking over these photos," began Kate. "The roll of film was only half used. Some images didn't turn out. However, there are several that I find disturbing. I called Sadie and she is bringing that detective over there to meet with me. I'll be there in a few minutes and we'll all have a look at them."

Chapter Forty-Six

EVIDENCE

"That is the sound of a sorrowful spirit"

Roselyn started a pot of coffee and instructed Maria to get ready for bed. She was determined to shield her children from the details of Megan's death. Soon, Sadie pulled up in my drive and she and Asher came to the door. Banyan opened the door and Sadie made introductions between the men. They shook hands and the three found seating in my parlor.

Roselyn carried a tray into my parlor just as Kate pulled up in her Jeep. Once she was in the group, all eyes looked anxiously at her. She laid a folder on the coffee table.

"I enlarged these to the five by seven sizes," she began; I thought it would make details clearer."

Everyone was on the edge of their chairs and I was trembling with excitement.

Kate opened the folder and scattered four photos out on the table. Every head leaned over them, peering closely.

I desperately tried to peek through, but I couldn't even get a glance.

"This first one was taken through a window, looking in from outside," explained Kate. "That's why it's blurry. Luckily, there's light in the room. That makes everything more visible. However, the lamp, back lights the images. That makes them harder to identify."

Asher took the photo in his hand and looked closely. Sadie put a hand on his shoulder and leaned over to see. Now I could make out the images. It appeared to be a man and woman. The lady was sitting in a chair, holding a martini glass. The man's back was to the camera.

"That's Dennis," confirmed Sadie, You can see he has curly hair and broad shoulders."

"So do thirty or forty percent of the male population," replied Asher. "This shows a man and woman having drinks. We have no idea who they are. All we know from this is that the owner of this camera was a peeping Tom."

"I'm sure that the woman is Megan's mother," offered Kate.

"Why?" asked Asher, "have you met her? Of course not. We can't know by this picture, that this is her mother."

Roselyn now held the picture. "The light is a bit on the right side of her face. She resembles Megan," she observed.

"How do you know?" asked Asher, "did you ever meet either of them? Just looking at one picture on a drivers' license and matching for resemblance to a blurred snapshot of a woman doesn't come close to evidence."

"Well," began Banyan, "we have a pretty good idea that the camera belonged to Megan. Common sense tells us that if she is taking a picture, it would probably be of her parents."

"You can't send a man to prison on common sense," said Asher. "This could be a capital case. The jury will want hard evidence before pronouncing him guilty. Let's see the other pictures"

Kate pushed the next one to the center. "This was snapped next, according to the numbering on the film."

I focused in. In dim daylight, a man carried a woman in his arms.

"There," said Sadie excitedly, "just like in my dream."

"If we could just know for sure it's Dennis," said Asher, looking closely.

"Too bad it was taken so late in the day, the shadows really make it hard to see faces," moaned Kate.

"But look how relaxed her body is," noted Sadie, "she is either dead or unconscious."

"That does appear to be the case," confirmed Asher.

"Hey," exclaimed Sadie, "look, you can see the house number."

"Shhhh!" cautioned Roselyn," You'll have all the kids down here if you yell like that."

"I'm not yelling!" defended Sadie.

"I think you may be right," said Asher. "Roselyn, do you have a magnifying glass?"

Roselyn got up and hurried to the fridge. Passing her hand over the top, she located it among all the clutter.

Returning, she handed it to Asher. Asher held the glass over the number by the front door. The entire house wasn't visible, just the front door and steps.

If only someone would ask that house. That's how the truth could be known.

"It looks to me like 1097, said Asher. "If we only knew the street."

"Does that number match the address on Megan's drivers license?" asked Kate.

"I intend to check that tomorrow," answered Asher. "Although we can't identify this man as Dennis, this does show a woman was carried out of that house. If this house number matches Megan's license, we are moving closer to proving her mother was incapacitated at some time or other."

Kate handed the third picture to Asher, "This," she said, "isn't clear. I think the picture was taken while Megan was in motion. It appears to have been shot through the back window of a vehicle."

"You're right," agreed Asher. "You can see the shape of the right side of the window and glare on the top of the glass."

He studied the picture closely. "Now this picture does show a good profile of the woman." He pointed at a woman's head in a side view.

"She is leaning over like she is passed out or too weak to hold her head up." Sadie pointed out.

"We just might be able to match this image with pictures in her driver's license." Asher said with enthusiasm. "I can get that pulled up at the police station tomorrow. How did she get a picture like this? This close, through a back window, is just plain impossible. Especially without being noticed."

"Not in a pickup," stated Roselyn "she could have slipped into the bed of the pickup after she took the picture through the window. When she saw her mother being picked up by Dennis, she probably ran to the pickup, jumped into the back so she would know where he took her."

"Exactly," agreed Sadie, "she might not have known he was going to kill her. Maybe she thought he was going to drop her off somewhere or tie her up. She wanted to know where she was, to be able to help."

"Why would she have been taking these photos on that afternoon?" pondered Kate.

Suddenly, thoughts I had sifted from Megan came back to me." I knew they wouldn't believe me, Mommy. I wanted to show them pictures of how he treats you, so they would take his power of attorney away."

When she sobbed these words while dreaming, they made no sense to me, now they did. I projected this to Kate.

Banyan was looking at the fourth photo and Asher, continued to study the third.

"I know what happened," Kate announced, "Megan was a repeated run-away. She didn't believe her word would be taken seriously by authorities. Her mother was considered mentally ill. She was probably not believed either. Megan was trying to get pictures to prove Dennis was abusive and manipulating her mother. She wanted to get help and she needed evidence."

I was impressed. Kate took my one sentence projection and developed it into a theory in nothing flat.

"So you need hard evidence?" Banyan spoke up, "How about a license number? That ought to stand up in court."

He handed the fourth photo to Asher. *I could see it clearly. There was a warehouse. The garage type door was half open as the image of a man stood in front. It appeared he was pulling the door down. From the inside, barely visible, was a pair of feet, dangling.*

"You can't see who the man is," Banyan continued. "But to the side, almost out of the picture, you can see the plates on the truck."

"Bingo!" said Asher.

I was stunned. I hoped the camera would provide evidence. Now that it had I could hardly believe it.

From the Greenroom, a soft, sorrowful groan began. The parlor group straightened in their chairs. Asher quickly stood. All eyes focused on the locked door. The noise evolved into a loud sob. Asher took several steps toward the sound.

Banyan shook his head. "No! Don't disturb it."

I was frightened. It's me that makes noises, calling on my store of memories. This wasn't me. I felt helpless.

The sobbing faded into a weeping gasp then stopped.

"What in Sam hill was that?" asked Asher.

"That is the sound of a sorrowful spirit," answered Banyan, softly.

Chapter Forty-Seven

EAST MEETS WEST

"You never know when fate sends another guest.
But then 'Fate' could be Sadie's middle name"

The following day, Banyan spent the morning working on insulation in my towers and attic. After lunch, he began preparation for his special dinner. Maria and her brothers were as excited as children on Christmas Eve. He restricted Roselyn from the kitchen.

"This is a surprise. You're allowed to see nothing," he warned. "It's a gift from me and your children."

He instructed Maria in preparing the fruits and nuts, desert tray and she busily peeled oranges, bananas, and papayas, sprinkling them lightly with lemon, sugar, and almonds. She placed them in the fridge to chill. When Banyan was ready to begin cooking, he carried in a box and a grocery sack from his vehicle.

Roselyn was presented with a steaming cup of coffee, new fluffy cozies for her feet, and a book of poetry to read. She was then banished from my kitchen and the door was closed. The wonderful aromas soon drifted through my rooms tantalizing her.

The three children stood anxiously at the counter with hands washed and faces alight with expectation

"What are we making?" asked Maria.

"My mother calls it Lentil Curry, but it goes by other names too." Banyan answered. "I'm cheating by using some canned vegetables. My mother would have used all fresh and cooked from scratch."

"Scratch?" repeated Ethan.

"Why does she scratch them?" asked Hunter.

"That isn't what he means, Hunter," coached Maria. "Just watch and listen."

Banyan opened the cardboard box and pulled out an electric rice cooker.

"Maria, please measure the rice and water according to these instructions." He handed her a paper. "We will be serving . . . . hmm, Ethan, how many people are eating dinner here tonight?"

Ethan began listing names by holding up fingers, "Mama, Grams, Banyan, Maria, Hunter, me, and Jack. Ahh, seven," he concluded looking at both hands of extended fingers.

"Old Jack's coming, is he?" asked Banyan, "Well, Maria, If we count seven, we'll plan for eight. You never know when fate sends another guest."

Maria began preparing the rice as Banyan unloaded the grocery bag. "Ethan, do you know how to operate a can opener?" he asked.

"Yes," answered, Ethan, jumping up on the counter and pulling the electric device forward.

"Here," prompted Banyan, "lets stand on a stool, that's safer. Now, open these cans for me, please."

Banyan placed two cans of red lentils, a can of diced tomatoes, and a small can of coconut milk near the opener.

"What do I get to do?" demanded Hunter, tired of waiting for his assignment.

"You have a crucial part," encouraged Banyan. "You'll be helping with the spices."

"Spices, "echoed Ethan.

"Why are spices important?" asked Hunter.

"With Indian cooking, there are a lot of spices. They add flavor but are also very healthy," Banyan explained. "See here, these are measuring spoons? You will be using only two of them.

Hunter pulled up another stool, climbed up on it. He studied the spoons. "They have their names on them," he commented. "This one says, one TB . . . does that mean tab?"

"No, it means tablespoon," explained Banyan. "Mostly, you will use this one, it's a teaspoon."

Banyan set down the spices in front of Hunter and named them; curry powder, turmeric, chili flakes, ginger, garlic powder, lemon juice, and sugar.

"Put in one teaspoon of each of these, except for curry and sugar," he set them aside. "You'll need a tablespoon for those. While you all do your part' I'll cut up the potato and onion."

Everyone was happily working together. I regretted that Roselyn couldn't see the harmony. I understood, however, that her presence often encouraged misbehavior from the boys as they competed for her attention.

I focused my attention back to her. She still reclined on the futon with pillows propping up her back. Her cup was half empty and the poetry book lay opened on her lap. A phone call had interrupted her reverie.

"I can't believe he confessed," she was saying to Sadie. "So how did that happen?"

"He was moved to the jail, this morning," answered her sister. "Once he was settled in there, he was questioned again by local police and by

Asher. When Dennis saw the pictures, he shrugged his shoulders and said "You've got me."

"Wow," was all Roselyn could think to say.

"They're going to have a trial about the assault first," Sadie explained, "then take him to Rock Springs for the murder case."

Roselyn sat up and dropped her cozy clad feet to the floor. "I really don't care anymore about the assault charge. I just want them to get the trial over with on the murder case." My ghost needs closure."

"Yeah, but it doesn't work like that," said Sadie with a sigh. "When assault charges have been made in Wyoming, it becomes a matter of the state. No one can change their mind or drop the charges. That prevents people from being bullied out of following through. He will have to face it here, and you will have to testify."

"Rats!" said Roselyn with emphasis, "I don't ever want to lay eyes on him again."

"Tell this news to Banyan, I'll bet he wants to know about the day's results," suggested Sadie.

"I can't," explained Roselyn, "I'm banned from my kitchen. He and the kids are making dinner with Indian cuisine."

"Yum," answered Sadie, excitedly, "I had that once in Cheyenne, I'll be right over."

"No, wait," started Roselyn, "This isn't really a big get together or . . ."

She was too late, Sadie had ended the call.

Good thing Banyan counted on the extra guest, sent by fate, I chuckled. "But then 'Fate' could appropriately be Sadie's middle name.

Back in my kitchen the smells were delightful. The rice was set and the brew was steaming in a pot. The lentils, tomatoes, potatoes, onion, and spices bubbled in a red liquid. Banyan opened the box again and pulled out a tea set and a bag of loose tea.

"What's that?" inquired Hunter.

"This is an old fashioned way to make tea," answered Banyan. "This tea pot and cups are from India."

"They're beautiful," cooed Maria.

"The cups are little," noticed Hunter.

"Little cups," agreed Ethan.

"Yes, mugs are more or less an American custom," said Banyan. "In India, tea time is an event, a time of sharing. People there don't pack their drinks around everywhere as we do here. Other countries have different customs."

Banyan poured boiling water into the pot. After it had sufficiently heated the pot, he emptied it and measured out the Indian classic Assam tea leaves. Placing them in the pot, he filled the pot again with boiling water.

"Now, we'll let it steep for five minutes while we serve up dinner," he said.

He stirred coconut milk into the lentil porridge and ladled the hot curry entrée into a large bowl. Scattering a handful of chopped cilantro over the top, he handed the container to Maria.

"Do you think you can carry this to the dining room table while I finish with the tea?" He requested. "Be careful it's heavy and hot."

Kate and Sadie drove into the driveway at the same time, Sadie in her sports car and Kate in her Jeep. As they entered my front parlor, Kate commented, "It smells absolutely divine in here."

Roselyn walked from my family room into my dining room as they entered from my parlor. "Look at the lovely table," stated Kate.

"The boys set it," boasted Roselyn. "I've done nothing in the preparation of this meal."

"Did you tell Banyan?" pressed Sadie.

"No, Sadie. We're trying to have a peaceful, spiritual, restoring meal with no talk of anything but love, peace and all things hopeful. There's time for all the drama and hype later"

As she opened the door of my kitchen she announced, "Ok, Mr. Chef, you can't keep me out any longer. I'm dying of curiosity."

Sadie looked at her mother, "I think she just told me to keep my mouth shut," she grinned.

"Yeah, that's how I took it," Kate answered with a smile. "I think I won't mention what I found out about our ancestry. Let's just fit their plans tonight."

Chapter Forty-Eight

SECRETS

"I realized that I now spent less time thinking about the old days
and more time caught up in the present"

It was a beautiful October. The trees that lined the distant river were multicolored red and gold. The small aspens Roselyn had planted in my back yard the first summer had thrived and their leaves turned a light lemon yellow. If the winds remained calm and no early snow storm arrived, the colors would last.

Hunter's pumpkins, planted around my porches, were large and orange. Every day, Roselyn reminded him to wait and not pick them until closer to Halloween. Every afternoon Ethan showed Roselyn his completed school work and answered questions about his day. His talking was evolving be on parroting and answering questions.

The bees were still in the cistern house. Banyan did not follow through with extermination and Roselyn didn't bring it up again. I knew from my long life in Wyoming that bees should be settling down for the winter by now. I wondered what delayed their retirement.

One warm October Sunday, the women, lounged on my front porch. Roselyn served hot spiced cider to compliment Kate's fresh oatmeal, raison cookies. Maria was visiting a friend.

"Do you think it will be too cold for the guys to enjoy the mountains?" asked Kate. "It can be really cold up at South Pass in October."

"I sent extra coats with Carl for the twins," said Carmen, "and a thermos of hot cocoa."

"Ethan and Hunter have their new parkas," added Roselyn." After browsing through the ghost town, they plan to stop for lunch in Atlantic City. They'll have opportunities to warm up"

"I think it's great that we have this time for girl talk," giggled Sadie.

"We haven't had much time to share with so much going on with the house, Dennis's arrest and all this romance," teased Kate, pretending to complain.

"I think there's a good chance that everyone here has a secret that needs to be shared with our Mom and sisterhood," said Carmen.

"Mom has a secret too," said Sadie with a smile. "I've been sitting on it so long I'm about to burst. She won't let me tell it."

"I just wanted to be sure I have all the facts," explained Kate. "Now I do, so I will tell my secret today."

"Tell us," insisted Carmen.

"I don't want to be first. I want to share last." said Kate.

"Ok, I'll go first," volunteered Carmen. "Carl and I will announce our formal engagement and plans tonight at dinner."

"That's all?" scoffed Sadie. "We've always known you two would marry."

"No, Sassy Pants, that's not all, "scolded Carmen. "I will be wearing a diamond tonight and we will announce the date for a Christmas-time wedding."

"That, great news!" exclaimed Roselyn. "Will it be a big one or a small one?"

"That's why I wanted to share with all of you first," began Carmen, looking at Roselyn. "I hope you will let us get married here. I planned to ask you that today."

"Here? Of course!" said Roselyn with enthusiasm. "That will give me a chance to finish the kitchen and family room so everything will be pretty."

"And that's not all," continued Carmen. "Carl wants to build us a house and a taxidermy shop on the south acreage. It's close to the highway, his business will have good access. He has lots of regular customers now."

"I guess I can stop looking for a house for you?" concluded Sadie.

Banyan says we can build what we want easier than changing something already built, and for less money too," she explained. "He and Carl have been looking at plans for log structures. We want something rustic."

"That will be such fun," said Roselyn, "we will be neighbors. When will you start construction?"

"He'll do some landscaping later this month, but construction won't begin until next spring, after the ground thaws." I want a good foundation."

I was excited. Not only would Carmen and her twins be nearby but I would have a new companion house. I wondered what I would name her. Maybe Carmen would name her. She would be a brand new house, just starting memories.

The women sipped the hot cider and nibbled on the cookies. They talked about the wedding. Carmen wanted an all blue wedding. Her sisters would be her maids. Kate would give her away. Soon, Sadie remembered there were other secrets to share.

"I'll go next," said Sadie, eagerly.

"You are not telling my secret, remember," cautioned Kate.

"I know," retorted Sadie. "Well, all of you may have guessed that I like Asher a lot."

The others looked at her and rolled their eyes.

"I kept it quiet while he was here working on the case. This is a small town and stories get started really fast and then take on a new twist every day," she explained.

"Well," said Kate, "you may have kept it quiet, but I've been asked by a number of customers if you were dating that nice detective," teased Kate, laughing.

"I am now admitting that I am in love with Asher Wilkes, "Sadie, continued, ignoring her mother's remark.

"It's too early to say if this will lead to marriage, but I can tell you, he's the first man I ever met that I would even consider commitment," she finished.

"I think Asher is a wonderful person," encouraged Kate. "I just hope he doesn't carry you away to Rock Springs."

"That's the rest of my secret," said Sadie. "He'll be leaving Rock Springs as soon as he's finished with Dennis's case. He's going to teach Criminal Justice and Criminal Psychology at Central Wyoming College."

My thoughts were in a whirl. Another of my girls would be getting married, I had no doubt. I hoped Sadie would marry here too. I wanted to be part of it.

As they discussed Sadie's plans, I became lost in my thoughts. I realized that I now spent less time thinking about the old days and more time caught up in the present events. Now I slipped back for the first time in months.

I thought of Miriam Gregg, the daughter of Johanna and David. Her little sisters died of polio, but she survived. They didn't think Miriam would walk again, but she persevered. Even with her severe limp, she lived a life to the fullest and had a loving marriage to Thad Carr. I remembered their little boy Jules. What a bright child he was. He looked a lot like Ethan and was just as loving.

Jules's daughter Rhoda would be the last of the family to share my space. While she was just a child, her father died and her mother moved away with her in the late eighties.

All of this history was still important to me but now I realized the history being made now was vital too. It is my lifeblood. Their heart beats unite to become my heart beat.

I pulled myself back. There were more secrets and I didn't intend to miss them.

Roselyn was just warming up for her turn to share news. "I know you all know my loan was approved by the bank," she announced.

They all nodded. Sadie picked up another cookie.

"With the pluming and electric passing inspection and the insulation completed, the house assessed for enough to secure a reasonable mortgage. I now have enough for complete renovation." She raised her mug of cider in a toast and her sisters followed her example.

"Banyan says we can start on the kitchen. After that, the rest of the ground floor rooms. Hopefully, that will be finished by your wedding, Carmen," she smiled at her sister. "Though-out the winter, we'll complete the second story. Those rooms won't be difficult."

"There was silence as the others watched Roselyn. They expected more news, *as did I.*

I had witnesses those tender kisses and embraces while the children were at school. I was putting my bets on Banyan to break through Roselyn's distrust of men. The lack of a loving father, disappointments in her first marriage, and the brutal abuse from Dennis had given her little reason for bright expectations.

"That's all?" demanded the ever impatient Sadie.

"No, actually Banyan is also going to restore the towers, so you will have to take your critters home, Carmen," she said. "He's turning the towers into a space for meditation and yoga."

Her mother and sisters stared at her. "I didn't know you were into yoga," said Carmen with admiration.

"I'm not, but Banyan is and he needs a quiet place for it. I might have him instruct me," she answered with a careless shrug.

Kate looked directly at Roselyn. "So, if he is creating a space for meditation and yoga, and he's the one most interested in it, is he planning to share more than lessons?" she asked.

Roselyn laughed. "Ok, I can't torment you any longer. Things are getting pretty serious with us. I'm not getting in a hurry. The kids are still adjusting to him and he's getting to know them. But by spring, when the inside of the house is completed, we should know for sure how we feel."

Kate raised her mug, "I propose a toast to a happy ever after for my daughters who are my best friends, and the mothers of the best grandchildren in the world."

After they all and touched their mugs together and sipped their brew, Sadie nudged Kate. "We've kept the best until last, spill it, Mom."

Chapter Forty-Nine

ANCESTRY

*"I was so stunned, I popped both my front and
back doors open to get air"*

Kate opened the folder she constantly packed around with her. Throughout the month, I watched her jot words, names and data in it as she searched her laptop screen. She often watched the boys while Roselyn ran errands or when she and Banyan went for supplies for my renovation.

Kate was intent on finding information about something. I was not able to sift all she was thinking but I concluded that search was for links to her birth mother

Today, on my front porch, she was ready to share her findings with her daughters. She pulled out several loose pieces of paper from the folder. "Remember when we found the birth certificate of my birth mother, Alfreda Rose?

Her daughters nodded, listening closely.

"I joined Ancestry.com the very next day. I simply typed in her full name and the dates of her death. A few weeks ago I was contacted by a first cousin. His name is Charles. He is the son of Alfie's twin brother Albert. "

She paused and took a long drink of cooled cider, finishing the last of the potion in her mug. "He knew all about Alfie having TB and dying in a sanitarium." She said. "He didn't know about me. He had never heard about Alfie's little daughter being adopted out."

"Are you going to meet him?" asked Carmen.

"Yes," answered her mother. "I'm flying out to Oregon next week to meet Charlie, his wife and children. Charlie is the name he wants me to call him. He's about five years younger than I am."

"Mom, that's so exciting," said Roselyn, wiping her eyes. "I don't know why I'm crying."

"Oh, believe me, I've cried happy tears after hearing from him, then sad tears for what might have been, and then tears of relief," answered Kate. "A week after we talked on the phone, he sent this chart of his, well my family tree. Read it Roselyn. Tell me if it reminds you of anything."

Roselyn looked at the listed names and dates for only a moment, "OH MY GOD!" she exclaimed. "You are a direct descendent of Duncan Kenyan.

I nearly collapsed. I popped both my front and back doors open to get air.

"Duncan an Amadhay Kenyon are the people in some of those old pictures," said Roselyn, touching their names at the top of the chart. "Amadhay was Cherokee. This says their son was named Augustus Kenyan."

"Right," confirmed Kate, "Charlie said Augustus or Gus as they called him, became a minister and pastored a church in Oregon. He was there his entire life. "

"So that's why there 're no pictures of Kenyons after the second generation," mumbled Roselyn. The sisters were now leaning over Roselyn, reading the chart.

I wished they would move their heads. They were making me sift and mesh for information rather than reading a long.

Sadie pointed to the paper, "Look, Gus married Mary Walking Thunder, That's a native name from around here. I've sold property to families with that name."

"That's true," confirmed Kate, "Charlie told me his grandmother was Native American from the Wind River Reservation and that his grandfather was half Scottish and half Cherokee."

"Wow, and we didn't even know we were part American Indian,' said Carmen.

"Or that we were part Scottish," added Sadie.

"See," said Kate, pointing to a lower block mid-way on the paper. "They had a son Alfred who married a German immigrant. Her name was Madeleine, but there's no last name. Charlie said no one knows what it was before she married Alfred."

"Alfred and Madeleine had twins and named them Alfred and Alfreda," continued Roselyn, moving her finger down the chart, "And then, there was you Mom, Amanda Rose."

Kate wiped a tear away and smiled, "Charlie said his sister always talked about having a daughter and naming her after their Cherokee, great grandmother, Amadhay. He believes Amanda was her modification of that name."

I was stunned. Every name they mentioned brought back a memory of a face, a laugh, comments, music, and events. To learn that these people of my memory were connected to my present family overpowered my emotions. I would need time to think this through.

Roselyn stood up and shut my front door that I needed opened to breath. "I don't want any pesky autumn flies filling up the house," she grumbled.

"Mom," began Sadie sharply, "if Duncan was Helen's brother, then that makes you also a relative of the Yingling's who built The Lady."

"I know," said Kate, "And you know what else?"

Her daughters looked at her expectantly. As did I.

"That means those graves out there on the old property are our relatives," she announced.

"I say we pay that little cemetery a visit," suggested Sadie.

"No reason not to," said Roselyn, "Dennis is locked up in Rock Springs, he's not going to hinder us from seeing the graves."

"I intend to take some really good photos of the cemetery and each grave stone," stated Kate, "especially if the names and dates are still readable."

"Why don't we run over right now? It's not that far. The kids are with Banyan and Carl, it's the perfect time." Sadie jumped up in her usual leader of the pack mode.

I want to go,' I protested as I projected to Kate.

"I almost wish I could take The Lady back and set her down where she was," said Kate, "but since I can't, I will make a lovely large picture and bring it to her."

I knew she got my message. I also accepted that her plan was the best she could do.

Sadie's cell phone rang. She pulled it out of her pocket and looked at the screen. "It's Asher," she informed the others, "Let me take this and then we can go."

She walked away from the porch and toward my north side. A shot exchange with her caller, she raised her voice to be heard from the others.

"Dennis is dead," she said. "He hung himself in the Rock Springs jail."

"What?" asked Roselyn in astonishment, "No way."

"Sadie returned her attention to her phone call.

Suddenly, I felt a churning throughout my north rooms. If a house could vomit, this is how it would feel.

The closed windows of the Greenroom began to rattle. The greenroom's door tried to open and jiggled roughly. A loud knocking could be heard from its inside space. I couldn't bring myself to focus on what was behind that door.

Sadie stared at the window from her position in my front yard. "What the . . . . ?" She yelled.

"Is this an earthquake?" asked Kate in alarm.

"Only for the house," said Roselyn, glancing around and seeing the ground was not shaking.

Then in a flash, one of the windows in the Greenroom burst. Shards of glass flew out like spears of ice. Sadie attempted to run backwards, tripped and fell. Her cell phone flew several yards away from her.

Asher's voice bellowed from it, "Sadie what was that? Sadie? Sadie?"

No one was listening to Asher, however, as the smoky colored funnel swirled out of the opening. Sadie laid down and covered her head as the twisting form whisked over the top of her. Daisy started barking and running in circles. Moonshine, who had been curled up and snoozing in a rocker, jumped straight in the air, yowled, puffed up her back and ran under Kate's Jeep.

The mini tornado rushed down the north side of my outer wall just as she had the day of Dennis's assault on Roselyn. The bees swarmed out of the cistern shed as though they were called. They meshed into the funnel.

The smoky blob then morphed into an image of a girl. Not one that appears as a real person, but rather, a feminine shape. The women were as frozen in their spots as solidly as I was in mine. The misty shape drifted off, bees and all, straight up like a helium balloon.

Sadie crawled over to get her phone to call Asher back. Kate and her other two daughters dropped back onto their porch chairs.

Roselyn found her voice, "I think that was my ghost."

"That would be my guess." agreed Kate.

"I believe it's safe to say, she's moved to the white light." said Carmen.

Sadie approached my steps, "Wow, that was scary," she said quietly. "Do you think my announcement about Dennis's suicide caused your ghost to wig out like that?"

"It all appeared to be connected," agreed Kate.

"I think the reason Megan's spirit was stuck here," began Roselyn, "is that she wanted to have justice for her mother's murder. She may have felt she had failed by killing herself before it was accomplished.

"She didn't fail," stated Sadie. "By leaving clues, she helped us finish what she needed done."

"Why did she kill herself?" asked Carmen. "She had the camera; she could have proven her mother was murdered."

"I don't believe she knew Dennis had come to Lander when she ran away," suggested Kate thoughtfully.

"She probably hitch-hiked to whichever direction she could catch a ride to go. Maybe she planned to go to the police and somehow learned that Dennis was living here. Perhaps she thought they wouldn't believe her and make her go back to him"

Sadie took a deep breath. "I don't know about the rest of you, but I don't think I want to snoop around any cemetery today. Let's put that off until tomorrow"

"Let's go to the church," said Kate. "Let's light candles and offer prayers for Megan."

"And for her mother," added Carmen.

"If we are Christians as we profess to be, "began Roselyn, "we will offer some for Dennis, as well. He's the one who will need mercy the most."

As they drove away, I prayed the prayer I first heard William pray within my walls.

'Heavenly Father,
Be in our presence and bless this our home.
Protect us from harm and from ourselves.
Lead us, and remind us to share your love.
Amen'

Kate's Family Tree

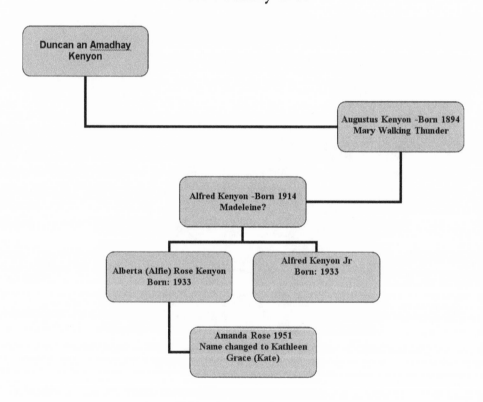

Duncan an Amadhay Kenyon

Augustus Kenyon -Born 1894
Mary Walking Thunder

Alfred Kenyon -Born 1914
Madeleine?

Alberta (Alfie) Rose Kenyon
Born: 1933

Alfred Kenyon Jr
Born: 1933

Amanda Rose 1951
Name changed to Kathleen
Grace (Kate)

Chapter Fifty

MORE REVELATIONS

*"Though he never practiced in India, his written words outlived him
and fulfilled his dreams"*

The months following Megan's release from my greenroom whizzed by. My mental and emotional health improved immediately. Megan's negativity with its lingering sorrow and regret disappeared. Harmony within my space continued uninterrupted.

Soon after my inner healing, the family of adults met in my parlor to discuss the events. This brought closure to all of us. They decided that the personal experiences we had with Megan would remain our secret.

"I don't want The Lady becoming a side trip for Halloween thrill seekers," declared Roselyn.

Kate added, "Or, have your children teased and harnessed at school for living in a house labeled as haunted."

"Not to mention the possibility of all of us being considered insane," said Carmen from remembering her medical perspective.

Sadie piped up with an interjection from her business sense. "Plus, it could lower the value of your property."

"That's not a worry. I'll never sell The Lady," declared Roselyn.

"All of these concerns are valid," said Banyan. "But I think the important thing to Carl is that this incident is a small frame of time in a long, rich history of The Lady's existence. The same is true of our lives. We experienced it; it had its purpose, and now it's over. We'll move on."

"I agree," said Asher, "and the best way to do that is to have no one from the outside keeping it all alive."

"Which means that what happened with Megan in this house, stays in this house," stated Carl.

And so it was decided and agreed. Only will my walls have recorded the story of Megan's courageous battle—to bring justice and her success in doing so. I can keep the secret safe.

Asher moved to Lander permanently. Sadie found him a small studio apartment over one of the downtown businesses. He said he didn't need much room and that was the case. All his time, when not preparing his courses for the spring semester, was hanging around Sadie's office or helping Banyan with my renovation. He kept us informed of the aftermath of Dennis's death and ill earned wealth.

Dennis had only one living relative. The money inherited from the murder of Megan's mother was not rightfully his. Therefore, it was not immediately handed over to his only brother. The land he moved me from was the same since it was purchased by a fraudulent source. The thirty acres on my east boundaries were less tainted and left to Donald Dickenson.

Don Dickinson took his brother's body back to Utah for burial. Dennis had long been estranged from his family due to many dishonest acts against them over the years. His brother, a complete opposite in character, set out to right the wrongs as best he could.

In late November, he came to Lander to seek Asher's help in resolving these issues. My family invited him to Thanksgiving dinner.

"I don't understand my brother," he explained. "As long as I can remember he was difficult. He had no respect for our parents. He had no interest in attending their funerals when he realized they left him nothing in their wills. They gave everything to charity. I've had my own success, I didn't need their meager estate, but Dennis always thought he deserved anything he wanted."

"It's commendable that you are taking an interest in wrapping up loose ends," said Kate.

"I hope I can," said Don. "I have several attorneys working on it and Asher has given me some great ideas. I want to set up a foundation to support run-a-ways. I would name it Megan's Gift. If I end up with any authority over the ranch, I will donate it to the historical society. I understand they want to build a replicate of Fort Brown and old Lander.

Excitement caused shivers throughout my walls, now covered with sheetrock and lovely wallpaper. This would be a wonderful accomplishment. My original' families' graves would not be desecrated. They would be cared for.

"Also, my brother bought the thirty areas on your east side for the unbelievably low price of back taxes. That isn't directly connected to the blood money," continued Don. I forced myself to pay attention.

So that'll be freed up soon?" asked Carl.

"I'm hoping that, by spring, I will have a clear deed. I understand that Dennis had visions of turning this area into an oil field, but I've checked that out. Its true there's oil here. However, there's even richer fields forty to fifty miles northeast, near Riverton. The companies with whom he consulted have chosen to invest there. That doesn't mean some oil tycoons might not show up someday and try to talk you into selling."

"The lady is not for sale," declared Roselyn.

"What do you think about wind power?" asked Don.

"Wind power is a excellent source of clean energy," said Banyan. "It's not in any short supply around here."

"I own stock in a small company called Airstream Wind Energy, would you be bothered by, say a half dozen wind turbines on that thirty acre hill behind you?"

"I would much rather have my back porch view consist of wind turbines than oil wells," said Roselyn.

"This is the perfect site for a small plant," explained Don. "The wind current from the mountains has you in a wind tunnel of sorts. Airstream would sell power, but I would insist, in my least to them, that you and Carmen have access to electricity without charge."

"When would this develop?" asked Carl.

"I would have it in progress next summer, but only if Roselyn and Carmen are sure they have no objections.

"Free electricity, from a clean source, without charge," questioned Carmen, "why would we object?"

From October through December, Banyan worked on my renovation four days weekly and attended his NOLS classes two other days. Occasionally, he has taken a few days for winter mountain hikes with the Leadership School. When he's away, Roselyn and one of the other women continued with projects he sets up for them. Asher's help really moved things along.

Snow arrived the same day as Halloween and continued unabated through Christmas. My indoor space remained toasty warm and Roselyn rejoiced over her lowered heat bills. My kitchen turned out beautiful. Roselyn ordered retro replicates and used a blue theme. She designed my kitchen after the forties era. I knew Johanna would have loved it. It's now where everyone gathers.

By the end of December most indoor renovation was complete. The wedding was the main focus. Carl wanted an all-western wedding and Carmen preferred ruffles and lace. She compromised and agreed to a denim wedding as long as the groom and groomsman agreed to wear pale blur, silk western shirts.

She wore a long denim skirt with a peasant blouse in soft pale blue silk. Her outfit was completed with a pair of white western boots. Rather than a bridal veil, she wore Kate's white lace chapel veil draped over her auburn hair. "This was for the something borrowed that every bride needs," insisted Kate.

Their cake was decorated with evergreen and pinecones made of sugar and a little log house sat on top. Guests were few. Besides our family, there were; Carmen's work chums, Sadie's boss Larry, Carl's family from Cheyenne, and Banyan's family from Montana. The Taylors fit in with us instantly. Maria instantly took to Lotus.

The Wedding was on the twenty-third so that Christmas could remain in tack for the children. Banyan's mother prepared an Indian meal for Christmas dinner. Everyone thought it was a nice change. The day after the holiday after the children were tucked into bed, the Taylors, Banyan and Roselyn settled into my new family room, now called the media room. A large leather wrap-a-round couch replaced the old futon.

Roselyn introduced the scrapbook she made about my life to Banyan's family. As she explained the history and pointed out various people in the pictures, Dr. Taylor said, "Wait, what did you say his name was?"

"William Yingling," answered Roselyn.

"Dr. William A. Yingling?" she asked looking closely at the picture.

"Yes, he was a doctor," said Roselyn.

"Just a minute, I have to show you something. It may not mean anything, but it seems to be more than coincidence," the doctor said as she sorted through a large bag she had beside her.

"In India, we studied medical literature from many countries and this booklet was written by a Dr, William Yingling, from America." She handed the small sized reference book to Roselyn.

Roselyn turned to the first page. There, was a black and white picture of an older gentleman. His hair was white and he wore a goatee. Dr. William A. Yingling was printed beneath the image. Roselyn flipped through the pages. This is pretty difficult medical writing," she commented, "I would love to show this to Carmen, she might understand it."

"That is a brief summary regarding women's health," explained Dr. Taylor." The information is still very relevant. There are others in this set; Emergency Care, Infant Care, Childhood Diseases, Men's Health, and several others. They continue to be printed in India. They are all in English, however. This is the only one I have with me."

Roselyn had turned to the back page and was read information about the author.

"Do you think this is your Dr. Yingling?" asked Mrs. Taylor.

"This says he practices medicine in Wyoming, USA, said Roselyn, It's my Dr. Yingling,"

She handed the small book back, but Dr. Taylor waved it away. "No, you keep it. I'll send you the others. I can easily get more. A full set belongs in his house."

As they slowly retired to their selected rooms for a deserved night's sleep, there was no rest for me.

I thought back to William, writing those manuscripts. He used a long pen, dipped in ink. He wrote carefully with a creative hand and flowing script. My William, the man whose dreams of India were dashed by rejection of a mission board. Though he never practiced in India, his written words outlived him and fulfill his dreams.

Chapter Fifty-One

THE PRESENT

"To appreciate joy, one must know sorrow, and to survive sorrow,
one must know joy"

Spring is never more beautiful than when it follows an unusually harsh winter. Its the last of May and snow continues to cling to the shaded areas on my north side. Banyan carefully filled all nicks and crannies on the cistern shed to prevent new bee swarms from settling in. It wasn't necessary as none have been spotted.

The sheep across the road are lambing. Hunter and Ethan visit after school, luring the lambs to the fence and allowing them to nibble their fingers. Moonshine has kittens that scamper around. They will soon go to new homes.

My rooms are completed and Roselyn runs a tight ship, insisting my spaces are clean and in order. The tower is a place for quiet time, meditation, prayer, or private counsel between family members. Occasionally, different individuals go there to watch the sunrise or sunset.

My old Greenroom is now Roselyn's office. The walls are papered in light colored beige with a scattering of tiny pink roses. My airy windows on two sides of this space are covered with pink lace curtains. An antique rolled top desk sets against my inner wall. Here she works on her billing for various medical practices and can be easily accessible to the boys.

Pictures of my first families are framed and hanging over the desk. Kate's skillful restoration is to be admired. The small closet that Megan used to conceal her wallet, camera and backpack was converted into an inverted bookcase. Among the books on these shelves are the medical writings of William.

This room, once an apothecary, a teacher's office, sewing room, and lastly music practice room, is again productive. Since she uses it for medical billing, it has made a full circle. But best of all, it's a happy room.

Banyan's words are true, 'To be truly healthy, there can be no secret hidden spaces left to decay in squalor. This is true for people as well as for houses.'

The past week has been involved in planning the improvements for my outer walls. I wanted white paint with red trim like my first design. Roselyn is adamant that frilly trims and lattices be added and painted several pastel colors. She says it in keeping with Victorian.

I relented. Love is not about getting one's own way and life is about compromise.

With good weather, the trim and painting will be completed by the end of June. Roselyn and Banyan will have an outdoor wedding during this month. Roselyn wants it to be Victorian theme. Kate is busily sewing from a pattern she got from Amazon. They will have a reception her

In August Sadie and Asher will be getting married in Las Vegas. They will have a reception here before taking a honeymoon in Hawaii. The landscaping is complete for Carmen's new log house. Construction will begin in July, when my renovation is complete.

Life, for the moment, is good. Every day, I lazily observe my family members live theirs. Sometimes I think back on the past but mostly I listen to the plans for the future. I know there will be times when sadness and grief will return. When it does, I will hold them in my love and try to project that lesson from long ago.

To appreciate joy, one must know sorrow, and to survive sorrow, one must have known joy.

My Muse Speaks

I have always loved old houses. They do not have to be fancy to be lovable. Each old home stands as a testimony to the spirit of the individual who planned, built, and cared for the structure. Long after the creator is forgotten, the building stands as a reminder of that person during a particular period of time.

I often sense energy in houses. Upon entering, I experience an emotional awareness of either positive, negative, or neutral force. This sensitivity can be contributed to my personal oddness, I suppose. It worked as my muse for this book.

'The Lady' is designed from a composite of several old houses.

1. Part of my childhood was spent in a hundred-year-old house in the Ozarks. My father spent years attempting to restore it, without success. He often complained that the building fought his every effort.

2. My mother spent much of her childhood in a house built in the 1800's by her grandfather, William Yingling. She loved the house, and its grand design. Her stories about it lend to the composite.

3. As an adult, with a grandson, I lived for a time, in an old home with a one year lease. The frightening experiences we had in that house led me to break my least in six months. I never solved the mystery of the noises, shadows and mists; the landlord was kind and understanding, releasing me from my agreement.

4. My final muse is a house purchased by my daughter. It is loved by all the extended family and now has its own persona of a sort.

All the above, when blended together, gave birth to 'The Grand Lady of the Valley'.

The characters, for the most part, are people of fiction. The only exceptions are William and Helen Yingling. These remarkable people were my great grandparents. Much of what is written about them is true, including the story of his desire to go to India and the eventuality of his medical books being used in that country. One book can still be purchased through Amazon.

William and Helen homesteaded in Kansas. However, much of my life was spent in Wyoming. Therefore, my story is set in Wyoming. The historical events related in the story regarding Wyoming history are true, and general knowledge in the state. However, I have taken liberties with the exact time line. This book is not intended to be a historical reference.

The female characters, Kate, Roselyn, Carmen, and Sadie, represent the multifaceted traits of womanhood. Kate represents creativity. Roselyn stands for maternal love. Carmen denotes healing and compassion. Assertive and resourceful, Sadie contributes strength.

The men, Carl, Asher, and Banyan are separate aspects of masculinity. Carl is sensitive and tenderhearted. Asher is direct, practical, assertive, and focused. Banyan is creative, introspective and spiritual.

Dennis, of course, is representative of the evil in society, which includes greed, insensitivity, disrespect, and violence.

The beautiful town of Lander and neighboring communities sets the stage for My Walls Speak. However, all names of people and businesses are fictional. Any similarities to real people or businesses are completely unintentional.

I hope you enjoyed my tale of a house that lived to tell her story about life.

CPSIA information can be obtained
at www.ICGtesting.com
Printed in the USA
BVHW090804071222
653622BV00001B/53

9 781499 017205